INSPIRED BY NIGHT

L.E. May

To Ada.
Happy 70th.

Enjoy

L.E. May

Published by Xcite Books Ltd – 2014

ISBN 9781783753192

Chapter One

August 2009

It was the knocking that woke me up: quiet at first, then more insistent. Who would want to speak to me at that hour? Hardly anyone ever called round; I sometimes wondered if anyone actually knew where I lived. If I died in my sleep no one would find me until the landlord came round to complain about late rent payments.

As I woke up fully, the knocking became louder and faster, interspersed with a gentle moaning noise. I groaned. My neighbour. I'd never met my neighbour but I knew more about her sexual desires than I knew of my own. I closed my eyes again and waited for the words. They were always the same: 'Faster, oh yes! Yes, just like that, fuck me, fuck me, fuck me.'

Sounds like he's doing just that, love, I thought.

I don't know what compelled me to lie in bed listening to my neighbour achieve her orgasm. Envy, perhaps? To say it had been a while was a major understatement – I was practically a born-again virgin. It had been so long since that door opened I was sure it had sealed over. It wasn't that I didn't get offers – well maybe not so much lately – but I was reasonably sure I could probably have had the varied, exciting sex life my neighbour enjoyed if I'd wanted to. I'd always found sex a bit awkward, though. I didn't really like talking about it; I verged on the prudish and for the last few years I'd found it less stressful to just avoid it completely.

I dragged myself out of bed and made my way to the bathroom. I'm not much of a morning person and working for myself usually gave me the freedom to roll into work whenever I wanted, but I was officially becoming an employer and I wanted to make a good impression. Well, not a good impression as such, the right impression. Not that I had any idea what that meant, exactly. I figured it couldn't hurt to be there before he arrived at least and appear as though I had this running a business thing down to a fine art.

I didn't, of course. When I started out, I'd had no intention of running the type of business that employed people but my last job got quite a bit of attention and suddenly I was the hottest programmer in London. Seemed stupid to turn down the work when it could be contributing to my early retirement fund, or that little house in the country I'd been secretly dreaming about sharing with Mr Right. But I could only take on so much by myself, so it was time to bring in reinforcements.

It always took me a long time to get ready for work. It wasn't that I took a great deal of care over my appearance, I could never be bothered doing anything with my hair, which is long and thick and hangs in that undecided limbo between straight and curly which borders frizzy. On a good day, I would throw my head upside down between my knees and scrunch a bit of spiral curl serum into the tresses, but most days I just piled it into a knot on top of my head. It had to be a really special occasion for me to get the hair straighteners out and even then, I had to plead with my best friend Ruth to straighten it for me. This was done with caution, however, because Ruth could never stop at my hair, and before I knew it I would be all trussed up like a doll and feeling pretty stupid, as though I was in fancy dress ... as a drag queen.

That's unfair actually. Ruth always looks good and tries her best to guide me with my fashion choices, but I just don't feel comfortable unless I'm in jeans and a T-shirt.

My main morning problem though, came down to

motivation. I didn't want to get out of bed, especially if I'd been rudely awoken by my noisily sexually active neighbour and missed out on a large chunk of my forty winks. Usually, when I did finally crawl out, I would stand in the shower far longer than was necessary, just enjoying the water. Warming my body on cold days, cooling and refreshing me on hot ones. I loved being in water. My dream country house would have a swimming pool and a spa!

Then, after I'd showered, I liked to sit wrapped in a towel staring into space while my body dried. Perhaps it was testament to just how lazy I was that I couldn't even be bothered to dry myself and instead waited for the air around me to do its work. Perhaps in my dream house I'd have servants who dressed me.

I realised my dreams had been tainted by BBC costume dramas. Perhaps sexually I belonged to those times, but my career was far more technologically advanced and I wouldn't swap that for all the tea dances in Derbyshire.

Eventually, two hours after I'd dragged myself out of bed, I got dressed. That didn't take me very long at all; my clothes lived on the floor at my feet and I just chose something that didn't smell too bad. Then I headed out the door and was on my way to my office.

On this day, however, I wanted to make a good impression. I wanted to be the best boss in the world. But I wanted to be respected too. I had no idea how to achieve that so I decided to aim for respectable and introduce laid-back Olivia afterwards. I drew the line at wearing a suit, though. I couldn't comfortably work in a suit so I decided on smart jeans and a plain T-shirt. I wouldn't be advertising my love of *Star Wars* or *Doctor Who* or *Batman*. I would be the busy and important owner of Inspired Programming.

Chapter Two

It was no coincidence that my office, in a converted school in Camden, was within walking distance of my flat. I commuted to work for four years before I went self-employed and wasted a lot of hours that I'd never get back. I don't know how it happens, but no matter where you travel to in London, it takes an hour. I vowed that I would at least live on the same Tube line as my office but when I found this place in Camden I knew it was where I belonged. Not just the building either, but the area. Camden reaches out and spreads its feel-good vibe, infecting everyone that walks within its boundary. Once I started working there, it was only a matter of time before I lived there too.

The school closed down eight years ago and the Church put it up for sale. They were about to demolish the building after six years, intending to sell the land when Dave stepped in. He bought the building, renovated the classrooms and converted them into office and studio spaces for creative artists and organisations. There was a sense of belonging to the building; even though we were all self-employed, it somehow felt like we were a team. Unsurprisingly I often got called on to fix the computers of some of the other tenants, and I helped out occasionally with designing flyers and websites and things like that for them. I enjoyed this because those favours provided a nice distraction from the more complex projects I generally undertook.

A knock at the door signalled the arrival of my new employee and brought me out of my reverie. I stood as the door opened and started making my way towards the kitchenette.

'Hi, Steven. Come on in. Would you like a tea or coffee?'

'Hey, Olly. Tea would be great, thanks. Milk, two sugars please.' Steven replied.

Olly? That's Miss Jones to you, young man, I wanted to tell him. Or at the very least Olivia! As the kettle boiled, I watched him dump his bag on his desk and sit in the chair, leaning back comfortably and swivelling in small half-circles back and forth while he waited for me to make his drink.

He was confident and relaxed. He wore black skinny jeans and baseball boots. A waistcoat was buttoned up over a casual, plain shirt, unbuttoned at the collar. His dark hair was short at the back, trained forward at the front and was thick and messy. He looked too cool for school, a far cry from the mass media portrayal of the average computer nerd. It annoyed me slightly. I remembered James fondly, and wondered if I'd made the right decision.

I'd interviewed four people for this job. In truth, I could probably afford to hire all four of them, but I was nervous about releasing full control over the work going out under my name and I wanted to ease my way in slowly. I'd devised a small test to find out how well they worked, their attention to detail, and techniques they used. Steven was quite cocky about the test afterwards, like it was nothing to worry about, while James had been nervous and over-analysed his work. I was childishly pleased that Steven had made a small error – nothing critical, but an error all the same – but James had made an error that was actually my mistake in the test design. When I corrected it, I found James would have been right.

Steven was confident, straight out of university and his training was completely up to date. The latest techniques, the latest software; he could probably teach me a few things. He also seemed likely to be good at schmoozing customers and clients – the one area in which I did not excel. Luckily, my work stood for itself, but I was sure I could bring more clients in if I could get the networking right and I had a gut instinct that Steven would be better at it than James.

I kept James's CV, though. If I decided being an employer was OK I thought I'd bring him in. I imagined I'd need someone else in the office who was more like me; Steven might just drive me insane!

I glanced over at him while I stirred the sugar into his tea and tried to swallow the feeling of annoyance at his confidence.

'OK, so first things first, there is a café in the front of the building and they deliver lunch to all the offices in here. You just have to get your order in by 10:30 a.m. and it'll be brought around by noon,' I said as I handed Steven a menu and picked up the phone to call Steph. It was answered on the second ring.

'Stephanie's, Steph speaking.'

'Hey, Steph, it's Olivia. How are you?'

Steph was the easiest person to talk to in the world; with so many customers in her café, she got so much practice that she could win prizes for small talk.

'Hi, Olly.' Steph exclaimed, 'do you want the usual?'

My usual was Chinese chicken and salad in a tiger-bread baguette with a bag of roast beef flavour Monster Munch.

'Of course. Hey, Steph, I have a new member of staff to add to your list. Steven Teller.'

I handed the phone over to Steven, and a flicker of uncertainty crossed his face before a huge grin spread across it and he spoke confidently into the phone.

'Hi, Steph. This is Steven, how are you?' He laughed at whatever she said and he looked across at me smiling. 'Yeah, she's made me a cup of tea and everything. I thought I'd be the one making the teas around here!'

I raised my eyebrows and muttered, 'Oh you will be.'

Steven finished his lunch order and replaced the handset. He grinned at me like he knew something he shouldn't. Damn Steph, what had she told him about me?

It was not going as I'd expected. Why wasn't he more scared of me? I was the boss, for goodness' sake!

I shuffled together the papers I had in front of me and handed them to him.

'Induction pack. There are a few forms to fill in and I need your bank details for your salary. I'll leave you to it; give me a shout when you're done.'

'Sure thing,' he replied, 'I have a form for you too from the university.'

He held out a booklet towards me. Really? *He* was giving *me* work to do? This was all wrong. I could feel the crease between my eyebrows forming.

'What is it?' I asked.

'It's to do with the internship programme; they need to know that I'm fulfilling the criteria set out by the programme organisers.'

Oh yes, that was the other reason I'd chosen him. Steven was on a fast-track intern programme, which matched up suitable graduates for twelve months' work experience. The salary was part subsidised by the programme so I got him cheap. I had not realised that this would cause me more work. I really needed to get an assistant.

'So what is he like?' Ruth asked me, tucking her feet underneath her body as she curled up comfortably in my armchair that evening. She knew I was stressing out about managing someone and was eager to find out how the first day had gone.

'He's annoying,' I sighed. 'No, he's not annoying, he's just young and cocky and sure of himself.'

'Aren't those last two the same thing?'

'Cocksure? I guess so. He called me Olly.' I folded my arms across my chest defensively and frowned.

She gasped, mocking me. 'That bastard, calling you by your name.' She laughed. 'Everyone calls you Olly.' Ruth was too reasonable sometimes; always saw the good side to everyone and everything.

'Yes but you know me. He should call me Olivia, or Miss Jones even.' I stopped when I saw the smirk on Ruth's face and started laughing, 'OK, maybe not Miss Jones, but you know, it's a little familiar to go shortening people's names before you even know how they take their tea. Not one single cup of tea did he make me today, I had to make my own.'

Ruth rolled her eyes towards the ceiling. 'How is that any different from all the time you've been working for yourself?' she asked sternly.

'Ah, but now I have to make two cups! I mean what am I paying him for if not to make me my tea?' I shrugged and let out a dramatic sigh. 'I don't want to go in tomorrow.' I grumbled.

'I'm absolutely certain he's not that bad. Maybe he was just nervous and hid it behind bravado. I bet he's not as sure of himself as you think he is.'

I pondered this for a moment.

'Well I'll be nice, but it's his bloody turn to make a brew!'

'So what does he look like? Is he cute?' Ruth teased, 'Or does he look like an über-nerd?'

'I don't know, he's about twelve or something,' I gasped incredulously, 'I didn't notice whether he was attractive.' I thought about what Steven looked like, 'He's quite trendy looking; all skinny jeans and big hair. Looks more like a gig promoter than a computer geek.'

Ruth's eyes lit up as she laughed. 'He sounds pretty hot, no wonder you hate him!' She threw a cushion at me. 'You should just start being nice to him,' she added in all seriousness.

I shrugged. 'I made him four cups of tea today. If I were any nicer it would be borderline sexual harassment.'

I grinned then and she laughed, regarding me quizzically. 'What on earth is wrong with your hair?'

Chapter Three

I vowed to get over my stupid prejudice toward Steven the next day, so when he arrived I made him a cup of tea and showed him where everything was kept so he could help himself. OK, maybe I was trying to hint he should get a round in once in a while, but I did it in the name of workplace fairness, not because I resented making him a drink.

We sat down at the meeting table and I spread out a few client files.

'These are the jobs we've got booked in at the moment. They are in various stages of development with the clients. I want you to start sitting in on future meetings so you'll be in a position to work on the coding.' I pushed the files towards him, 'Have a read through them and if you have any questions give me a shout. I want to go through the new contract with you this afternoon. It's a big job, the reason I had to expand, so I want you involved from the beginning.'

There now, that wasn't so hard. No employment tribunals heading my way any time soon. I found it strange sharing my work space with someone, especially someone I hardly knew. I kept thinking he was going to get up any second, thank me for my time and leave so I could get on with my work. It's like having a visitor who doesn't know when he's outstayed his welcome. I knew I would need to find a way to feel comfortable working while someone was there. I was sure that in time, when we got used to each other, I would wonder how I ever worked alone.

The door opening signalled the arrival of lunch.

'Hey, chicken!' Steph called, a hint of laughter in her

voice.

I groaned as she started singing, 'Chick chick chick chick chicken,' and then laughed at Steven's bemused expression.

'I'm sorry, chick. Your song was just on the radio while I was making chicken butties, it got stuck!' She placed my usual lunch on my desk and wandered over to Steven to deliver his sandwich bag.

'She doesn't like to talk about her music career,' Steph whispered as she placed his food on the desk. Steven's eyebrows shot up and he turned to stare at me, torn between his own curiosity to know what she meant and Steph's warning not to ask me. He opened his mouth to speak, unsure what to say and stuttered for a while. I shook my head at Steph and then nodded towards the wall. Steven's gaze moved to, and settled on, two frames, the first setting off a computer animated character called Jerk Chicken, the second displaying a gold disc.

'You created Jerk Chicken?' he whispered.

'I'm surprised she even eats chicken any more, she's so sick of that thing!' Steph said, grinning.

'Jerk Chicken wasn't the problem – it was that stupid song. I don't know why I agreed to it.' I shook my head.

'My cousin wanted a Jerk Chicken plush toy,' Steven mumbled.

'Well there's a cupboard full of them over there. Help yourself, you'll be doing me a favour,' I laughed.

Jerk Chicken was a 3-D character I created for a project while I was in my final year at university. A slack-jawed, stupid chicken singing, "Chick chick chick chick chicken." A few years later, I uploaded it to YouTube and within a week, it had over a million views. It went viral; I even received the link myself by email on twenty-three separate occasions.

Then I got a call from a record label wanting to release a single, a dance remix with Jerk Chicken sampled throughout it. They wanted me to make a video to go with it, of course. At the time, I was in shock that my stupid university project had become so infamous, but then I received the draft contract from the record company and I couldn't believe the amount of money they were offering me. I didn't have to think long to realise I could leave my job and set up on my own, knowing this song would earn me more than enough money to live off for a few years while I was getting my business started.

As it turned out, I needn't have worried; Jerk Chicken made my CV look pretty good and work had been regularly knocking on my door since I started three years ago. But the song was everything I hated about music and it remained a constant source of embarrassment to know that all the merchandise and licensing agreements for Jerk Chicken, which earned me so much money, stemmed from that record.

Steven continued staring at me in, what was that? Awe? I felt a flush creep up over my face, which made Steph laugh as she left the office, whistling the tune to herself.

'Wow,' he said finally, 'I mean don't get me wrong, the song was awful, obviously.' I shrugged my shoulders and nodded in agreement as he continued, 'But when I first saw that YouTube video, seriously, I could not stop watching it. I can't even tell you how many people I sent that link to,' he grinned. 'Wow, I'm working for Jerk Chicken!'

'I hope that my track record following Jerk Chicken is far more impressive than my university project piece?' I scowled at him.

His eyes widened and he stopped grinning.

'Oh sure, yes of course, I mean I've played your games and they're some of the best game apps I've played,' he trailed off and I sighed.

'Yeah, but it's Jerk Chicken. I know,' I threw a plush toy at him. 'Why don't you honour your newly respected leader with a cuppa?'

'Coming right up, boss,' he grinned and bounced towards the kitchenette.

Steven placed a mug of tea and a plate of cookies in front of me and sat down. 'Homemade,' he said by way of explanation. They looked amazing – soft and chewy with big chunks of chocolate. I could feel my mouth watering and my stomach clearing a path for the inevitable influx. I mostly follow a 'seafood' diet, as in, I see food and I eat it.

'They look amazing,' I mumbled as I reached out to take one, trying to be a little calm about it and not just shovelling it into my mouth like I wanted to. The smell alone was driving me crazy; they were so fresh. I will never think badly of Steven again. I bet James wouldn't have brought these little pieces of heaven to my door.

'I made some notes about the current projects. I hope you don't mind?' Steven said, forcing me to concentrate on work and not biscuits. He pushed a sheet of paper towards me. He'd made some good points about the brief for a mobile phone app, currently unresolved between myself and my client Jack, mainly because he wanted a level of interactivity I didn't think was possible within the brief.

'It's quite a new technique that I was working on in my final project and I think it could work with this,' Steven finished up and I realised I'd missed half of what he said, but recognised he was offering a solution that would please the client. That would also mean having to hand over a large chunk of the project to Steven because I hadn't updated my skills yet. *Damn it.* I knew I was being stupid feeling resentful and even perhaps a little bit jealous, but I couldn't help it. This was my project, I'd worked hard to win it, and to hand it over to someone else made me feel inadequate. But isn't that why you hired him, I asked myself. Because his skills are completely up to date? And because I had too much work coming in to do alone. I *had* to hand some of it over. I bit into another cookie. Oh homemade cookie, I sighed inwardly, if only everything were as simple and lovely as you. I nodded at Steven.

'Congratulations, kid, you just won your first job. Can you put together a plan of how this will work, and we'll meet with Jack later this week?'

Steven stared at me, then shook himself.

'Yes, yes of course, thank you. Wow, are you sure?'

'Of course I'm sure, now take these away from me before I eat them all.' I reluctantly pushed the plate of cookies towards him and stood up.

'Do you still want to go through the new contract with me?' he asked, reminding me why we had sat down at the meeting table together. Humph! I grumped inwardly. So you can steal that away from me too?

'I do, but I'll put together an overview and email it to you tomorrow. I think if you can get your plan started this afternoon and we can go finalise it with Jack you can get cracking on this as soon as possible. I was going to have you share the new contract because I wouldn't be able to do both by myself, but if you can take this one off my hands I'll be able to do more of the new one.'

I grinned then, as I realised we were embarking on two big pieces of work at the same time: quite an achievement for a small time developer. In the past, I'd worked on a client project for six months and then worked on something of my own, dividing my time between commissions and developing something I *hoped* would sell and earn me lots of money. Taking on two clients at once was a big step, but seeing Steven's enthusiasm made me feel excited about expanding. Maybe I'd take on some more staff, after all. Someone who would make the tea, for instance!

Chapter Four

The familiar notification sound clicked on my laptop signalling an instant message. I was updating my Facebook status and accepting some friend requests. Steven had added me on Monday night but I was only just checking my account three days later. The instant message was from him, thanking me for adding him as a friend. I debated whether to reply or just ignore it. On the one hand I didn't really want my employee intruding in my life outside work, but on the other hand I didn't want to be rude. I typed, *You're welcome, see you tomorrow*, and hit enter. Then I closed my laptop and switched on the television. No doubt there would be a message waiting for me next time I logged in that I wouldn't need to reply to.

The following morning, Steph arrived early with our sandwiches and sat down on the sofa, closing her eyes for a few moments' respite from the rush of the café. Friday mornings were always busy, with everyone treating themselves to breakfast, although lunchtimes were often quiet with people going out to the market or the pub for lunch.

The office was an old infant classroom which had areas built in which would have served as a play shop or play house. There was also plumbing built in for a cleaning area for arts and craft activities, which Dave had used to build in the kitchenette.

Being on my own for so long, there was very little furniture in here other than the sofa for less formal meetings, a table for formal meetings, and a couple of desks. I had added the second desk as soon as I placed the job advert a few weeks ago. A bookcase and filing cabinet stood in the second alcove, along with the Jerk Chicken cupboard to complete the set-up.

The sofa was big, green, and swallowed you up if you sat on it for too long. It was the best sofa in the world. Cosy and warm in winter, I spent as much time as I could on the sofa under a blanket.

'We are heading to The World's End after work tonight, Steven – I hope you'll join us.' Steph informed him, opening her eyes. Steven glanced across the room to me and I shrugged.

'Friday night, drinks after work. It's sort of a thing they do,' I explained.

'You really get to know a person when you go out drinking with them, don't you agree?' Steph asked casually, 'It's a miracle we ever got to know this one of course, bloody hermit.'

'I'm not a hermit, I'm just slightly anti-social,' I corrected her. Steph snorted.

'You go home and play video games. Don't you get tired of video games?' she asked, shaking her head.

'Just checking out the competition,' I grinned at her and she sighed.

'Well now if it's work, maybe you should be playing video games during office hours,' Steph suggested.

'That is not a bad idea, especially now I've got someone else here to do all the hard work for me,' I grinned at Steven, who pulled a face at me.

Steph stood up and touched his arm.

'Come the pub,' she implored him, 'we usually head over at 4:30. Try and drag this one along with you, it's been too long since she went out and getting tipsy would do her some good.' She leant in closer to him and whispered, 'Getting laid would do her even better, but that's just my opinion.'

'I heard that, Stephanie.' I folded my arms and turned

my face away, pretending to be offended, but she laughed at me.

'You were meant to. Make sure you take your staff to the pub, don't be mean and leave him to drink with strangers. It's your duty as a good boss to get him drunk, especially on his first Friday.'

I sighed and nodded. Why not? It's been ages since I went to Friday night drinks after work. I realised it would be good to catch up with everyone and get to know Steven a bit better outside the office. Besides which, everyone knows the best times are had when you don't plan for them. I felt a flutter of excitement deep in my belly and realised I was looking forward to having a night out.

When we entered The World's End on the corner of Camden High Street the rest of the tenants were already there. They gave a cheer when we arrived and I heard lots of exclamations about how they never see me out. It was nice actually, to feel such a welcome and I wondered briefly why I didn't come out for a least one drink after work more often. Steph was probably right that it would do me good to socialise more. Ruth was always inviting me out to gigs and for drinks with her friends but I always declined. I just can't be bothered with the small talk of meeting new people and I find myself longing for my sofa and my PS3 or my DVD box sets. I felt a flush of shame as I realised that all the people sat around the table welcoming me were people I knew. Meeting people at work somehow made it easier to get to know them and I had no excuse for not socialising with them. Steven touched my arm.

'What are you drinking?' he asked, leaning in the direction of the bar. I shook my head.

'No, it's your first week, let me buy you a drink. What are you having?' He grinned happily at me and straightened himself up.

'Pint of lager would be smashing, cheers.' He made his way towards the table and I watched as Steph waved him over to a spare seat next to her. I smiled to myself. Steph clearly had a crush on Steven. I ordered our drinks and turned my attention back to them while I waited. I could see why Steph would like him; he was easy to be around. He found a common ground quickly and maintained a flow of conversation. It was hard to feel uncomfortable with Steven; there were no awkward silences. He knew when it was right to be quiet and he knew how to fill a conversational void before it became tense.

It occurred to me that despite all the easy conversations, I didn't know much about him. Well, if Steph was willing to share his attention perhaps tonight I would get to know him better. I carried our drinks over to the table and found a seat opposite Steven and Steph, pushing his drink towards him. He winked at me in gratitude. Winked! I resisted the urge to roll my eyes and tried to smother the flicker of annoyance. If I was younger than him I'd find him patronising. The fact that I'm the elder just made him irritating. I hoped that in time I would get used to his little ways and stop finding it annoying – after all he was a brilliant programmer, an excellent designer, and he was fitting in nicely around my work routine. I just wish he acted his age and treated me like I were mine.

'Not often we see you down the pub, Olly. To what do we owe the pleasure?' Dave asked, nudging me. Dave was the only person, besides Steph, that I saw on a daily basis. He was a good guy, lots of fun to be around, supportive of all his tenants, offered us all great advice. He had been particularly helpful to me in the early days when I was puzzling over the legal status of my business. I'd read so many websites talking about Companies House, directors, partnerships, and shareholders, I'd had no idea what I was doing. Dave was lying on the sofa in Reception when I arrived one morning and called me over, so I'd sat down on the sofa opposite him with a big sigh.

'That is a big sigh. What's up, Olivia Jones?' I'd told him where I was up to in getting my business off the ground which, given that I still didn't know what my legal status was, wasn't very far off the ground at all. He asked me three questions: Do you own this business? Have you put up the money to get it started? Where will the profits go? To which I'd replied, 'Yes, it's all mine, and the profits go to me to live off.' He'd shrugged and said, 'Seems to me you're a sole trader.'

This was a relief because from everything I had read online I didn't need to do anything to register as a sole trader. I could register as a limited company and be the sole director and member, but that seemed like a lot of obligatory annual paperwork for no reason. So I opened a bank account as a sole trader and got on with the important job of designing a mobile game app to introduce Inspired Programming to the world.

I grinned up at Dave, glad that he was in the pub.

'Well you know, now that I'm an employer I thought I should bring my new member of staff to the pub and introduce him to everyone properly.'

Dave smiled and nodded, and regarded me with a look of pride and winked. Dave is allowed to wink at me because he is ten years older than me and has been my mentor for several years.

'Staff, eh? Look at you!' He nudged me again and as I straightened up he threw his arm across my shoulders in a congratulatory hug. I rolled my eyes, embarrassed at the attention.

'So, Steven, how's your first week been? I hear your boss is a real bitch?' Dave grinned at me and then leant forward to focus his attention on Steven.

'Oh I wouldn't say she was a bitch, a tyrant at times

maybe, but she's OK.'

I narrowed my eyes at him in mock warning and he laughed, 'I've had a good week, I don't think I could have asked for a better first job. I think I will learn so much more from Olly than I would have learned elsewhere, much more hands on, she's already entrusted me with a big project.' He smiled at me appreciatively. Steph giggled.

'Hands on? You should tell her to keep her hands to herself!'

I raised my eyebrows at the veiled warning from Steph. As if she had anything to worry about from me – aside from the fact I'm his boss and considerably older than him, she was beautiful, funny, and easy to be around. I wouldn't have been surprised if the Monday morning gossip was that Steph and Steven ended the evening together.

Steven and Dave continued talking, about how the centre had come about and what they both wanted from the future. I decided to take a breather and made my way to the quiz machine in the corner. Steph followed me and stood watching, waiting for me to make conversation. I concentrated on the game. It was childish of me but I'd moved over here to have a much-needed moment and Steph was well aware that I required regular alone time. I glanced round at her and followed her gaze back to our table, more specifically Steven.

'He seems nice?' she said, looking up at me. 'You must love having him around the office.' I sensed this was a question rather than a statement so I shrugged again.

'It's nice to share the work load and have someone around who understands what I'm saying.'

'Is he single?'

'I have no idea. I don't actually know anything about his personal life,' I shrugged.

'What have you been talking about all week?' She asked unable to conceal her surprise.

'Work mostly. I'm not paying him to be my friend, I'm paying him to do the work I don't have time to do.' I grinned at her then, and shrugged, 'I was hoping to get to know him a little better tonight but I haven't had a chance to speak to him since we arrived.'

Her cheeks flushed with embarrassment.

'I think he's cute,' she admitted.

'No, really? Oh wow, I had no idea,' I said, my voice heavy with sarcasm. She blushed again.

'Am I that obvious?'

'Only to me, love.' I put my arm round her shoulder. 'I promise I will see what I can find out for you, OK?' She nodded, smiling as we made our way back to the table. Dave was at the bar and Steven was chatting to Tracey, a singer who ran a chain of community choirs. I felt Steph bristle next to me and I sighed as I noticed Tracey looking up at Steven through her eyelashes, smiling and playing with her hair. I groaned inwardly, realising my office was going to be like Clapham Junction, with all his admirers finding excuses to stop by. Steph sat down next to Tracey to join their conversation and Dave returned, distributing drinks around the table. He smiled as he pushed a pint my way and sat between Steph and me to listen to what Tracey was saying, still directing her words at Steven, pretending no one else was there. Steven looked up at me and grinned. He touched Tracey on the arm and said he'd catch up with her later and then he came to sit beside me on the double seat at the end of the table. He leant back and turned his head to face me.

'Hi, didn't I arrive with you?' he asked, frowning. I nodded, smiling. 'I thought I recognised you.' He indicated the rest of the table. 'These guys are cool – not as cool as you of course, but pretty cool.'

I laughed out loud.

'You don't have to sweet talk me you know. You got the job already and I have nothing more to offer you.'

'What? No! I mean it.' He grew serious. 'Honestly, I was expecting my first job to be taking notes for some guy in a suit. You are actually letting me loose on your projects, and trust me, I can deliver, I promise you, but I never imagined I'd be given the chance to prove myself so soon. That's cool, you're very cool.' He smiled shyly then smiled his wide, goofy smile. 'And let's not forget ...' he began, and I shook my head.

'I created Jerk Chicken?'

He nodded, grinning. I looked at him closely while we chatted. He really was an attractive man, and close up he didn't look that young. He had a maturity about him; perhaps he had been around older people a lot and had a more grown-up outlook. I remembered my promise to Steph and was just about to ask him when I heard him groan as he looked towards the door. I followed his gaze and saw an attractive blonde girl weaving her way through the crowd which had grown considerably since we had arrived. I was about to ask who she was when I felt his breath on my ear. I froze.

'Olly I need you to promise me something,' he said quietly. I nodded. 'If it looks likely that I'm going to leave with that girl, please, *please* stop me.'

I looked at him out of the corner of my eye and he returned my look with pleading eyes before continuing. 'I sort of knew her at uni. I worked behind the bar so pretty much everyone knew me. We bumped into each other a few weeks ago and I haven't been able to get rid of her since. She seems to know where I am all the time. I don't know how she does it but every time I go out she turns up, she somehow insists on sharing a cab and then before I know it I'm back at her place.'

'Tell her you're not interested.'

'I have, so many times.' He squeezed his eyes shut and shook his head. 'Just watch, she'll find me and I will be rude to her but she won't give up, she's as thick skinned as they come.'

'Well surely if you're not interested it should be easy to not go home with her,' I pointed out, confusion evident on my face.

He chuckled at my apparent innocence.

'If only that were true, Olly. She will wait 'til I'm drunk, she will ask to share my taxi and make me feel sorry for her. I will be adamant that I'm going home but then ...' he stopped and looked at me, his face full of shame, 'she'll put her hand down my pants and there's just no way I'm not going home with her. She says she knows I don't want her but she knows how to get me anyway.' He put his head in his hands and sighed. 'I hate it, I hate myself for it, and I just want to get away from her.' He looked back up at me, 'Please, promise me, no matter what I say, don't let me leave with her.'

'I will try my best,' I promised. He took hold of my hand and kissed it.

'Thank you.'

I heard her before I saw her again; it was a perfectly rehearsed gasp.

'Steven? Oh my God, what are you doing here?' She was smiling as she tried to squeeze past me and force herself into a non-existent space between us. She ignored me, despite half sitting on my knee, as she smiled up at him.

'Go away, Melissa,' he said irritably. I watched with interest as both Steph and Tracey became aware of Melissa. Steph took in the blonde hair, the tight top, and the cleavage and glanced down miserably at her work clothes. Tracey tried to set her delicate features to hide the distaste she felt and anyone who didn't know her would be fooled, but I could see through her frozen smile. I looked at the back of Melissa's head and listened to her pointless chatter.

'I can't believe you're here, I just decided to pop in for

a drink and see who was about. I had no idea you would be here,' she flicked her hair over her shoulder, swatting me in the face. 'I am so glad you are, though,' she murmured, looking up at him through her eyelashes. I cleared my throat.

'Excuse me, hi,' I said, smiling politely.

She turned to look at me, scowling. It wasn't an attractive look. Her face was caked in make-up and her false eyelashes had been covered with thick liner, framing her eyes and making her look like Miss Piggy.

'He's here with me tonight and we were in the middle of something, would you mind?' I raised my eyebrows questioningly and waited for her to reply. She looked me up and down slowly, her face displaying a commentary as she got the measure of me, and seeing nothing that worried her she stood up and squeezed past me again. She leant across the table to Steven.

'I'll see you later,' she whispered, blowing him a kiss as she straightened herself up and sashayed away to the bar.

Steven looked mortified so I punched him lightly on the shoulder.

'Hey, round one to us. Do you want another pint?'

I watched his face as he narrowed his eyes, watching Melissa, then he jumped to his feet, grabbing my hand.

'She just entered the ladies, can we get out of here?' he asked. 'Quick before she comes back?' he insisted.

I stood up, aware of Steph watching me, a frown on her face.

'I'll text you where we've gone. Follow us when you've finished this round, OK?' I shrugged apologetically as Steven pulled me towards the door; I kept an eye on the ladies' toilet, hoping Melissa wouldn't emerge and spot us trying to make a run for it. We stumbled out into the street and ran across the road towards Camden Town tube station and out of sight of the pub.

'She will notice as soon as she opens the toilet door,' he said, a hint of panic in his voice. 'Where can we go?'

'The Mixer?' He nodded and started running across the road towards the Good Mixer. I loved The Mixer, it had a bit of a history as a pub that cool bands had frequented.

We slipped inside, found a corner table and sank into the seats, breathing heavily. Steven looked tense but I was feeling something else, an adrenalin rush maybe, it was really quite thrilling. Running away from a stalker might sound scary but when it's not your stalker it's just fun. I thought back to my childhood nightmares of being chased by the Terminator and reasoned that this was probably like that for Steven; a relentless being with a single mission. For me it was nowhere near as frightening as being chased by a merciless android so I was finding the whole thing really quite exciting.

'Pint?' I asked standing up after my breathing had returned to normal. He nodded, watching the door in trepidation. I realised it wouldn't be that difficult to work out which pub he might have gone to, there are not that many after all. 'Tell you what, my flat is a two minute walk from here. We can go there, you can call a cab and be home long before she even comes looking for you?' I suggested.

Relief washed over his face and he nodded, smiling. I held out my hand to him and pulled him up. We must have looked like a dodgy pair sneaking out of the pub, looking all around. I was trying to take it seriously for Steven's sake but I kept pretending I was Jack Bauer, whispering, 'I'll check the perimeter, you cover me. OK it's clear, head to the next corner.' By the time we reached my flat, Steven was grinning.

'We are at the rendezvous point, location is secured.' I giggled as I unlocked the door.

'Copy that, Agent Jones.' He glanced around one last time before following me through the door.

I collapsed on the sofa, giggling. Steven stood in the doorway, watching me.

'I'm sorry Steven, I know it's not funny, it's just that –' I giggled again '– well, it sort of is funny, if you think about it. Running away from some woman because she wants to have sex with you.'

'Well I suppose when you put it like that, it must seem pretty funny,' he agreed, 'but she's relentless. I just want her to leave me alone. I mean, can you imagine me trying to actually meet someone with that constantly turning up all the time? She'd scare everyone away until there was only her left.'

I wandered into the kitchen, grabbed a couple of beers from the fridge and sat back down on the sofa.

'She was pretty, though. I mean, crazy stalker tendencies aside, why aren't you into her?' I asked, curious.

Steven took a long drink of his beer and sighed, wiping the back of his hand across his mouth. He leant back into the sofa and looked at me.

'I'm a nerd, Olly. I did a degree in video game programming, I take computers apart for fun, I have the entire DVD collection of *Star Trek* and I sometimes sit around my house wearing a Stormtrooper helmet,' he explained.

'I can see why she likes you so much, you are a catch.' I clinked my bottle against his and took a sip. He pulled his tongue at me and I realised he thought I was teasing him, when I was actually being serious. Best not to think about that too much, Olivia Jones.

'It's a bit different at uni – you start off living in a student house or halls with a random set of people and it doesn't matter what you study, you just bond over the shared experience. I also worked behind the bar at the student union so everyone knew me without knowing I was this big nerd. And then someone in their wisdom decided to make The Doctor all handsome and sexy and easily accessible to a mainstream audience. For the first time in my life, no one was calling me a speccy twat any more. All these apparently popular girls were hanging around the computer rooms looking for their latest fashion accessory to hang off their arm.'

'OK, but that doesn't explain why we're sneaking round the streets of Camden trying to lose a girl who's apparently really into you.'

'She knew me from the student union, and she had a thing for me, that's all. But she was studying fashion design, she likes Take That, she watches *The X Factor*.' He paused to check my reaction. I nodded. 'You see? I can't have a conversation with her, we have nothing in common; she wants to be out partying every night, she wants to be meeting celebrities. I want to play video games and drink in old man pubs. Do you want to know what my fantasy is?' he asked suddenly. I raised my eyebrows and shrugged, inviting him to continue. 'I fantasise about having a girlfriend who opens her door to me on a Saturday night and says, "You know, I don't really feel like going out tonight, can we just stay in and play *Lego Batman*?"'

I glanced sideways at the *Lego Batman* cover on the coffee table and laughed.

'Wow, I actually *am* spending this Saturday night playing *Lego Batman*, and that is why I don't have a boyfriend. You know, if you were a few years older I'd probably be stalking you myself!' I smirked at him.

'If you spent your weekends playing video games you wouldn't have to stalk me.' He looked at me then, a small smile tugging at the corner of his mouth, his eyes exploring my face. I felt a prickling sensation creeping up the back of my neck as his words sunk into my mind. Shit, he was going to try to kiss me. I started to panic and, breaking away from his gaze, I pushed myself off the sofa and busied myself in the kitchen, pouring a glass of water and wiping down the sink. He watched me for a few minutes before joining me in the kitchen.

'Is it my age?' he asked.

'I'm sorry?' I feigned ignorance at his question, but my heart rate increased slightly. Were we really having this conversation? I supposed it was better now so we could pretend we didn't remember it when the hangover kicked in. Monday was going to be awkward.

'Cards on the table time, Ols. I like you, you're cool, you're funny, beautiful, nerdy, you don't over-think things, except maybe now you're definitely over-thinking whether or not you should let me kiss you.' He smiled and moved closer to me, raising his hand to touch my face.

I closed my eyes, fighting the urge to go with the moment and sink into his arms. I took a deep breath and using all the resistance I could muster, I stepped away from him and refilled my glass with water. I searched his face as I drank it down slowly, deliberately stalling before I had to speak. His face betrayed no feeling of disappointment or rejection. He was smiling, the confidence of youth, I suppose. Perhaps in his mind it was a foregone conclusion that something would happen, but what? What was he expecting, a one night stand with his boss? A relationship?

I wiped the back of my hand across my mouth and took a slow deep breath.

'It's not just your age. I'm your boss, I hardly know you yet – how do I know you're not angling for a sexual harassment suit, to put me out of business and skip off with all my clients?'

He stared at me, his confident air visibly shaken. I don't think I'd hit a nerve; he was genuinely shocked at my suspicion. I felt guilty.

'I'm just saying, we haven't known each other long enough to be more than just work colleagues yet,' I explained.

'If I didn't work for you, if you had just met me tonight and everything that followed still happened, would you be kissing me right now?'

Yes! My shoulder sagged and I sighed. I closed my eyes and covered my mouth with my hand before nodding my head. I heard him exhale and opened my eyes, regarding him sadly. I felt bad, had I offended him? Was he upset? Was Monday morning going to be the most awkward day in the history of office experiences? He looked like he wanted to say something but changed his mind, shrugging instead.

'Thanks for tonight, I owe you one. Can you call me a cab?'

I nodded and picked up the phone, relieved he was leaving. I wanted to think over all his comments and everything I'd learned about him. I was feeling confused about Steven; one minute he was annoying me, the next he was making me laugh. He was too young and yet he always behaved older. I fought an urge to reach over and run my fingers through his hair.

'Ten minutes,' I told him as I settled down next to him again on the sofa, the moment long past when I feared he might kiss me. Did I want him to kiss me? *Maybe.* No, my explanation was valid, not that I'd thought about it before I said it, it just came to mind in the moment, but it was a worry all the same. I wanted to get back to the easy conversation we were enjoying before all this. I didn't want him leaving in a bad mood, worrying about facing each other at work on Monday.

'So why don't you take Melissa to your place and let her see your true nerd? Maybe that will put her off once and for all,' I suggested.

He contemplated my suggestion but dismissed it.

'I don't think she cares about talking. I think she wants the arm candy.' He grimaced and shook his head. 'I can't believe I'd even qualify as arm candy. It's bad enough that The Doctor became a poster pin-up, but since when did nerds become sexy?'

'Nerds have always been sexy. Just because the non-nerds have only just realised it doesn't mean we weren't all aware of it already.'

He clinked his bottle against mine.

'You are so right!' He grinned. 'So I assume you're partial to a nerd yourself then? Come on, Ols, what's your story, what do you go for?' I felt my cheeks flush and he laughed. 'Come on, I won't tease you. I promise.' I shook my head and he was distracted by a car horn beeping outside.

'Ah your taxi awaits. Do you want me to go sweep the perimeter, make sure she didn't track us here?' I offered.

Steven laughed and shook his head, following me to the door. We descended the stairs and I held open the door to the street, waving at the taxi to let him know we were there. Steven threw his arms round me and squeezed me.

'Thanks for tonight, Olly, and thanks for hiring me.' He walked backwards down the path, pointing at me. 'Best. Boss. Ever!' He grinned, 'Oh and I will find out who your dream man is.' He waved out of the window of the cab and was gone.

I walked back into my flat and filled another glass with water. I leant against the sink looking at the fridge, and smiled at the picture of the current Doctor – David Tennant. Good job Steven didn't see that, he'd be most disappointed. Shaking my head again, I turned off the light and went to bed.

Chapter Five

'It was a disaster!' I exclaimed the next day when Ruth arrived for lunch, eager to hear about Friday night drinks and how I had survived the first week with an employee.

'Is that arsehole still calling you by your name?' she teased.

I felt a flush of shame at how I had described Steven on Monday – after last night I felt very differently toward him.

I told Ruth about the night; Steph and her attempt to claim him, Melissa, hiding in The Mixer before making a dash for home. I smiled to myself as I recalled us pretending to be secret agents. I told her everything I had learned about Steven, skipping over the brief moment when I thought I might want him to kiss me. She wasn't fooled though, she could see through me like my skin and skull were made of glass.

'So not an irritating little shit anymore?' she asked, regarding me with a knowing look. 'He sounds pretty awesome actually. Tall, dark, handsome, wants to stay in with you and play video games.' She raised her eyebrows questioningly and I shook my head.

'You're forgetting young, annoying, and my employee,' I said, ticking them off on my fingers. She rolled her eyes as I continued. 'Besides which, he seemed pretty scornful of women who fancy David Tennant and let's face it, I'm a big fan of DT.' I pulled my mouth down into a grimace and shook my head. 'And let's not forget that I was very drunk last night, so anything I thought I might be feeling was just down to alcohol and I'm just glad I was sensible enough to make sure nothing happened,' I finished, remembering his intense gaze after he said I wouldn't have to stalk him and feeling my cheeks flush. Ruth narrowed her eyes at me.

'There's a small part of you that is vaguely interested though, isn't there? Come on, Jones, admit it.'

I closed my eyes and sighed.

'I'll admit to being a little confused,' I said, raising my hand holding my thumb and forefinger a centimetre apart. 'A little,' I stressed.

She grinned at me, bouncing on the balls of her feet in excitement.

'A little confused is good, it's been too long since you had even a vague interest in a real human being.' She took in my expression and saw I disagreed. 'No, Olly, TV characters do not count as real people, nor do the actors playing them. Whatever you day-dream about, I can assure you that Alexander Skarsgård is not going to bump into you in the corridor outside your office and fall madly in love with you.'

'You know stranger things have happened,' I sulked.

'But that won't,' she said firmly. 'Olly, the point still remains. Even being a little confused about Steven is a good sign; you're returning to the real world after your disappointingly doomed romance with Brian.'

I winced. I hated talking about Brian. I don't know what I was thinking when I got involved with him. We had been hanging out with each other since we were kids, grown up together; he was like a brother to me. When we both returned to London from university, things were a bit different, we'd both changed and it became obvious that he found me attractive. I didn't feel the same way at all but he was still my favourite person to be around. I continued spending all my spare time with him until it became clear I had to make a choice between leading him on and being with him. I guess he had reached an age at which he had no interest in just being friends with a girl.

The first time he kissed me was quite nice actually; I had realised that not having him around was worse than kissing him. But then naturally he expected more. The first time we had sex was a disaster, I was nervous about him seeing me naked after all these years and I actually had no desire to see him naked.

The whole thing was messy. I found excuses not to have sex; headaches, periods, whatever I could think of. We only actually had sex when I was very drunk. I feared I was stuck in this relationship, because we were friends, we had so much history, our parents were friends and ecstatic that we were together, talking about our families merging. It was too much pressure and whenever I imagined the future, I felt depressed. In the end I broke up with him and I haven't seen him since.

'You know you shouldn't have taken it to heart what he said?' Ruth was telling me. 'He was just upset and wanted to hurt your feelings, and besides which even if what he said was true, it's only because you didn't fancy him.'

'He said I was as passionate as a wet lettuce,' I laughed, 'and that he got more enthusiasm from a blow-up doll.' I offered a small smile.

'Wow, do men really use blow-up dolls?'

'Would it surprise you if Brian did?' I asked, shrugging.

She considered the question and shook her head.

'Nope, he always was a bit of a perv, wasn't he?'

I laughed. This was the first real conversation I'd had about Brian in five years and it was making me feel much better.

'He also said I could stand to lose more than a few pounds,' I said, frowning.

'Like he could talk!' she snorted in my defence. Bless Ruth; she always knew what to say.

'Well maybe back then he was just being a dick, but if he saw me now, blimey he'd be relieved at his lucky escape, I think.'

I was aware that my sedentary lifestyle had resulted in my belly becoming a little soft around the edges. I had lost so many hours of my life to video game programming and playing that most days I ordered takeaway and forgot to exercise. I hadn't weighed myself but I definitely had to wear bigger clothes these days.

I looked at Ruth and took in her figure. At 5'4, she was petite, her waist was not much bigger than my thigh, and she was dressed immaculately, nails perfectly manicured and her strawberry-blonde hair hung in soft curls across her shoulders.

'You just need to wear the right clothes, Olly. You cover yourself up in big baggy ones. You want to show off your figure a bit more.'

'You mean my big belly and my fat arse? I stick out at the front and I stick out at the back. I look like a duck,' I moaned.

'You do not look like a duck.' She laughed. 'Right, come on, we are going shopping.'

'I hate shopping,' I groaned.

'I know you do, and that's why you slob about in oversized hoodies. Come on, we'll get you something nice to wear on Monday.'

'What's happening on Monday?' I asked, searching my memory for any plans I'd made.

'Your hot new employee will be sitting in your office all day long and you want to give him no reason to be looking at Steph or thinking about Melissa,' she grinned at me, excited about dressing me up. I sensed this was going to be both embarrassing and expensive.

'No,' I shook my head, 'I don't want to play dress-up for Steven, it's ridiculous. I'm his boss. I'm older than him, and even if I did find myself a teensy weensy bit attracted to him, I doubt he would be attracted to me because I'm his boss, I'm older than him, and my arse is twice the size of his.'

'We are going to make your arse look fantastic. He won't be able to keep his eyes off it,' she grinned.

'I doubt he could keep his eyes off it now, it's so big it's always there intruding into his field of vision,' I laughed. 'Seriously, Ruthie, I don't want to attract this guy, I want to bury any small attraction I might have and concentrate on maintaining a good professional relationship.'

Ruth's face fell, disappointed, and I felt guilty.

'OK how about this – you can take me shopping, on the condition we get lunch in Burger King?' I offered.

Ruth wrinkled her nose in disgust but after some consideration she nodded.

'And I don't want anything that is designed to make me attract someone I don't want to attract,' I warned her. 'Deal?'

'Fine, deal.' She widened her eyes, innocently, 'besides, whether we are trying to attract anyone or not I'm going to make you look hot. The sexy older boss lady.' She grinned, waggling her eyebrows at me.

The shopping trip was as expensive as predicted but I had to admit, some of the clothes I had bought were nice. Ruth had made me try on things that I wouldn't have dreamed of trying, but she was right about everything she suggested. A larger dress size meant I had no unattractive bits of flesh hanging over the top of my jeans. She found trousers with a high waist and a control panel that gave the illusion of a flattened stomach, and she made the most of my otherwise hourglass figure with T-shirts that hugged my sides, drawing the eye away from the belly and focusing on the waist. All in all I was impressed. I looked nice without looking like I'd made an effort to dress up. Most of the T-shirts were superhero related, but rather than my oversized men's sizes she had insisted on the ladies' sizes, emphasising the shape of my breasts and waist. Even though the dress size had increased I still looked good. I was pleased. So at least the packaging looked good. As long as no one peeked inside!

Ruth was inspecting my wardrobe, throwing items on the bed she wanted me to throw away and replace with the new clothes. I eyed the pile as it grew, knowing that, as soon as she left, most of it would go back in the wardrobe.

'So do you have any photos of Steven?' she asked. 'Is he on Facebook?'

'Yes he is – actually I accepted a friend request from him on Thursday.'

I retrieved my laptop from the lounge and settled back on the bed. I pulled up his Facebook profile and turned the screen towards her. She whistled through her teeth.

'Jesus, he's pretty cute,' she agreed. 'How do you concentrate?'

I laughed.

'Well up until last night I just thought he was highly annoying and hadn't really thought about him being cute,' I sighed, 'and I don't intend to think of him as cute. He's just Steven, someone I pay to do the work I can't do. I have a responsibility towards his wellbeing in the workplace but other than that I have no interest in his life outside of the office.'

'Yeah OK,' Ruth replied, her voice heavy with sarcasm. 'He's posted something on your wall, by the way.'

I turned the screen back to me and looked at his profile. His last activity was a comment on a photo I had been tagged in. I clicked on the image link and recognised a photo Steph had taken of all the tenants around the table in The World's End. I smiled at his comment: *Really nice to meet everyone last night, I love my job!* I clicked on my notifications link and clicked through each one. I'd been tagged in several photos from the pub, including one of me and Steven on the double seat at the end of the table, laughing together. If I remembered correctly, he had just told me I was cool.

I noticed a couple of comments underneath the photo. One was from a guy called Chris Knight, which said *Wow, Steven, who is this beautiful lady?* I felt a blush creep over my cheeks and moved to the next comment from Steven that said *She's my boss, Olivia.* I felt a stab of disappointment that he didn't describe me as anything other than his boss. Clearly, whatever had passed between us last night had been down to alcohol or just my imagination. Another comment followed from Chris Knight. *Wow, she's cute, how do you get any work done?* I smiled – that's what Ruth said about Steven. I looked for a response from Steven but there wasn't any. I sighed.

'Well forget Steven, I have another admirer!' I smiled smugly and pushed the laptop to Ruth. She read the comments and raised her eyebrows at me.

'I wonder if Chris is as cute as his friend?' I pressed my finger to my lip in mock contemplation, wondering what I wanted him to look like. 'He has no photos!' she exclaimed. 'Who has a Facebook profile with no photos? That's weird.'

'He's a vampire!' I laughed. 'Or maybe his profile is private.'

'You have a friend request,' she said, pushing the laptop back to me. 'Who's it from?' she asked when she saw my surprised expression.

'Chris Knight,' I laughed, 'should I accept?' I was dubious about accepting a friend request from a stranger who had just posted a comment on my photo. It felt predatory but I also felt quite excited that someone was attracted to me. I reasoned that it was harmless enough, an anonymous person in cyber space. Besides which, he was a friend of Steven, not a complete stranger.

'Yes! Even if it's just to see his photos!' Ruth was

bouncing on the bed in excitement, all her earlier thoughts of Steven dismissed in light of a new interest, one who wasn't my employee.

I clicked accept, and shut the laptop.

'Well look at you, putting yourself out there!' she laughed. 'Good job we went shopping!'

Chapter Six

My phone buzzed later that evening with a notification from Facebook. I flipped open my laptop and logged in. Steven had posted another comment in answer to Chris on the photo of us. It said: *Yeah she is pretty awesome.* I felt my heartbeat quicken and my cheeks flush. I was about to close the lid again when a chat message popped up from Chris Knight.

Chris Knight: *Hi Olivia Jones, thanks for adding me.*

I was curious about this guy. Why had he added me in the first place, what was his connection to Steven, could I find out more about Steven through Chris? I decided to reply.

Olivia Jones: *No worries. I'm curious, though, why did you add me?*

Chris Knight: *Because you're very attractive and Steven says you're pretty cool. And because there's no such thing as strangers, only friends we haven't yet met!*

That made me smile. My mum had a decorative wall plate with that same statement written on it. I had always thought it was a nice sentiment.

Olivia Jones: *That photo caught me in a good light, I'm really not attractive at all.*

Chris Knight: *So modest. But I wouldn't expect anything less. Steven said you are a bit of a hermit, seems a shame to deprive the world of your beauty.*

Olivia Jones: **Sticks two fingers down throat* Whatever! If you want to believe I'm beautiful you feel free. God knows no one who actually meets me thinks that.*

Chris Knight: *That simply is not true. Steven finds you very attractive.*

My face flushed and my heart thudded loudly in my chest. *Really?*

Olivia Jones: *Steven likes that I created Jerk Chicken, that doesn't mean I'm beautiful.*

Chris Knight: *Well beauty is in the eye of the beholder, you should just accept it if someone finds you attractive. I bet you don't fancy all the same blokes your mates fancy, do you? But they like them, just like men find you attractive even if you don't think you are worth it.*

Olivia Jones: *Wow, look at you, Mr Maturity!*

Chris Knight: *I've had enough years' experience – I'm 32.*

Hot older man? I don't know why I suddenly hoped he was attractive, not like it would make any difference. I frowned at his profile photo – a cartoon drawing of a weightlifter.

Olivia Jones: *Oh fair enough, then, I suppose you know what you're talking about. I suppose you got your education from the university of life and all that nonsense?*

Chris Knight: *Actually, I'm at university at the moment, as a mature student of course. That's how I know Steven.*

Olivia Jones: *So you're in Edinburgh, then? Are you a fellow nerd?*

Chris Knight: *I am indeed in Edinburgh but I'm no nerd. I'm studying law. Can you be a law nerd? I shared a house with Steven until he moved to London this summer.*

He would definitely have some stories to tell about Steven if he lived with him.

Olivia Jones: *I see, so I guess you know him pretty well then? Anything you care to share with me?*

Chris Knight: *Ha! What happens at uni stays at uni. ;) Besides, I'm more interested in hearing stories about you.*

Olivia Jones: *I imagine you've probably heard everything you need to know about me from Steven. There's really not much more to tell. I'm really pretty dull.*

Chris Knight: *Steven doesn't seem to think you're dull.*

Olivia Jones: *Steven is a nerd; he's straight out of a computer games design degree and his ambition is to do what I've done. I'd be offended if he wasn't at least a little impressed by me, but I'm really only of interest to a small minority of people.*

Chris Knight: *I loved that Jerk Chicken video by the way.*

Olivia Jones: **rolls eyes**

Chris Knight: *Haha! Steven said you would do that!*

Olivia Jones: *He's learning!*

Chris Knight: *Right, on that note I will let you get back to your Saturday evening. Any plans?*

Olivia Jones: *I'm playing* Lego Batman *on the PS3.*

Chris Knight: *On a Saturday night?*

Olivia Jones: *Told you I was dull ;)*

Chris Knight: *Hmmm I think there's more to you, Olivia Jones. I look forward to finding out what makes you tick!*

Olivia Jones: *I think you will be disappointed, sir.*

Chris Knight: *We shall see. Speak to you soon, Liv.*

I felt a stab of disappointment that the short conversation had ended, but I had a feeling I'd be hearing from him again. I wonder what he means about finding out what makes me tick. I shook my head smiling to myself and switched on the PS3.

Chapter Seven

All too soon, the weekend was over and I found myself opening up the office at 9 a.m. Having staff had certainly made my timekeeping more consistent. Steven was an early bird, or maybe he was just making a good impression. I yawned loudly as I made a mental note to speak to him about his preferred start time. I'd certainly like an extra hour in bed!

His voice interrupted my thoughts, making me jump.

'That was a big yawn. Must've been a good weekend?' There was a hint of teasing in his voice, mixed with surprise. I shook my head.

'Whatever impression I gave you last week, I'm not a morning person. I usually roll in at 10 a.m. at the earliest. The joy of being the boss!' I smirked.

'Well you never did tell me a start time, I just assumed it was 9 a.m. I would be more than happy to come in at 10 a.m.,' he suggested, almost pleaded.

I bristled slightly with annoyance that he was trying to set a later start time and then scolded myself. Be nice, Olivia Jones. You already decided you wanted him to come in later. I swallowed my irritation and reminded myself that Steven didn't annoy me any more; maybe I should just give him a key to open up? I couldn't decide whether I was ready to trust him with keys to the building. Maybe in a few weeks.

'Yeah, good plan. Starting tomorrow!' I made my way to the kitchenette to make a cup of tea and settled on the sofa.

'Come sit for a minute,' I called over before he sat down at his desk. He wandered over and took the proffered mug of tea from me. He looked wary as he sat down; perhaps he thought I might say something about Friday night. Maybe he thought I was going to kiss him. *Ha! As if!*

'Good weekend?' I asked, much to his visible relief.

'Yes, it was good. Quiet after Friday night. Wow those guys sure can drink. I expected Friday night drinks after work to finish by seven; there's some serious drinking going on there, does that happen every week?' I nodded and he whistled through his teeth, then grinned. 'Good, I enjoyed it. And why not finish off a hard-working week with a few beers? Will you come again?'

'Oh, I don't usually bother with all that,' I waved my hand dismissively.

'But you had a good time?' he asked insistently.

'Well yes, I did, although the best bit was sneaking home pretending to be secret agents!'

He laughed at the memory.

'You did me a huge favour helping me hide from Melissa, thanks,' he said warmly.

'No worries. I saw Steph's photos on Facebook.'

Steven's cheeks flushed slightly and I wondered if he was embarrassed by his comments about me.

'That Chris guy sent me a friend request,' I added. He didn't seem too surprised by that.

'Chris spends a lot of time online, he likes to add to his ever-expanding network of friends. Plus, he will want to see more pictures, check if you're as hot as he thought you were in that photo!'

'Well I expect he will be disappointed then. We had a brief chat actually, he seems interesting.' It was more of a question than a statement. It suddenly seemed important to me that Steven had a good opinion of him.

'Yeah he's great; I lived with him at uni. I grew up a lot when he moved in.'

I noticed the tone of his voice, telling me he was more

mature than his years, not that his age was my only issue. My mind returned to Monday morning and a thought occurred to me;

'Oh shit, I forgot to text Steph, she's going to be so mad at me.' I looked up at him thoughtfully and smiled my brightest smile. 'Can you do me a favour?'

'Anything, Ols. You're the boss remember?' he teased.

'OK, well I was meant to text Steph, let her know where we had gone to on Friday night. I forgot. Thing is, she's a bit into you so she might think I took you away to keep you all to myself or something.'

A small smile twitched at the corner of his mouth, his eyes warm with contained laughter.

'But I didn't tell you that, obviously,' I flushed. 'So anyway, she's going to be mad, can you phone up the lunch order? She won't be mad at you, tell her what happened and get me off the hook too if you can?'

'How much to tell though? Will she still be mad at you if she knows it's you I want, not her?'

My eyes widened and I froze. No! He didn't just say that out loud? I blinked and he laughed.

'Relax, Ols, it's not a big deal. I like you, if you don't feel the same or feel some need to deny you feel the same, that's cool. I know I need to prove myself to you.'

I didn't know what to say so I nodded and, pushing myself up off the sofa, I made my way to my desk. I needed to get an office built in; I didn't think I could cope sharing a room with Steven. I listened in while he made the lunch order to Steph. By the end of the conversation, he was laughing and I knew I was off the hook. He didn't tell her he tried to kiss me of course, he's not stupid and he knows the extra generous portion sizes are because of her attraction to him and the hope of something more. I still couldn't believe he was so open about his feelings, but then I reasoned; he is a nerd, and nerds do deal in facts and evidence. His feelings were out in the open and he knew where he stood, no confusion, no distractions. I envied him his simple outlook. He seemed content, not in the least bit embarrassed or upset by my rejection. He was sure enough of something between us that he felt able to wait around for me to trust him. Could I trust him? Or was this just part of his long game? This was a problem of being self-employed, no one to ask about the rules. If I had a boss above me I could go and talk to my boss, be open about it, and just see what happened. Maybe I just need witnesses. Should I take on more staff? Could I cope with that many people? Yes if I had my own office!

My mind started drifting, picturing myself in a little office, comfy swivel chair, sturdy desk with a new iMac. A name plate on the door. Staff working in the open-plan office outside. Steven walking in, locking the door behind him and striding across the room, kissing me, laying me across the desk …

'Ols, you're doing it again.' Steven's voice broke through my thoughts, bringing me back to reality.

'What?' I asked, slightly disoriented and disturbed by the direction my mind had gone.

'Staring at me. You can't tell me you don't want me then sit staring at me longingly,' he teased. How is he so comfortable talking about this, I wondered. He grinned at my obvious discomfort. 'May I inquire as to what you were thinking?' My face reddened, causing him to laugh. 'Must've been something good. Were you thinking about me kissing you?' he asked hopefully. *Bingo!* I frowned and shook my head and he pretended to look disappointed. I scrabbled about in my mind for a subject.

'I was thinking about Edinburgh …' I said. *Oh really, Olivia Jones, and what about Edinburgh were you thinking?* 'There's a conference there in a few months, networking, workshops, latest developments, that sort of thing. I thought you might like to go? You'll be great at the networking, I'm not very good at it at all, and it's about time we got out there.' Really? A conference? Where had that come from?

'You'd let me loose as the representative of Inspired?' he smiled. 'That is very trusting of you.' There was a note of sarcasm to his teasing voice as he emphasised the word 'trusting'.

'I'm trying,' I said quietly, and his face grew serious. He smiled and nodded.

'Sounds great, I can show you all my old uni haunts.'

I shook my head.

'No I'm not going. I never go to these things. One of the reasons I hired you was to go to these events for me. Use that abundance of charm you've got and win us some more clients.'

He looked disappointed. Maybe he thought he could sneak into my hotel room late at night and seduce me. A tingle ran down my spine and I felt a flush of heat through my lower body. I couldn't believe this was happening to me, this was not helping me forget about him. How was I going to maintain a professional relationship if my body kept betraying me like this?

'OK,' he replied, shrugging his shoulders and returning his attention to his monitor, 'if you're sure you can trust me to represent you in your absence.'

I watched him for a moment. I couldn't work out if he was irritated or amused by the conversation. I realised I was sending out mixed messages. What was I thinking? One minute I'm telling him I'm scared he's plotting to sue me for sexual harassment so he can ruin my business and steal my customers, and the next I'm inviting him to go off to conferences to meet potential clients. Well if the former turned out to be true then the latter was just me handing my business to him on a plate.

Edinburgh. What was I thinking? Of all the things I could've said. I should have just said, 'Yes, I think about you kissing me all the time,' in a sarcastic tone of voice.

Chapter Eight

That evening I was wrapped up in my dressing gown, fluffy slipper boots, and a blanket. I opened up the laptop and did a search for some programming conferences. The idea had occurred to me after I'd mentioned Edinburgh. Part of my reason for hiring Steven was to network, despite my earlier reservations I knew deep down he wasn't out to get me. While I still found it hard to believe that he would be attracted to me considering my age and appearance, I didn't really believe he was trying to sabotage my business and steal my clients. The truth of the matter was that I found his presence distracting, he was very present in the room – even when he was quietly working away I was aware of him and I couldn't concentrate. I would need a long-term solution of course, but perhaps sending him off to conferences would at least give me some respite in the office.

As I was searching, a Messenger window popped up. I haven't used Messenger for a long time; I'd forgotten I was even logged in.

Chris Knight: *Good Evening, Liv. How was your weekend?*

Olivia Jones: *It was wonderfully quiet. I completed the story mode of* Lego Batman.

Chris Knight: **shakes head* You should get out more. Pretty girl like you should be going out and meeting people, not hiding away behind a video game.*

Irritation shot through me. Who was he to tell me how I should be spending my time? I thought about ignoring him – he clearly had nothing of interest to say to me and I had better things to do than justify my lifestyle to him. I continued browsing the web, making a note of conferences and upcoming event dates. The message icon started flashing again.

Chris Knight: *Sorry, did I offend you?*

Chris Knight: *I used to moan at Steven all the time for wasting his life playing video games. If he wasn't doing his college work or working at the bar he was playing games. I just didn't get it. I still don't. But he seems to be making a living from it as, of course, do you. So who am I to judge?*

Olivia Jones: *You probably wonder why I would spend my weekend playing video games after spending all my week working on them?*

Chris Knight: *Well yes. Where's the social life? You have to enjoy yourself too, can't be working all the time.*

Olivia Jones: *I got into programming because I loved playing video games. I wanted to know how they worked and I wanted to create things that addressed all the complaints I had about other video games. But I still love playing them, and it's hard to play a game you've created yourself; there is no excitement, no surprises, and no puzzles to solve. I spend my week working on a game and then I relax by playing something someone else created, I get the all-round experience.*

Chris Knight: *Sounds like something Steven would say! I guess you two are all-round video game nerds!*

I smiled at that – partly I liked that he had thrown us together as a pair, but partly I liked that he understood our passion for video games.

Chris Knight: *I do have one question though, if I may?*

Olivia Jones: *I assume I'm going to hate this question, the fact you've sought my permission to ask it. But go ahead.*

Chris Knight: *When was the last time you had a boyfriend or went on a date?*

It took me a while to respond, not because I didn't want

to answer but because it had been such a long time that I'd been on a date it took me a while to remember.

Olivia Jones: *My last relationship ended five years ago.*

Was it really that long? What had I been doing with my time?

Chris Knight: *Are you serious? Why? The men in London can't be that bad?*

Olivia Jones: *I really like the way you assume it's because I'm picky and not because there's something wrong with me.*

Chris Knight: *Well I can see there is nothing wrong with you; you're smart, you run your own business, successfully I might add, you seem to be quite witty, and your pictures suggest you're very attractive. I should definitely say it is an error on the part of the male population that you haven't been snapped up.*

Olivia Jones: *I suppose it would help if I didn't stay home playing games and watching TV though.*

Five years? It has been a long time.

Chris Knight: *So the question now is: why? I don't think it's just because you're too busy. Do you have to be that busy?*

Olivia Jones: *I guess when I first started my business I spent my days programming and my evenings trawling through business stuff. It was necessary, but now I spend my evenings watching TV because I like it and my weekends playing video games because I like it. I prefer staying in than going out.*

Chris Knight: *Aren't you lonely though?*

Olivia Jones: *Well I have been thinking about getting a cat.*

Chris Knight: *So you are lonely then?*

Olivia Jones: *I don't know, I didn't think so. My best friend Ruth comes over a few nights a week, I'm not a total hermit.*

Chris Knight: *Well that's a relief. So when was the last time you had sex, then?*

What? I couldn't believe he just asked that. I also couldn't believe I was replying, but I knew the answer would be a shock and it made me giggle anticipating his reply.

Olivia Jones: *About five-and-a-half years ago.*

Chris Knight: *How long were you with your ex?*

Olivia Jones: *About eight months.*

Chris Knight: *And for the last six months of that you didn't have sex?*

Olivia Jones: *Nope.*

Chris Knight: *Jeez, what was wrong with that guy? If you were mine I'd be ripping your clothes off every chance I got.*

I felt my cheeks flush. My body wasn't used to all this sexual excitement that seemed to have been awakened since the weekend and the slightest thing was setting me off. *It really has been a long time!*

Olivia Jones: *I didn't want him to. That was the problem. And after that ended I lost my confidence and by the time it was making a return I'd started* Inspired *and was too busy to think about it.*

Chris Knight: *Wow. So what was the problem? Why didn't you want to sleep with him?*

Olivia Jones: *Too much history I guess. We had been friends forever and it just never quite felt right being with him, not sexually anyway. I guess while I loved him as my longest, oldest friend, I just wasn't physically attracted to him. I thought maybe the friendship part was enough but in the end I realised I wanted a full relationship, sex and all.*

Chris Knight: *Quite right too, sex is great.*

Olivia Jones: **rolls eyes**

Chris Knight: *Lol but it's true, it's a big part of expressing your love and it feels good and it's something* *that should be shared with someone you love. Sex can be amazing but you need to trust someone to put yourself in their hands, so to speak, to be able to let yourself go, give yourself over to the wild abandonment required in the pursuit of sexual pleasure. So it's right you should end a relationship with a guy you don't feel you want to have sex with. You'd be giving up a huge part of your life otherwise. Poor guy, I bet he was gagging. I almost feel sorry for him.*

Olivia Jones: *Well he got his own back. He was pretty cruel at the end; caused me to lose my self-confidence and probably explains why it has been five years.*

Chris Knight: *What did he say?*

Olivia Jones: *Told me I needed to lose weight and that he hadn't fancied me anyway – sort of tried to make it sound like he was the one not having sex with me, despite the obvious attempts he had made. I guess he was just trying to make me feel the way he was feeling; rejected, unattractive. But he's pretty thick-skinned so he got over it and moved on. I didn't. I comfort ate, got really fat, and now I wouldn't dream of getting naked in front of someone – which kind of hinders the libido somewhat.*

Chris Knight: *Turn the lights off. Wear a skirt and just remove your pants. You don't have to get naked, Liv, to have sex.*

Olivia Jones: *I don't know what to do either; he said I was rubbish in bed.*

Chris Knight: *Of course you were – you had no desire for him, no passion towards him. That doesn't mean you won't be excited and passionate with the next guy. What do you fantasise about?*

This guy has no boundaries; I can't believe he's asking me this stuff.

Olivia Jones: *Erm, celebrities I guess. I have a bit of a crush on The Doctor.*

That was an understatement!

There was a long pause before Chris replied,

Chris Knight: *OK so imagine you're in bed with David Tennant.*

Olivia Jones: *No!*

Chris Knight: *Why not?*

Olivia Jones: *It's weird, he's The Doctor. He's family friendly, rated U. It's morally wrong.*

Chris Knight: *OK just imagine you're in bed with someone you fancy. Then compare it to how you felt in bed with your ex. I bet there is a world of difference.*

I giggled to myself as I tried to imagine myself in bed with someone; trying to stick a face on a body. I pictured someone getting impatient with me while I decided, looking at his watch; *'Come on, Olly, who do I look like?'* I could only imagine Steven and I didn't want to think about Steven. But even a slight glimpse in my mind of Steven, half naked, covered only by plain white linen sent my pulse racing. If only Brian had looked like Steven!

Olivia Jones: *Yes, I think you are probably right.*

Chris Knight: *So who do you think about, you know, when you masturbate?*

My eyebrows shot up almost off my head. This guy didn't have any boundaries whatsoever.

Olivia Jones: *Jesus! What kind of a question is that?*

Chris Knight: *Lol, I'm curious. Come on Liv, everyone does it, not many admit to it, but everyone does it. You are only human, and it has been five years. I don't believe you haven't had an orgasm in five years.*

Olivia Jones: *Haha, I suppose so. Besides, if I didn't please myself I would never have had an orgasm.*

Chris Knight: *Again – are you serious?*

Olivia Jones: *I don't think it's that unusual, is it?*

Chris Knight: *Do you mean penetrative? Or just in general?*

Olivia Jones: *Erm, both I guess. I mean I accept I'm never likely to have a penetrative orgasm, but men are a* *bit lazy in my experience, they just don't know how to touch a woman. They get bored and then they just climb on in till they finish and fall asleep.*

Chris Knight: *This is shocking. You should feel comfortable enough to be able to direct him a bit if necessary. How many fingers?*

Olivia Jones: *I'm sorry?*

Chris Knight: *How many fingers do you insert? When you pleasure yourself I mean.*

Eww gross! I could feel my cheeks burning with embarrassment the longer this conversation went on.

Olivia Jones: *I don't.*

Chris Knight: *So you use a dildo?*

Olivia Jones: *No!*

Chris Knight: *Vibrator?*

Olivia Jones: *No!*

Chris Knight said: *How do you do it, then?*

Olivia Jones: *Apparently I do it wrong!*

Chris Knight: *Lol, no not wrong, just not the way I expected. Maybe you never come through penetrative sex because you're only used to it from clitoral stimulation. You might be able to train yourself ... buy a dildo! :-)*

I was beginning to feel uncomfortable with the way this conversation was going. Why was I talking about my non-existent sex life with a complete stranger? Perhaps the sense of anonymity made it easier – like talking to a therapist, someone impartial. He asked questions that made me think and gave me time and space to sort through my thoughts. It was quite refreshing, actually. But still it felt a little too familiar. Like Steven calling you Olly? I smirked at the memory and felt a flush of shame as I imagined Steven starting a conversation like this on his first day!

Olivia Jones: *I don't know about that.*

Chris Knight: *Exploring your body and what it wants is nothing to be ashamed about, Liv, it'll make you better* prepared for sharing the experience with someone else. Might make you more confident too.

Olivia Jones: *Knowing how my body feels doesn't change the fact I have a body I don't want to show to anyone.*

Chris Knight: *Only you can change that, Liv. But hey, I am a fitness instructor so if you want any advice I'd be happy to help you.*

Olivia Jones: *Really?*

Chris Knight: *Yes, I was a fitness instructor before I decided to go to uni and study law. I want to represent athletes and sports people. I work part-time in the gym to cover my outgoings.*

Olivia Jones: *Wow! OK, what do I need to do?*

Chris Knight: *Apart from the obvious eat less, exercise more, I can't really say without seeing you, but if you send me some details I could work out a plan for you, if you wanted?*

Despite being ridiculously lazy and uninterested in exercise, I suddenly felt excited. I could certainly stand to lose some weight and I suppose, if I did eventually give in to Steven and allow myself to fall into his arms, he might want to do more than just kiss me. Would he run a mile if he saw my horrible figure up close? How could I feel confident and comfortable with him if I couldn't even bear to look at myself in the mirror?

Olivia Jones: *I would really appreciate that, thank you. What do you need me to send?*

Chris Knight: *Your measurements: weight, height, age. Keep a food diary for a week, every single thing you eat and drink, and any exercise you do. I will base a programme on all that. Starting today. Make a list of everything you've consumed and carry it on. Send it to me next Monday.*

Olivia Jones: *OK that sounds easy enough.*

Chris Knight: *What did you have for dinner tonight?*

Olivia Jones: *I ordered pizza, hasn't arrived yet. I am starving though, hope it comes soon.*

Chris Knight: *You'll have to cut that out if you're going to lose weight.*

Olivia Jones: *Are you going to expect me to cook?*

Chris Knight: *Yes! You can't live off takeaways every night.*

Olivia Jones: *You can't? But they're so easy and tasty.*

Chris Knight: *And full of fat and salt, clogging up your arteries and damaging your heart.*

Olivia Jones: *Boring.*

Chris Knight: *Lol. But it's all true. You stop eating takeaways and I promise you'll see the weight drop off!*

Olivia Jones: *Sounds hell. Is there no other way?*

Chris Knight: *You could eat takeaways every day but you'd need to punish yourself in the gym daily to burn some of it off.*

Olivia Jones: *You're mean!*

Chris Knight: *You don't have to listen to me. But if you're serious about losing weight you would be advised to!*

Olivia Jones: *Oh, pizza is here. I shall be sure to savour every bite.*

Chris Knight: *Lol. Goodnight, Liv, speak to you soon. X*

Chapter Nine

I was much more awake when I arrived at work the next morning due to the extra hour in bed. Steven was relaxing on one of the sofas in Reception chatting to Dave when I arrived to sign in. He grinned at me.

'I forgot!' he shrugged, rising to join me. Dave smiled up at him.

'Good chatting to you, Ste. Olly, you should get him a key cut,' he advised me.

'And let him loose in the office without me? Not sure about that!' I said laughing, although I was only half joking. I knew deep down that he was a good guy, but the fears I had confessed to him were valid. On the one hand, if his scheme was to ruin my business and take my clients, he would benefit from having access to the office in my absence. On the other hand, if he was genuine and trustworthy, he would probably be doing me a favour, getting ahead of his work load and freeing me up to work on Inspired in-house products. So confusing.

The worst thing about it of course, was that none of this had crossed my mind until I was drunk and needed to explain why I couldn't get involved with him. Maybe I was just naturally suspicious; I had already found it difficult to relinquish control over my work – I wanted to be the one who did it all. But I recognised that to grow, I needed to expand. Perhaps an internship wasn't the best way to go – of course he would be ambitious, he would want to learn as much from me as he could and then go off and be a big success. But it wasn't like I was the only programmer in the world, I certainly wouldn't be the last. So what if he did leave after a year and set up his own business? And who knew? Maybe he would want to stay at Inspired. I guessed only time would tell. Or would it …? If he were playing a long game, he'd no doubt be able to keep up the pretence of being attracted to me indefinitely. Maybe I needed to see a therapist to deal with my paranoia!

'Earth to Ols.' Steven was teasing as he poked me in the side, causing me to jump out of my thoughts and back into reality. 'What were you thinking about?'

'I was thinking about conferences actually, there are loads of them all year round. I want us to start being represented at them.'

'OK, does that mean by me?' he asked, cautiously.

'Yes, I'm not a people person – I want to win clients, not scare them away! I'm also considering hiring more staff, but I'll need to build an office because I can't work in an open-plan room, not if it's full.'

Steven raised an eyebrow sceptically but said nothing.

'I want us working on commissions and in-house projects simultaneously. And I want someone else to do the boring paperwork!' I finished up grinning.

'Wow, Olivia Jones, taking over the world one app at a time!'

'Well you know, Steven, if you are planning on slapping me with a sexual harassment case, I'd better make sure I've got enough in the bank to pay you off, hadn't I?' I smile sweetly at him and he laughed with me.

'Well, if I'm the inspiration behind expansion, then I'm glad!' He frowned, 'although realistically, you could probably fire *me* for sexual harassment.' He smiled awkwardly. 'I should stop making my intentions so clear, shouldn't I? Especially if we are going to have company.' He smiled then and I was relieved he was back to his carefree self. I motioned to the sofa, inviting him to sit with me.

'How did you find your first week here?' I asked in all

seriousness. I was aware I had paperwork to complete for his intern organisers.

'It was great, Ols. I really enjoyed it. Glad I'm here.' His voice was warm, honest.

'Do you have any future plans, Steven? Have you thought beyond the twelve-month internship?' We regarded each other thoughtfully. I had no idea what he was thinking but I knew what I wanted him to say.

'I guess my only real aspiration at the moment is to impress you enough that this turns into a permanent job at the end of my programme,' he shrugged. His eyes never left mine as he spoke; I sensed he was trying to prove he was telling the truth, proving I could trust him.

'I love the fact you're a small, independent company competing with the big boys and holding your own. Sure it would be fabulous to run my own one day, but do we really need another independent games company in the market? I'd rather work on the games you're putting out – which will get bigger and better as you expand, than try and compete on my own,' he concluded.

'I got lucky; Jerk Chicken paid for Inspired, not many people get that kind of chance,' I smiled. 'Let's make Inspired the preferred choice for game apps development then, shall we?'

Steven grinned and nodded.

'If it keeps me in a job, you have my full support, boss.'

At lunchtime Steph arrived to deliver our sandwiches. 'Dave asked me to pass this on,' she said, holding up a parcel addressed to me. I nodded towards Steven.

'Management decision – Steven is now in charge of the post.' I grinned at him and took a bite out of my sandwich, sighing loudly in appreciation.

'What did you order today? Sounds amazing. I'll have one of those tomorrow, Steph.' He grinned at Steph who peered at him over the side of his desk, smiling and fluttering her eyelashes at him.

'Chicken with basil, mozzarella, and tomato,' she informed him. She frowned as Steven pulled out a piece of paper and wrote it down. 'Wow, you're really writing it down!'

'Oh, this is for Olly; she has to make a note of everything she eats this week.'

Both Steph and I stared at him, Steph waiting for a reason and me wondering how he knew. He looked at me and smiled.

'Chris emailed me. He doesn't think you'll remember to write everything down so he asked me to,' he explained.

Steph looked at me for further clarification.

'His friend Chris is a fitness instructor; said he'd help me lose weight.'

She raised an eyebrow in understanding.

'OK, so who is he?' She demanded.

'Just someone Steven lived with at uni'

'No not him, the guy? The guy you're contemplating sex with.'

I choked on my sandwich and Steven stared at his screen, I could see him fighting back a smile.

'What are you talking about?' I asked wiping my mouth with a napkin. I could feel my cheeks burning. Steph turned her attention to Steven to explain.

'Olly never dates because she's scared it might end up in bed and she's too ashamed of her body to get naked! If she's trying to lose weight, she must have her eye on someone.' She looked back up at me, 'come on, Olly, who is he? Who are you shaping up for?'

'No one,' I shrugged. 'I just realised it's been a long time and maybe I need to think about getting back out there – might as well be ready just in case Mr Right turns up. Can we not talk about this please?' I felt irritation shoot through me that Steph was being so open with my secrets in front of Steven, and mortified that Steven was getting a glimpse into my pathetic dating history.

'As long as he's not Mr Always Right like your last boyfriend.' Steph shook her head sadly and Steven looked at her quizzically. 'Oh, she doesn't like to talk about it,' she whispered behind her hand. Steven nodded, looking serious, but there was a twinkle in his eye and he turned to me smiling.

'So come on then, what does this Mr Right look like?' He asked innocently.

I felt my face flush and I knew Steph would blurt it out.

'Oh, The Doctor, obviously, the ultimate nerd,' Steph said without even thinking about it.

Steven turned to stare at me, I couldn't read his expression, but I was mortified. Hadn't he already said he couldn't take anyone seriously who fancied The Doctor? I took a deep breath and without looking at Steven I gathered up my sandwich wrapper and threw it in the bin.

'OK, Steph, same time tomorrow?' I said firmly. She grinned and left.

I walked to the sofa and sat down, focusing my attention on a proposal I had drafted. I heard the sound of Steven's chair rolling away from his desk, the creak as he stood up. I sensed him making his way towards me but I couldn't look up. I felt ridiculous. For all my protests and arguments for being sensible I couldn't bear the thought of Steven having a bad opinion of me. Thinking of me like any other mindless girl with a crush on The Doctor. Maybe this is for the best, I told myself. He won't want you now anyway. I raised my head and peered at him, he stood staring at me, his hands clenched in fists at his sides. I felt a prickling sensation creep up the back of my neck and fought the urge to go to him, put my arms round him, and ask him to forgive me. I remembered that feeling as a child when my mum was angry with me; that if I could just get her to hold me I would know she still loved me. I knew it would be for the best if Steven didn't love me, but I wanted him to. I realised in that moment that I did want him to want me because I know I want him. But I knew I couldn't just rush into something – we needed to take the time to get to know each other properly. And the time for me to lose weight and feel comfortable in bed.

'So, The Doctor, then? He's your dream man?'

'Sorry.' I mumbled.

'What are you sorry for?'

'After everything you said, about them making *Doctor Who* sexy to appeal to a mainstream audience, I thought you would be disappointed.'

'Oh that's different, Olly. I bet you fancied the Ninth Doctor too. I'd expect a she-geek to have a crush on all of the Doctors, really.'

I frowned.

'Even Hartnell?' I asked, surprised.

'OK maybe not all of the Doctors,' he smiled, 'besides which, it bodes well for me that you're attracted to a sharp-dressed nerd with lots of hair. In fact it's taking every ounce of my restraint not to kiss you now. Give me a reason why I shouldn't. Can you deny that you find me attractive?'

My eyes widened in surprise. I shrugged slightly. I closed my eyes and shook my head. He was there in a heartbeat, perched on the edge of the sofa, one arm reaching around my body, the other hand touching my face. I stared at his triumphant face and shook my head, warning him not to.

'What? Are you saying you don't like me?' He asked dropping his hand, confusion replacing his triumphant expression.

I shrugged.

'I'm saying I don't know you. OK, you like all the same things as me; you make me laugh, you're very attractive, and if I wasn't the owner of this business – if I wasn't your boss – I'd kiss you right now. I would want to date you. I'd give it a chance if that's what you wanted.'

'That is what I want, no one can predict if a relationship will work, Ols; you just have to give it a try.' He sounded exasperated.

'And what if it doesn't work? Coming in here every day, seeing each other all the time? Guess how many of my exes I've seen since I broke up with them? None. I cut them out, whether I end it or they do, it's over. I don't want to see them again.' I sighed.

'You were younger then, I'm sure you would handle it differently now.' He looked hopeful.

'And you are young now,' I pointed out. 'I'm looking for Mr Right, and while you're looking like a contender for Mr Absolutely Perfect, you're not at an age for settling down. You'll pursue me until you get me and then start looking for the next chase.'

'You're definitely right about one thing, Olivia: you don't know me at all, if that's what you think.' He snorted.

I shrugged apologetically but glad I'd at least made my point, even if it had offended him.

'I have to think about the business, this is my life. It has been for three years. If I take on more staff, will they complain that you get treated better because of our romance? Will you expect more from me as the boss? If it doesn't work out, will you think I'm treating you unfairly? There are a lot of risks, and for peace of mind, why can't we just get to know each other for a few months? If we still feel this way about each other, then fine, we can think about taking that chance. If not, we'll have saved ourselves a lot of awkwardness.' And a lot of naked embarrassment. I wondered if six months would be enough to lose sufficient weight for me to be comfortable with my body.

He scrutinised my face for a long time. I was starting to feel uncomfortable and I couldn't look at him anymore. He sighed.

'Is this weight-loss nonsense anything to do with me? Because you should know I don't give a shit about that stuff, you're beautiful and sexy to me exactly as you are.'

My stomach did a somersault and I felt a rush of heat flushing my face. I shook my head.

'I appreciate that, Steven, but it's my hang up, my self-confidence. It's not why I want to wait though, if that's what you mean.'

He nodded reluctantly and stood up.

'OK then, I'm going to ask you out to dinner once every month. When you know me well enough, you can say yes. Deal?' I smiled and nodded. He held out his hand to help me up.

I don't know how it happened, I felt his hand under my elbow steadying me then his arms were around me and his mouth was on mine. In a split second, he was kissing me. His hand reached up to my face, his tongue was brushing against my lips, looking for an entrance into my mouth. I resisted and tried to step away, but he held me tight against him. His body was warm, his smell a mixture of laundry detergent and aftershave – a clean, comforting scent. He was planting swift, insistent kisses on my lips, like knocking on a door to be allowed access. I felt my body relax, defeated, and I parted my lips. His tongue found its way into my mouth, exploring my lips and my teeth, before mingling with my own tongue as they danced together. His arm released me and his hands took hold of mine, placing them around his body, before holding my face; running his fingers into my hair, his thumbs massaging my temple and my eyebrows. My head was screaming at me to stop responding to his touch but I couldn't. I'd been thinking about this all weekend and I wanted it so badly. This mustn't change anything that we had talked about. The situation was the same, our agreement in place. He kissed my lips once more before trailing kisses along my jaw towards my ear.

'Stop thinking about it, and just enjoy it,' he whispered.

He trailed kisses back towards my mouth and my hands moved to his face pulling away from him to look him in the eye. His eyes were full of lust, but a hint of fear appeared – a worry I was going to stop him. His lips were parted and his breath heavy. He looked beautiful. His dark eyes searched my face for a reaction. I relaxed my hands and his mouth was covering mine instantly, our tongues writhing together. My legs buckled but his arms held me tightly, steadying me, crushing me against his body. My hands found his hair, running my fingers through it, tightening it in my fists. His hand cupped the base of my head, tangling his fingers through my hair.

There was a knock at the door and we leaped apart. I threw myself onto the sofa and he busied himself at the sink filling the kettle as Dave walked in.

'Good afternoon, Inspired, how are you all today?' I scooped my dishevelled hair up into a ponytail and massaged some feeling back into my tingling lips. Steven turned around grinning, his dishevelled hair not looking any different to his usual look. He held up the kettle.

'Hey, Dave. Tea?'

Dave shook his head and I stood up from the sofa. I'd asked Dave to show me some empty units to help me with my expansion plans.

'Is now a good time, Olly?' he asked. His expression gave no hint that he suspected the conflicting emotions running through my head.

'Yes, we're done here.' I said glancing at Steven to make sure he understood I was talking to him too. He nodded imperceptibly. I followed Dave out the office and shut the door behind me, without a second glance at Steven.

Dave led me into a small room next door to my office. It had two doors, one on each side, and a large window.

'This would make the perfect office for you, Olly, because the doors lead straight to the rooms on either side.' I had always wondered what was behind that locked door in my office. Dave unlocked the door to the next room: it was the same size and shape as my room but had obviously been used as an IT suite during its days as a school. All along the walls were regularly spaced power sockets and two rows of floor sockets. The floor had removable panel strips for wires and plugs. I pictured a bank of staff, working at computer terminals, and briefly recalculated the time in which we could finish a project, if we worked together. I noticed another door.

'That's a store cupboard,' Dave explained, opening the door to show me a perfect space for a server room. I smiled as I started imagining the possibility of expansion and nodded at him.

'I want them both. I need to draw up a business plan for expansion, but I already know I want them.'

He grinned at me, proudly and patted my shoulder.

'Who would have thought it, eh? Olivia Jones with staff?'

I shook my head grinning.

'Not me, that's for sure. Can I move into the office right away?' I asked, serious again. He regarded me curiously. 'I find it difficult to get any work done, sharing a room is distracting.' I explained.

'You're the boss, Olly, tell him to shut up and get on with his work.' He was smiling as he said it, but I felt a surge of protection towards Steven and defended him.

'It's not that, he's a great worker, programmes faster than I do, and he plugs in his headphones and I don't hear a peep from him.'

'So what's the problem?' Dave frowned.

I sighed and shrugged helplessly at him.

'I've got my perfect man sitting in my office, Dave. That's pretty distracting!'

Dave roared with laughter, so hard that pretty soon I was laughing with him.

'Have you got a little crush on him, Ol?' He loudly sighed, when he finally calmed down. He frowned again, 'what aren't you telling me?' I hid my eyes and grimaced.

'He likes me too. He told me he likes me, wants to take me out on a date. And I look at him, all charm and good looks, perfect hair, nice clothes, and I badly want to say yes. But I keep saying no, because I'm his boss and I barely know him.' I looked up at Dave for reassurance and confirmation. 'Right? That's the right thing to do?'

Dave shrugged non-committally.

'That's really up to you to decide, Olly. There's no law saying you can't date your employee. And I seriously doubt your interest in him is purely based on his looks.' I raised my eyebrows, questioning his theory. 'You have a crush on The Doctor, regardless of who plays him, right? OK, David Tennant might be particularly attractive, but you still kind of fancied the Ninth Doctor, because the point of those regenerations is that it's still the same man – different face, different body, but the same brilliant mind. He's still got gadgets, he's still a genius, and he's still a massive nerd. You like Steven because he's the first bloke you've met who you can talk about your work to without having to dumb it down. He likes all the same nerdy stuff as you. You can be yourself with him. And you would like that, regardless of what he looked like,' he concluded.

I sighed. But my heart rate sped up, I thought I'd wanted Dave to agree with me, tell me I was right, but this felt like the permission I was after to go for it. I shook my head.

'Feels too risky, Dave. If it doesn't work out, what happens? I can't fire him, could he sue me for something? Sexual harassment? Constructive dismissal? I don't know. Will the rest of my staff think I treat him more favourably? Will I treat him more favourably?' I looked at him

71

pleading for an answer. Dave put his arm around my shoulder.

'Who are they to question it? Put him in a role where there's no risk of apparent favouritism. The main thing is, if you expect it'll end before it even starts, I'd say leave it. But if you think it's got legs, Ol, then there's a risk in any romance. Just enjoy it. And if it ends – at least now you have an office to hide in!' He grinned squeezing my shoulders, 'I'll say one thing, Ol; while I think you're wise to take it slow and get to know him a bit first, seeing you this last week, you look more relaxed in his company than I've ever seen you.'

'I just don't get why he would like me; I'm old, overweight, and I look like I get dressed in the dark,' I pointed out.

'It's the person, not the packaging. If he's as into you as he says he is, then regardless of how you see yourself, he will think you're the most beautiful woman on the planet.'

I nodded. 'Most beautiful woman on the planet? I can live with that.' I grinned. 'And just for the record, I never fancied the First Doctor.'

I returned to my room after collecting the keys and signing a new lease for the additional units. I was intent on ordering furniture for my new office and packing up my desk. Steven would probably be offended, but that was just tough. It was for the best; putting some distance between us would help on a daily basis.

I paused at the door, my hand on the handle. Memories of the kiss crossed my mind and I felt a rush of warmth through my body. I needed to get this out of my head before I saw him again. I took a deep breath and composed myself.

Steven looked up as I entered, nodded his head in acknowledgement, and continued working. He had his headphones in and his fingers were flying across his keyboard. Good, he was busy. I walked to the locked door joining my office and unlocked it with one of the three keys Dave had given me. I stood in the room getting to know its space, its smell, and its atmosphere. I looked out of the window and tried to decide how I wanted to furnish the room.

I jumped when he spoke, lost in my own thoughts.

'I was wondering about this door,' he said, dragging me from my thoughts.

'My new office,' I said looking around. 'And through there,' I nodded to the door opposite him, 'is our second office, which I intend to fill with app testers.'

His eyes never left me as he crossed the room and opened the door. He glanced through the door and gasped.

'Perfect, isn't it?' I grinned.

'It really is,' he agreed. 'So you're doing it then?' He asked surprised by the sudden progress of my plans for expansion. I nodded.

'Still need to plan it out properly, but I'm making a start. It will take a few months to get the rooms ready and recruit staff, but yes. I'm going for it.'

He smiled at me, amused by my obvious excitement. He looked like he wanted to say something, but he made his way back towards his desk instead. I followed him in and sat down at my desk, digging the measurements out of my pocket and opening up a web browser to search for office furniture. I could at least make a start on getting my office sorted and then think about my required staff team and office equipment. I made a mental note to warn Reception to expect lots of deliveries, when I remembered about the package Steph had delivered. Not wanting to disturb him I peered over at Steven's desk to see if he had opened it. He noticed me and a smile flickered over his lips. Does my attention make him smile? I felt a surge of affection for him at that thought. He paused mid keystroke and removed an earphone from his ear, looking at me in anticipation.

'What was that parcel Steph delivered earlier?' I asked, not seeing the package anywhere on his desk. His face turned red and he looked away from me embarrassed. He opened his side drawer and pulled out the box, handing it to me.

'You can open your own parcels in future,' he grimaced. 'Putting in some practice?' he asked teasing.

I frowned; I had no idea what he was talking about. I hadn't ordered anything; I had assumed it would be a show reel from a prospective employee or student. I opened the box and gasped, dropping the package on the floor.

'Oh my God!' My hand flew to cover my mouth. 'I don't know anything about this, who sent it? Was there a note? Why would anyone send me that?' I picked up the box and sank into my chair. Curious I pulled the vibrator from the box examining it with disgust. The packaging was a lurid pink colour, a big star on the front claimed "three speeds" and the image displayed a slim black vibrator decorated with pink hearts. I searched through the box for any hint of the sender but there was nothing in there. Why would someone send me a vibrator? What kind of a sick joke was that? I glanced over at Steven and noticed a smile tugging at the corners of his mouth. He was amused and I was aware he probably thought my reaction was an act. As if I would forget ordering a vibrator, for goodness' sake.

'When I find out who sent this I'm going to …' I paused, brandishing the vibrator at Steven.

'What? Vibrate them to death?' he grinned. 'It's OK, Ols. I won't tell anyone.'

I felt my cheeks redden, 'Seriously, I have no idea who sent me this, but I know for certain that it wasn't me!'

I scowled as Steven replaced his headphones and turned his attention to his screen, trying to hide the big grin on his face.

Chapter Ten

The rest of the week passed by without any more major events. I had made a start on getting my office ready, painting the walls and doors ready for the furniture, which arrived on Friday morning, and I spent the day arranging the desk, filing cabinets, and shelves to create a comfortable room to work in. By the end of Friday I had moved the contents of my desk into the new office and made sure I would be ready to get stuck into programming again the following week. Steven was true to his word and didn't make any further reference to his feelings for me, my feelings for him, or that kiss.

That kiss had been replayed from every angle in my mind every evening since. I wanted it to happen again and was relieved that Steven was being more restrained. Working in my own office couldn't come soon enough. The distraction his presence made was more than I could bear.

Did I really say six months?

Steph burst through the door at 4 p.m.

'Come on, you two, it's Friday, it's four o'clock, it's time for the pub.'

I curled my top lip and shook my head.

'Well, I didn't really expect you to join us, Olly,' she snorted. She turned to Steven. 'You're coming though, right?'

'Yeah definitely, I'll follow you over when I've finished here,' he grinned.

'Oh come on, it's Friday, come now,' she pleaded. 'Olly won't make you stay late, will you, Ol?' She turned to face me.

I shrugged and shook my head. Steven smiled warmly at me before addressing Steph.

'I'm just in the middle of a particularly tricky piece of code and I don't want to leave it; it's not something for a Monday morning!' he smiled. 'I'll be there by six at the very latest, will everyone still be out by then?'

'I'll wait for you, regardless. Promise.' She said winking at him. She grinned at me as she left, raising her eyebrows optimistically. I felt a stab of guilt. I hadn't given Steph's feelings a second thought this week. In theory, it would be a good thing if Steph could hook Steven – it would make everything so much easier. But I knew I'd be gutted at the same time. Not that I could blame him, if he went off with someone else. I suppose that's another risk – he wouldn't wait forever, and I wouldn't expect him to. He could meet someone tomorrow who removed all thoughts of me from his mind. Things change, feelings change.

'Oh, Steph, don't tag me on Facebook if you check in at the pub.' Steven asked suddenly, as he glanced at me looking thoughtful. Steph looked surprised waiting for an explanation.

'That's how Melissa found me last week. She saw the photo you tagged me in.'

'Oh you mean that girl you were hiding from at Olly's place?' She threw me a look of disapproval.

'Yeah, her. I hope she doesn't turn up again tonight, especially if Ols isn't coming to protect me.' He smiled at me conspiratorially and I felt a giggle threaten as I recalled sneaking home. 'Can I not convince you to come tonight?' He addressed me. 'You know, for the benefit of my wellbeing at work?'

'Your wellbeing in the pub isn't my responsibility,' I informed him.

'But it's drinks after work, so it's implied that it's an

extension of the work place, surely?'

I glared at him, avoiding Steph's eyes boring into me. I had to admit I did want to hang out with him, and what better way to get to know him than in the pub over a pint? I'd learned so much about him last week. I knew Steph would hate me playing gooseberry, but then again, I wanted to play gooseberry! I shrugged.

'Well, I'll see how I feel when I'm done here.' I conceded. Steven grinned at me. Steph rolled her eyes and made her way out of the office. I smiled to myself. It occurred to me that Dave might be right, I certainly felt a lot more relaxed about socialising since Steven had joined me. I wondered briefly if it was obvious that there was some connection between us. Steph didn't seem to notice it the same way Dave had, but maybe she was wilfully ignoring it. Even though I was determined to keep some distance between us, I was enjoying the occasional feeling of solidarity.

As it turned out I decided not to go to the pub. I wanted to get home and shower, I was feeling pretty grotty after all the furniture moving; packing and unpacking boxes and getting the office straight. I couldn't face sitting in the pub. I had been careful not to let Steven get too close to me in case I smelled sweaty.

Steven seemed disappointed when I told him. I walked with him to the pub and continued on towards home. I was worried he would end up coming back to mine and I didn't trust myself to be alone in my flat with him under the uninhibited influence of alcohol. A reckless part of me wanted to use drink as an excuse to kiss him again. A flush of warmth radiated through me as I remembered that kiss and my inner demon glared at my smug angel.

I ran a hot bath and eased my tired aching body into the water, feeling all the tension fill the bubbles and drift away. Moving furniture is hard work. I wondered briefly if that counted as exercise. I could certainly justify a nice takeaway, especially on my last weekend of food freedom, before Chris set my fitness plan. *Chris*. I hadn't thought about Chris all week. I wondered if Steven had told him anything; apart from apparently finding me attractive and thinking I was cool. I felt a prickle of embarrassment as some of his messages flitted through my mind. And that's when it occurred to me. Chris sent the vibrator. It had to be Chris; hadn't he talked about it the previous weekend? He had said I could teach myself to orgasm through penetration. I felt a mixture of emotions, my angel was irritated and disgusted that a man I'd never met had been so presumptuous in sending me such a private, personal, *embarrassing* gift to my place of work. My devil was thrilled, aroused, and, for the first time, suggesting I try it out. My angel frowned at the devil. I was naturally reluctant about anything sexual, even masturbation. As much as I might enjoy it at the time, I always felt a bit guilty afterwards, dirty. I never planned to do it. It just happened occasionally, in bed, in the dark, late at night. The thought of using a vibrator disturbed me. It suggested a certain amount of forward planning; acknowledged the fact of masturbation that I wasn't comfortable with. Chris's words drifted through my mind, my devil whispering in my ear. *Exploring your body and what it wants is nothing to be ashamed about.*

I finished my bath, wrapped my dressing gown around me, and ordered some food. I grabbed a beer from the fridge and settled on the sofa, turning on the television and opening up my laptop. It pinged immediately and I knew it would be him.

Chris Knight: *Good evening, Liv. Home alone on a Friday?*

Olivia Jones: *Hello, Mr Knight. Speak for yourself!*

Chris Knight: *Lol but I'm a student, I'm going out later.*

Olivia Knight: *Well I'm a grown up with a busy job, I'm tired.*

Chris Knight: *Staying home to play with your toys?*

I flush of embarrassment shot through me. Did he mean his present? I decided to feign ignorance.

Olivia Jones: *Friday night is for TV, Saturday is for video games.*

Chris Knight: *That's not the kind of toy I meant. ;-)*

Olivia Jones: *Oh.*

Chris Knight: *Did you like my gift?*

Olivia Jones: *No! It was highly inappropriate. I have staff who open my post.*

Chris Knight: *Lol. That's made me chuckle. I bet Steven got quite a shock.*

Olivia Jones: *Not as much as I did.*

Chris Knight: *I imagine it probably turned him on.*

Olivia Jones: *I doubt it.*

Chris Knight: *It's pretty hot. A beautiful woman pleasuring herself, men pay for that kind of thing.*

Olivia Jones: *That's disgusting!*

Chris Knight: *So innocent, Liv. Lol. The porn industry thrives on men wanting to watch women touch themselves. Magazines, films. Personally I'm not interested in seeing some guy's hairy balls banging against a woman's arse cheeks, I'd rather watch her fuck herself with a dildo.*

I felt my cheeks flush with shame. I was disgusted but fascinated. And slightly aroused. *What? Gross! This shouldn't excite me, this man is disgusting.* I wondered briefly about him. Was he really a fitness instructor? He could just be some pervert sat at home jerking off to numerous porn films. No, Steven had lived with him. He was who he says he was.

I guessed that as a fitness instructor he was surrounded by beautiful skimpily clad women all the time. He probably didn't need porn.

Olivia Jones: *I suppose you see enough fit bodies in*

the gym? Isn't it distracting?

Chris Knight: *Not at all. It's fun actually. Sometimes a lot of fun ;-)*

Olivia Jones: *I don't see what could be fun in a gym.*

Chris Knight: *That's because you haven't been to the gym with me!*

Olivia Jones: *I imagine being bossed around by someone, making you do ten more reps, would be the complete opposite of fun.*

Chris Knight: *Not if he gives you a nice reward afterwards.*

Olivia Jones: *Cake?*

Chris Knight: *No not cake. So innocent, Miss Jones. Lol.*

My cheeks flushed as the penny dropped. Does he have sex with his clients?

Olivia Jones: *Gross. At the gym?*

Chris Knight: *That depends how desperate they are to fuck me I guess. Sometimes in the locker room, the shower, the car park. Sometimes I drive them home.*

Olivia Jones: *Is that ethical?*

Chris Knight: *Haha! I'm in the business of making women feel good about themselves and their body. If fucking them improves their self-confidence and body image, I see that as an extension of my job.*

Olivia Jones: **Rolls eyes* Of course, you do it for them. How very selfless of you. I bet you don't fuck the fat ugly ones though?*

Chris Knight: *The fat ones don't come on to me – at least, not until they are thin.*

Olivia Jones: *Not that you would notice.*

Chris Knight: *Harsh, Miss Jones. I think you have a low opinion of me. I'm really not so bad. I'm a grown up and so are they. They take their newfound body confidence and explore their sexuality. They road test their attractiveness by flirting with me. And I comply. I'm only* *human after all. I'm training to be a lawyer and I'm working to pay for it. I don't have time for a girlfriend, but I'm a hot-blooded male with needs. I'm not hurting anyone.*

I snorted. I wondered how many hearts he'd broken. Thankfully, we would never meet so it didn't matter. I frowned at the thought that crossed my mind wondering if I would ever meet him. I couldn't explain why I felt a pull towards him. He disgusted me mostly, always talking about sex so openly and yet it excited me. Sex was a natural thing, but it had never come naturally to me.

Olivia Jones: *Well, I hope you're not expecting the same kind of recompense for helping me.*

Chris Knight: *Of course not. Steven would be very upset with me for one thing and for another, you're at a very safe distance from me and my predatory ways. I take it that's what you think of me anyway?*

Olivia Jones: *Is that not the case?*

Chris Knight: **Sigh* no, Liv, it's not. They come after me. Anyway back to the point. Have you road tested your new toy yet? ;-)*

Olivia Jones: *No I have not!*

Chris Knight: *Would you like me to explain how to use it?*

Olivia Jones: *Absolutely not. I have no intention of even getting it out of the box.*

Chris Knight: *Oh, Liv, you're missing out. Trust me, you'll love it. Seriously, what's the worst that could happen – your orgasm is no better than before? But it's more likely to be a hundred times better.*

Olivia Jones: *My orgasm is none of your business.*

Chris Knight: *OK, Liv, I understand you're not comfortable talking about sex. But you should be. It's not a bad thing. You're just a little repressed is all.*

I wanted to argue, but I couldn't. He was right. I was completely repressed. I grew up with very religious parents who didn't believe in sex before marriage. The shame I felt whenever I thought about sex stems from that. Every time I had sex in the past, it was tainted by the disappointment my folks would feel if they knew I was fornicating.

Olivia Jones: *Never thought of it like that before, but you're right. Strict upbringing, I guess. Even though my folks have passed on, I'm still influenced by them.*

Chris Knight: *Parents can fuck us up! But we all reach an age, Liv, when we realise that we are capable of our own thoughts and beliefs, and we don't have to follow those of our parents. In this day and age, we don't have to do as our parents did. We have access to technology and information. We can make our own choices.*

Olivia Jones: *I know. That knowledge and technology is my life blood. But it's hard to throw off the guilt that stems from disappointing your parents – even if they're not around to see it.*

Chris Knight: *Well, you have to try, otherwise you'll never be truly happy; you'll never reach your full potential in life if you hold back for the sake of others. Live your life, not the life they dreamed for you. On that note my dear, I have to go. Enjoy your lonely Friday night in. I look forward to receiving your food diary on Monday. I expect it to be hideously saturated in fat.*

Olivia Jones: *Oh it is. I've been reassuringly bad with my food this week – making the most of my last suppers.*

Chris Knight: *I can't wait to whip you into shape, Miss Jones.*

Olivia Jones: *Pervert.*

Chris Knight: *;-) x*

Chapter Eleven

To: Chris Knight
Sent: Monday August 10th 2009
From: Olivia Jones
Subject: Food Diary

Hi Chris,
Here goes …
Height: 5ft 9
Weight: 11st 3lb

Monday
Breakfast – two pieces of toast with butter.
Lunch – ham and cheese panini
Dinner – pepperoni pizza (takeaway)
Six cups of tea with semi skinned milk

Tuesday
Breakfast – sausage toastie from the café.
Lunch – chicken, mozzarella, and tomato baguette
Dinner – chicken and mushroom Pot Noodle. Two custard
doughnuts
Six cups of tea

Wednesday
Breakfast – Crunchy Nut cornflakes
Lunch – Chinese chicken salad roll
Dinner – fish and chips (chippy)
Six cups of tea

Thursday

Breakfast – Crunchy Nut cornflakes
Lunch – chips and curry (chippy)
Dinner – cheese sandwich from the garage
Six cups of tea
Three homemade cookies (Steven's mum)

Friday
Breakfast – sausage and fried egg toasted sandwich
Lunch – tuna melt panini
Dinner – Chinese takeaway – chicken chow mein, spring rolls, prawn toast, crispy seaweed, spare ribs, prawn crackers
Four cups of tea
Three beers

Saturday
Brunch – bacon, sausage, mushrooms, two eggs scrambled, tomatoes and two toast
Dinner – chicken tikka masala (takeaway), garlic naan, poppadum, mango chutney
Five cups of tea
Three beers

Sunday
Brunch – bacon, sausage, mushrooms, two eggs scrambled, tomatoes, and two toast
Dinner – microwave roast dinner
Victoria sponge cake
Six cups of tea
I sort of exercised – I moved furniture around the office on Friday. I was a big sweaty mess … I hope that counts for something,
O X
Olivia Jones
Inspired Programming

I had heard from Chris again that evening. He'd told me that my weight was fine for my height, that my BMI was 23.6 which was in the ideal range although not perfect, whatever that meant, but he expressed surprise that based on my food diary I didn't weigh a lot more. I guess I had failed to mention the fact that I weighed significantly less not so long ago. He warned me that if I continued to eat with my usual gusto my weight would continue to rise and the journey back would be longer and more difficult. I was convinced. Although I sensed I wasn't going to like his regime. I was half-relieved that he lived so far away and wouldn't be around to crack the whip. The thought of Chris cracking a whip sent a thrill coursing through my body that was both pleasant and disturbing at the same time. I was confused enough about Steven without adding feelings towards a virtually anonymous man at the other end of a computer.

Chris was actually really helpful in between his constant teasing; he gave me a simple set of exercises to complete daily and sent me links to websites which demonstrated each exercise. He sent me a link to an online calorie tracker which counted the number of calories eaten and worked out how many I had left. He had already calculated the number of calories I had been eating, and what I should be eating to maintain my current weight. I optimistically decided I would eat a bit less to try and lose a little bit of weight but Chris seemed confident that exercise would tone up the bits I wasn't happy with.

The best thing was that he said I could eat whatever I wanted as long as I stayed within the limit. Unfortunately I can't count the calories if I don't know what they are so I should avoid eating things that don't display nutritional information; takeaways were out. I was going to have to learn to cook!

The following morning I scrutinised the packaging on the Crunchy Nut cornflakes. It informed me there were

131 calories in a 30-gram serving. That was OK. One hundred and thirty one down, one thousand, six hundred and eighty six to go. I started pouring the cereal when I remembered Chris had said I would need to measure and weigh things. I had no idea what thirty grams of cereal looked like. I rooted around the kitchen cupboard until I found some scales, dusting off the layer of dust and setting the weight of the bowl to zero. Thirty grams was reached in no time. Really, I thought. That's all? I reasoned that I could afford to double it and measured out 60 grams. I grabbed the milk and noticed the nutritional sticker. One hundred millilitres equalled fifty calories. I found a measuring jug, and measured out 100 millilitres and poured it over my cereal. I frowned and poured another measure. Better. I could live with that. I usually had the milk right up the top of the bowl so I could drink the leftovers at the end, the milk tasting of honey and nuts from the cereal. One meal down, 362 calories spent, 1455 remaining. Plenty of calories left.

I made a mental note to ask Steph if she knew how many calories her sandwiches contained and which had the lowest amount.

Chapter Twelve

I arrived at work early; I wanted to be in my office and working when Steven arrived. Last week had been physically busy and active and had been a welcome distraction. Steven had so far been true to his word and not mentioned anything about 'us' since he had pounced on me. I wondered when he would ask me out on a date and occasionally found myself practicing my responses, ranging from rolling my eyes and shaking my head, sighing, and saying 'too soon', to screaming at him in exasperation.

I knew it was what I wanted and that I should be relieved he'd finally listened to me, but a part of me couldn't shake the feeling of disappointment that he had stopped relentlessly pursuing me.

I heard the door open and the sound of his chair rolling away from his desk.

'Hello?' He called. I opened my office door and popped my head around the edge. I faltered as I saw him. His hair had that 'just got out of bed look' that other men spend hours perfecting and he was wearing black jeans that hung off his hips and fell to the floor, his Converse peeping out under the frayed edges. He was wearing a patterned shirt, open at the neck, his sleeves rolled up revealing slightly tanned arms. He probably spent his weekend outdoors and caught some sun. The colour suited him.

'Oh hey,' he grinned, 'I forgot about your executive office space. Are you all settled in now then?'

'I am. It's swanky. I like it.' I laughed. Swanky was hardly the word for it but it was nice enough. It was my space again, a miniature replica of the main office that had been my sanctuary. I had a large heavy desk in front of the window and I'd treated myself to an executive chair, more expensive than necessary but comfortable. I'd have to be careful I didn't find myself snoozing in the afternoon.

I'd acquired a black and white chequered rug for the floor and I'd painted the walls a warm cream colour to make the pictures stand out. I'd had canvas prints made of all the various apps I'd programmed over the last three years. A leather sofa matching the chair filled the wall next to the main door with a small coffee table for meetings. I never had understood why meetings should be formal, uncomfortable affairs sat around a table. Why couldn't we relax on a sofa and chat over a brew?

Steven popped his head around the door and whistled through his teeth.

'It's nice. Of course it's not as big as my office,' he laughed sweeping his arm indicating the main room, 'does that make me more important that you?'

'Of course,' I smirked, 'you're the one who does all the work!'

He laughed and shrugged.

'Better make a start then, but first, can I get you a cup of tea, madam?' He asked theatrically.

I grinned and nodded.

Steph sounded strange on the phone when I spoke to her and I remembered about Friday night. I wondered if anything had happened and was displeased by the stab of jealousy that shot through me as I considered it a possibility. She laughed when I asked her if she knew the number of calories in her sandwiches.

'Olly, I work with food every day, it's my life, of course I know how many calories are in my sandwiches. If you ever bothered to come in and look at a menu, you'd know too.'

'Awesome, can you bring me a menu at lunch time?

Today I'll just have my usual.' I had thought checking calories would be difficult but it was turning out to be really easy. All the food packages had them printed on and Steph included it on her menu. Perhaps she recognised there was a whole market of calorie counters and that's why she's always so busy.

'What's the boy having?' she asked; her tone was almost too disinterested to be genuine. Something must have happened on Friday. I was slightly relieved that whatever had happened wasn't something Steph was excited about. My jealous head crawled back to its crypt. I had no right to be jealous anyway.

'Not sure, I'll put you through to him.' I pressed the transfer button and dialled his number. It had taken me ages to work out how to programme these phones over the weekend and I hadn't had a chance to tell him about it yet. I doubted he had even noticed the new phone on his desk. I could see him through the open door and noticed his amusement when he saw the phone. He glanced up at me puzzled as he answered the phone.

'Inspired, Steven speaking,'

'It's me. Got Steph on the phone for you.' I pressed the transfer button again and replaced the handset. He was still watching me through the door, his bemused expression making him look adorable. I shook my head and looked away.

I was working on the new business plan when he appeared in my doorway, his eyes smiling in amusement.

'Everything's changed,' he said, 'new swanky office, new phones. What's next?'

'We're getting a server put in next month, shared drives, all that stuff, it'll make it easier for multiple staff to work on the same project. I figured my haphazard ways were fine when it was just me but if I'm going to attract a good team, I need to have better systems in place.'

'I hope it won't get too streamlined though, I kinda like

your haphazard approach.' He seemed almost sad and I wondered if I was in danger of losing the identity I'd built up. I dismissed that notion, after all the systems were about control, the staff increase was about expanding production, and I would need to be able to monitor the progress of everyone. I held his gaze for a while and smiled.

'I sort of feel like you've been here a lot longer than two weeks,' I frowned. 'I should've done all this before you started, then you wouldn't have known any different.'

'I guess you didn't know if you could cope with staff before I started, though. I'm quite flattered actually.' He cocked his head to one side and smiled at me, his eyes twinkling. I could see thoughts passing through his mind, things he wanted to say, but he stopped himself each time. I returned his smile and put him out of his misery.

'You'll still be my favourite, I'm sure.'

His grin widened across his face, he stood looking relaxed against the doorframe, but his clenched fists betrayed his struggle to restrain himself from crossing the room and demonstrating his feelings.

'I was going to request that you only hire women but I realised it might make me sound a bit like a pervert, when I actually just want to eliminate any competition.'

'Competition is healthy though, I know I have my fair share of it.' I raised one eyebrow wondering if he might shed some light on Friday night. I didn't want to bring it up but I was curious about Steph's mood. Instead he shrugged and backing away from the door he challenged me.

'Maybe you should hurry up and grab me before someone else does then?'

I shook my head, smiling, and returned my concentration to the business plan. I hated business planning. It was so dull. I never quite understood why I had to spend so much time writing down my intentions when I could just be getting on with the work. I let my thoughts wander and realised I was feeling content since my little exchange with Steven. Nothing had changed. He still wanted me.

I heard the door burst open as Steph's trolley clumsily forced its way through into the main office. I stood up and leant in the doorway of my room and watched her as she followed it through.

'I hear you're expanding?' She smiled with interest at me, ignoring Steven as she handed him his sandwich. He had removed his headphones and was frowning at the obvious snub. I smiled to myself as I watched his face fall with disappointment when he opened his sandwich, expecting the generous helping he'd received before and saw the standard portion the rest of us were used to. His eyes met mine and we both shrugged slightly.

I took my sandwich off her and nodded towards the office to show her.

'Wow, it's fancy. Look at you Miss Olivia Jones, executive manager boss lady.'

I laughed at her description.

'We acquired the next room too, same size as this one.' I indicated the main room and continued, 'I'll have lots more lovely new customers for your lunch rounds soon!'

'Ah now that is what I like to hear!' She agreed. Finally she glanced over at Steven who was watching our exchange with an expression of mild confusion. 'How's your girlfriend?' She asked him coldly. He frowned and shook his head, the corners of his mouth moving down into an upside down smile and he shrugged for good measure. I felt a prickling sensation on the back of my neck as she continued, 'Melissa? Is that her name? The girl in the pub on Friday.' Steven closed his eyes and breathed out slowly.

'That girl is relentless, she's like a zombie,' he said bitterly. His eyes met mine and he shook his head. 'I didn't go home with her though. I definitely woke up alone in my own bed on Saturday morning.' Relief flooded through me, but I had no idea how he had managed to avoid her. I looked at Steph to see if she was going to say anything more and she laughed angrily.

'No, she dragged you off to the toilets and had her wicked way with you there.'

Both Steven and I looked at her, horrified. His face flushed red and he avoided my gaze. I tried to remind myself that he was young, single, attractive, male, and human. I had no right to feel hurt, betrayed, or angry. But I felt all three.

'Yeah Dave was worried about you and sent me in to check you were OK.'

He watched her for a long while to see if she would continue. I grew impatient, I don't know why I wanted to hear it but I did. I wanted to know exactly what had happened.

'And?' I snapped. She looked at me surprised and I tried to smile with an air of mild interest.

'He was fucking her over the sink.' I saw Steven drop his face into his hands, my own face registered blank confusion, Steph sighed, 'from behind. She was watching him in the mirror. He didn't actually look like he was particularly happy about it, mind you.' she looked over at him with disgust and then shook her head at me.

I shrugged, shaking my head.

'Maybe it's true what they say about men's brains being in their trousers huh? Must be liking a homing missile, always able to find a landing pad no matter how much the heart is saying no.' I saw Steven slump further onto his desk as he heard my words.

'The most disturbing part was the way she looked at me when she saw me in the mirror. She was so smug, getting caught clearly turned her on, she was so noisy.' Steph shuddered, 'Slut!'

'I wonder how many people saw them?'

'It was pretty late, there weren't many people left, but I would imagine a few.' We watched Steven replace his headphones, drowning us out, not wanting to hear anymore. I turned to Steph.

'How do you feel?'

'Honestly? On the one hand I felt disgusted, totally put me off him. On the other hand, I sort of wished it had been me he'd fucked in the toilets. Although,' she glanced behind her at his face filled with horror and shrugged 'I'd prefer he remembered it and was happy about it too.

'Was he particularly drunk?' I asked. Steph considered it for a moment and shrugged.

'Well, I guess he was sober enough to know what he was doing, but apparently drunk enough to have forgotten about it.'

'Well he escaped her last weekend. She clearly wasn't letting him do it again.' I concluded.

My jealousy evaporated and was replaced with sympathy. I wanted to go to him, comfort him, but I couldn't until Steph left. I sensed his grief was worsened by my knowledge of the incident. I wanted to reassure him but it occurred to me that this could help put a bit of distance between us. I was confused once more about what to do and decided to just wait and see what feeling took over. I moved towards the kitchenette to make a cup of tea. Tea, the nation's healer, made everything better.

Steph handed me a menu.

'I take it the great diet starts today?' she teased. I nodded, 'OK, well I usually give you more generous helpings but for my average customer these calories are true so I will start making yours to this standard in future if you prefer.'

'Thanks, Steph,' I squeezed her shoulder as she turned to leave.

I took longer than necessary to make the tea. I placed

both mugs on the table by the sofas and made my way to Steven. He knew I was there but he wouldn't look at me. I took hold of one of his hands, forcing him to stop typing and look up me. His eyes were heavy with sadness and shame. I removed his headphones and nodded my head to the sofa. He pushed himself up and let me lead him the sofa. Sitting down I pulled him down into the seat next to me and put my arms round him, hugging him. His body was tense and I kissed the top of his head, stroking my fingers through his hair and rubbing his shoulder in soothing circles. He eventually relaxed, defeated, and slumped against me sighing.

'I'm so sorry,' he whispered in my ear. I shushed him gently. I couldn't bear the thought of him with her, or anyone else for that matter, but he'd done nothing wrong, weird maybe, but not wrong, not to me. He had nothing to apologise for. His distress was palpable, but I couldn't fully understand it. It's not as though sex with Melissa was a new thing. A warning played in the back of my mind; if he was so susceptible to Melissa, could I trust him to be faithful to me if we were together? I made a mental note to be sure she was off the scene before I considered anything between us. I needed to be sure about him and he needed to sort out his baggage.

I loosened my grip on his shoulders and reached across to the table, handing him his cup of tea. He wouldn't meet my eye but thanked me and took a sip. He kept his head bowed but I could see he was looking at me, not quite able to lift his gaze to my eyes. Finally he spoke.

'Fucking Melissa,' he spat viciously.

'Literally,' I teased. He looked up at me in horror.

'This isn't a joke, Ols. I seriously have no idea how to get rid of her. It was the same routine, but I was determined I wasn't going home with her. She asked me to just have one drink with her and went to the bar. She promised she'd go away after that. But then Dave got another round in, I kept drinking, to avoid talking to her more than anything. I remember going to the bar and she followed me, I think we started arguing. In my wisdom I followed her into the toilets to avoid making a scene, but ended up giving in to her advances. I had no idea anyone saw us. When I woke up Saturday morning, with a killer hangover, I was just so happy I was alone in my own bed. I knew I hadn't completely avoided her but it felt like progress somehow.'

'Ever considered a restraining order?'

'Seriously, what am I going to say? I want this girl to stop turning up and making me fuck her?'

'She's stalking you, making it difficult for you to live your life. I mean it's not a particularly enticing prospect is it? Date me, don't mind my crazy stalker who I occasionally fuck in public toilets when she pisses me off, I doesn't mean anything, it's you I love.' His eyes met mine for the first time and disappointment registered in them. I nudged him. 'Come on, what's done is done. Not the first time you've shagged Melissa, probably won't be the last time either if she has her way.'

'I wish you'd been there.' His voice was heavy with remorse.

'But what could I have done?'

'You would have helped me run away while she was at the bar.' I felt a brief flutter of guilt but dismissed it. This was not my doing. Melissa needed to be dealt with but it wasn't my problem to deal with.

'I think reporting her is the only thing you can do. I'd at least avoid going the same pub on Friday night.' He filled his cheeks and puffed a breath out, shaking his head.

'I'm not going out this week. No chance,' he glanced up at me and smiled sadly, 'I'm sorry.'

'What are you apologising for?' I was still confused by this.

'I'm trying to prove you can trust me. Then I go do

something stupid like this.'

'You have nothing to apologise for, you are a single man, you can do whatever you want with whoever you choose. It's nothing to do with me.' I was secretly pleased to see that he looked disappointed by my assessment. I took pity on him. 'I'll admit to feeling a little bit jealous, but that's not your problem. I need to snap you up before someone else does, right?' I tried to tease a smile out of him and eventually I succeeded. 'But until then, you're fair game and it's none of my business.'

Chapter Thirteen

I handed Ruth a beer that evening and curled up on the opposite end of the sofa from her. I'd filled her in on everything that had happened with Steven so far and she was grinning like a Cheshire cat.

'Told you I'd make you look hot, didn't I?'

'That's the main thing you got from my story?' I laughed. She looked at me with mock confusion.

'Well yeah, that was the main point, wasn't it?' she grinned at me and raised her bottle to clink mine. 'Progress, at least now you're admitting you like him even if you won't do anything about it.'

'It's the right thing to do.'

'But you already know you're going to go for it eventually right? He sounds amazing.' I knew she meant he sounded amazing for me and I agreed with her.

'I don't know. People change. He might lose interest in me in next to no time at all and my caution will have saved me a lot of heartache.' It was a relief to be able to talk about my feelings; get them out and examine them properly.

'He doesn't sound particularly fickle. And he seems certain, he must know his own mind, surely?' I shrugged.

'Haven't we all fallen in love and believed it was the "one" as soon as it happened, only to lose interest in them a few months later?' I reasoned. Ruth rolled her eyes, 'and he's young, remember?'

'But when you know, you just know.' She regarded me for a moment, searching my expression, 'do you know?' she asked, referring to whether I felt something more for Steven than I was admitting. I closed my eyes and searched my feelings.

'I see him in my future. I'm doing a lot of planning at work and I see him being a big part of it.' I shrugged. I doubted if that meant anything.

'I want to meet him. Are you having drinks after work this week?' Her eyes were sparkling with excitement and mischief. I shook my head and she pouted.

'After Friday night I doubt he'll go out in Camden for a while.' I reminded her.

'Not even if you're there to protect him?' She wheedled, staring at me with big eyes full of hope. I rolled my eyes. She was so difficult to say 'no' to. And it would be good to get her opinion of him. Ruth is much more observant than I am, she notices those imperceptible signals people give off, the looks when they think no one is watching ... Ruth is always looking, she doesn't miss a thing. She's an excellent judge of character.

'OK I'm not planning for it, if the subject comes up I will agree to go for a drink with him and let you know where we are.' She grinned satisfied.

'What are you going to wear?' She disappeared into my bedroom and I heard her rummaging through my wardrobe. I held my breath while I waited for her to find the old clothes I promised to throw away, but she returned with a couple of hangers. 'You should wear these. You'll look really pretty.'

'Just a drink after work, he'll find it odd if I suddenly dress up on a Friday.' I eyed the outfit dubiously. It was pretty though, long tailored shorts and a layered vest. It wasn't too dressy, but it was nicer than what I usually wore to the office. Maybe it would be nice to make an effort, make sure it was me he was looking at, even if Melissa did turn up and start jerking him off under the table. I shuddered at the thought.

'Did you hear any more from vampire guy?' She asked, dragging me away from my thoughts.

'Who?'

'The guy with no photos, Chris?'

'Ah the mysterious Chris Knight. He actually has loads of photos but none of them are tagged so I'm none the wiser as to which one he is. There is a photo of Steven with someone who I'm assuming is Chris, hoping actually, he's pretty hot!'

'Like celebrity crush hot?' She asked, grinning.

'He looks moody, like Angel.'

'So he is a vampire!' She laughed, 'have you heard from him again?'

'Yes, he's helping me lose some weight in fact.' Ruth raised her eyebrows, impressed as I continued, 'He's a fitness instructor. Well actually he's a law student, he lived with Steven in Edinburgh for two years.'

'Interesting.' She whispered as I nodded in agreement.

'Indeed. Anyway he's been advising me about exercise and diet.'

'So what is he like?' She asked interested, and mildly amused that I suddenly had two men in my life to talk about.

'He's a bit forward. Asks a lot of personal questions and stuff.'

'Such as?'

'Well he asked me about sex and stuff and,' I couldn't even say the word, Ruth was waiting with anticipation, 'masturbation! He sent me a vibrator. To my office. Steven opened the post!' Saying it out loud made it seem a lot funnier a week after. Ruth's jaw dropped and her eyes widened before she roared with laughter, 'Chris said Steven would've been turned on by the thought of me using it.' I shook my head grimacing, 'in actual fact he looked completely mortified!' I joined her in laughter for a while as the memory crossed my mind. I'd been absolutely stunned and couldn't even look at Steven but looking back it was quite funny. We calmed ourselves except for an occasional sniff of laughter.

'If there's one thing I've learned over the years about men, it's that they know what they like. If he says Steven would be thinking about you using it, you can damn well bet your money on it.'

'I hope he shaves a few pounds off me in his mind, I don't want him picturing this body!' I laughed.

'Does this Chris guy sound like he knows what he's talking about?'

'Well he's thirty-two and he sleeps with his clients to make them feel good!' I raised an eyebrow sceptically at her. She giggled.

'So yes, pretty experienced then?' She stated.

'He said he's in the business of making women feel good about their bodies and if that means fucking them then it's all part of the service.'

'Wow, what a hero!'

'Suits him I suppose, he's too busy for a girlfriend but wants to get laid a lot.'

'I wonder if his clients all wear skimpy gym gear once they start shaping up a bit. I bet they start out in oversized sweat pants and baggy T-shirts. That, to me, is what the gym is like. It smells of sweat and it's a bit gross.' She wrinkled her nose up.

'Yeah but I bet you wear the skimpy stuff, making us fatties jealous.' I teased her. She shrugged guiltily.

'I suppose if you had this handsome fit guy showing you how to work out, pressing up against you as he guides your movements, you'd probably get a bit turned on. Brilliant incentive to keep going back, and to get in shape to attract him.'

'He said once he's screwed them they stop flirting with him, like they've achieved everything they wanted and don't need him anymore.'

'Or he's really shit in bed!' She suggested. I pondered on that suggestion for a few minutes then dismissed it.

'As he's virtually unreal, I'm going to assume he's really handsome and amazing in bed. He offered to explain how to use the vibrator.' I giggled.

'Oh let him! That would be hilarious.'

'It's so embarrassing, I feel my face flush every time I chat with him.'

'Well it has been a long time, Olly, it's natural you'd be a little, frigid.' I gasped.

'I think repressed was the word we decided on.' I grumbled. She giggled again.

'Maybe this Chris will liberate you and turn you into a wanton sex machine ready to pounce on Steven.'

'Whenever I think about sex with Steven I feel sick.' I said sadly. Ruth looked horrified, 'with nerves, I mean.'

'Oh well that makes sense,' she shrugged.

'I can't remember what to do. It's so long ago, I don't even remember if I ever enjoyed sex. And I hate my body and I don't know what he will expect.' I could feel panic rising just thinking about it, 'Pubic hair? Should there be pubic hair?' I asked desperately, 'should it be shaved, trimmed, or natural?'

'Erm, well,' her eyes flickered briefly towards my crotch and she frowned. I laughed.

'I'm not saying I haven't groomed since I last got naked with a guy, because obviously it would be down to my knees by now. But how trimmed should it be. Completely bare? Trimmed short? How does Andrew like it?' Andrew was her husband, they'd been married two years and met when they were at university. She shrugged.

'Andrew likes it however it's presented to him.' She smiled and shook her head at my questions. I'd never had the guts to ask such questions before, but if there was anyone I could ask it was Ruth, 'I suppose as a general rule, you don't want to be transporting a pant moustache but stubble is probably a bit painful on their bollocks,' she shrugged, 'so maybe a little hair is good?'

As she was leaving Ruth hugged me and after scrutinising my face she said 'I'm glad you're getting back out there. I think even talking about sex with Chris will give you more confidence about it, you'll be fine when it happens.' I nodded, but still, just the suggestion of it brought thousands of butterflies swarming into my belly.

I went to bed thinking about it. I had been so busy over the last few years, so dedicated to my work that sex hadn't crossed my mind. Apart from my over active noisy neighbour, but that was merely a disturbance, it didn't make me want sex particularly, just the intimacy of being close to someone. Lately though, I was feeling things I'd not felt in a long time. Since Steven had arrived I found myself feeling aroused and it was building up, winding me up, and I felt ready to explode. It was becoming difficult to concentrate, my mind was constantly drifting, exploring scenarios that lead to us falling into each other's arms and making love. My mind drifted to the vibrator. I'd brought it home because I was worried it might get misplaced during the move, I should have just thrown it away but something compelled me to throw it in my bag. It was still in the packaging, hidden in my bedside cabinet.

I opened the drawer and pulled the box out. My nose wrinkled in disgust. Surely it couldn't hurt to just take it out of the box, though? I held the cool moulded plastic in my hand. It was heavier than I expected, felt smooth and hard. I pressed the button at the end and it started buzzing gently, with a slight vibration. I felt stupid lying there holding a vibrating stick in my hand and even more stupid when I moved it down my body towards my crotch. My body jumped as it reached the lower edge of my pubic bone heading towards my clitoris. Hundreds of sensations fizzled through my body, my lower back, my legs, all rushing to one point. I held the vibrator against me for a few moments, my breathing becoming shallow. My hips started instinctively moving, trying to grind more sensation. I pressed the button again and the vibrations increased. My body convulsed at the sensations as I moved the vibrator back and forth against me. I felt the sensation building and building inside me, tingling through my body rushing to the same point, every nerve concentrating on one spot at the centre of attention. The sensation was building, growing bigger with each roll of my hips, grinding my clitoris against the shaft of the vibrator. My orgasm burst out, I let out a gasp as it broke like a wave, my hips bucking and grinding myself against the vibrations wringing every last sensation out of my body. It lasted a long time, far longer than any orgasm I'd ever experienced before. My body was exhausted, my breath ragged. I allowed myself to enjoy a moment of awe and wonder before the inevitable guilt and shame kicked in. I marvelled at how quick it had been. I felt elated. Perhaps it had simply been so long that it was necessary, no guilt needed. No guilt came.

I got out of bed to use the toilet, my legs were shaking and I found it difficult to walk straight. I giggled to myself as I stumbled through the hallway to the bathroom. I felt light and free after carrying around weeks' worth of pent-up frustration. I made my way to the kitchen to get some water and as I passed my laptop I decided to open it up. I knew he would be there. He was a night owl.

Olivia Jones: *I just road tested my new toy.*

Chris Knight: *And?*

Olivia Jones: *Best orgasm I ever had.*

Chris Knight: *Wow. Wish I'd been there to see it.*

My face flushed and I felt the familiar creep of shame wash over me.

Chris Knight: *But then, if I was there, you wouldn't need a vibrator.*

Olivia Jones: *But now that I have a vibrator, I won't need a man.*

Chapter Fourteen

I was distracted all the following day in work. I couldn't explain it to myself but I was looking forward to chatting to Chris again. I'd logged off last tonight after saying I wouldn't need a man anymore. I smiled to myself as I remembered and wondered what his response would have been. I had a feeling he would have plenty to say on the subject today. I had realised that it was completely out of character for me to have started the conversation the way I did. To be so open about sex was a new thing for me, and I wasn't completely comfortable with it. Perhaps it had been the talk I'd had with Ruth that had somehow empowered me or maybe I was just overcome by the amazing orgasm I'd had. I felt the familiar flush of shame as I remembered. There she was, the repressed Olivia I knew. I closed my eyes sighing.

There was something about Chris that affected me. His shameless acknowledgement of sex, his openness about his thoughts and his desires, it made me feel excited. Maybe it was just because it had been so long or perhaps it was because I was attracted to someone for the first time in five years, but I found myself feeling aroused by the things he was saying. *I wish I'd been there to see it.* His words ran through my mind and sent a fizz of excitement through my stomach. I couldn't imagine someone watching me, I'm sure I'd feel stupid but his simple statement made me feel desirable and sexy in a way I'd never felt before.

Steven popped his head round my door.

'I'm heading home, Ols,' he said, smiling tightly. I was startled out of my reverie.

'Is that the time already?' I'd had no idea it was so late,

it felt like I'd done nothing all day but daydream.

I arrived home, switched on the oven to heat up, and grabbed my shorts and vest to do my exercise routine in front of the bedroom mirror. The first day had been hell. I had felt so hungry but today I had changed my eating habits and worked out my calories to spread them out more evenly and so far so good. It showed great restraint on my part that I switched on the oven that evening instead of calling a pizza. Was it really only four days ago that I last had pizza? It felt like months!

The exercises were difficult. I had sweat dripping off my face, although I took that as a good sign and my legs had a satisfying ache.

I put some chicken into the oven and threw myself on the sofa. I eyed the laptop and wondered whether Chris was online yet. I decided to check and sure enough he was there. His message came through before I had chance to finish typing mine.

Chris Knight: *How frustrating you are, Miss Jones, I was thinking about you and your vibrator all night.*

Oh my. I felt my muscles contract and I squirmed in my seat, smiling to myself.

Olivia Jones: *Well, that doesn't surprise me at all, Mr Knight, you big perv.*

Chris Knight: *LOL. But anyway, you agree I was right?*

Olivia Jones: *About what?*

Chris Knight: *The far superior orgasm you had. You could even say that I gave you.*

Well he did buy me the damn thing, I reasoned, but I knew he was just trying to get a rise out of me.

Olivia Jones: *You wish.*

I couldn't believe I wrote that. Something about this man made me feel liberated in some way. I liked being cheeky and flirty with him.

Chris Knight: *Are you flirting with me, Liv? I must say I like this new slightly less innocent you.*

Olivia Jones: *I suppose talking to you has been quite an education.*

Chris Knight: *Oh, there's still plenty left to learn yet;)*

Olivia Jones: *I'm intrigued.*

Chris Knight: *Good, I like an eager student. Now how is your fitness regime going?*

Olivia Jones: *Good. I stayed below 1600 calories most days. I've been exercising every day. I was just about to take a shower after tonight's session.*

Chris Knight: *Which exercises are you doing?*

Olivia Jones: *Squats, crunches, push-ups, though I'm never sure if I'm doing them right.*

Chris Knight: *What do you mean?*

Olivia Jones: *I can never work out whether my hands are in the right place and whether my knees are shoulder width apart or not.*

Chris Knight: *Well as I can't see you, I have no way to advise you. Just out of interest, what do you wear when you exercise?*

Olivia Jones: *Shorts and a vest. Why?*

Chris Knight: *So I can think about it later ;-)*

Olivia Jones: *Pervert!*

Chris Knight: *How short are the shorts?*

Olivia Jones: *Very short.*

Chris Knight: *Are they loose or tight?*

Olivia Jones: *Pretty loose.*

Chris Knight: *Excellent. :-) Of course if you could send me a picture that would help.*

My eyes widened in disbelief but I felt a shiver of excitement course through my body and settle in a fuzzy tingle around my crotch.

Olivia Jones: *You want to see a photo of my shorts?*

Chris Knight: *Preferably with you in them.*

My face flushed while I considered it. I could take a

photo from behind, he wouldn't see my face, no one would ever know it was me. I was enjoying this line of conversation and wanted to see where it would go to rather than stopping it dead by refusing. I searched the kitchen drawer for my digital camera. The batteries were still working thankfully so I glanced around the room to decide the best place to set it up. I set the timer for thirty seconds, set the camera on the book case and stepped forward into the line of fire and waited. I heard the camera click and I went to check the image. It was quite grainy and far away. I placed the camera on a lower shelf and tried again standing closer this time. The photo was a close up shot of my backside. It actually looked fairly good. I flushed as I thought about what I was doing – sending a photo of my bottom to a stranger on the Internet.

Really, I wondered. Is this really what I'm doing? I told myself he wasn't like a complete stranger, being friends with Steven. I uploaded the image to my laptop and sent it across to Chris.

Olivia Jones: *There you go then. Enjoy. I'm going to take a shower.*

I closed the laptop and, after checking the progress of my chicken, went to wash off the sweat from my workout and cool my suddenly overheated libido.

Chapter Fifteen

My plans for the business expansion were coming along nicely. I had finally worked out the job roles I wanted and had sent out job adverts in all the local press and programming magazines. I already knew I was going to hire James and just needed to decide when to call him.

I was standing in the testing room that Friday afternoon, admiring the new layout, when Steven found me. He whistled through his teeth in admiration.

'This place looks awesome,' he said. There was a hint of admiration in his voice and I felt my heart swell with pride.

'It's really coming along, isn't it?' I agreed.

Steven opened the door to the server room and grinned back at me.

'Is it all up and running?' I nodded. 'They're going to run the connections through over the weekend and we will be connected to it on Monday.' The server was going to make team working much easier. Not something I'd ever had to think about before. It would also make remote access possible too: I could connect to it from home, not that I wanted to spend every waking minute working but it would allow me to work from home if I felt the need to be away from so many people once in a while ... or one particular person.

I remembered my promise to Ruth about going for a drink.

'Not having a quick one after work tonight?' I asked him, 'I think this deserves a celebration.'

He smiled sadly, shaking his head. He'd been quiet the rest of the week after Steph's revelation.

'Can't help noticing that no one invited me this week.'

'You don't need to be invited, you just turn up.' I told him. Steph had only made a point of inviting him last week because she had particularly wanted him there. Clearly that wasn't the case this week.

'I don't think it's a good idea anyway,' he shrugged.

'Are you sure? You kinda look like you could do with a pint.'

It broke my heart to see him so torn between wanting to go for a drink and wanting to get home to safety away from Melissa.

'I could use a beer, but I guess I'll just have one at home.'

'Not even with me there to protect you?' I grinned at him. Steven shook his head.

'Thanks, Ols, I appreciate that, but I just want to get home and get this week behind me.'

I nodded in understanding and watched him leave.

As I walked home, I pondered on my feelings for Steven. There'd been a change in the atmosphere this week, particularly after the revelation about Melissa. He'd been quiet and moody ever since, looked at me sadly; perhaps he thought I was disgusted with him and was upset by it. Was I disgusted? I didn't think I was. I felt jealous as hell that he had been with her last Friday night but I also recognised it for what it was. I missed the confident, flirty Steven although I had to admit it was also good that he wasn't distracting me so much. Instead I was feeling distracted by Chris Knight. The anonymous Chris Knight. I shook my head. Swapping a gorgeous man who was right there in my office for an unknown man on the end of a computer who I would never meet. It was insane. Or maybe it was just the distraction from Steven I needed.

As soon as I opened up the laptop that evening, a message arrived from Chris.

Chris Knight: *You did it again, Liv, putting ideas into my head and leaving me dangling.*

Olivia Jones: *I don't know what you're talking about.*

Chris Knight: *Thank you for the photo, I'll be keeping that with me at all times. Nice ass, by the way.*

I smiled as I felt my heart rate increase and my face flush with a warm glow.

Olivia Jones: *It still needs some work but thanks.*

Chris Knight: *Not at all, it's perfect. I've been thinking about you doing your push-ups in those shorts.*

Olivia Jones: *I doubt that's a pretty thought, my big fat arse sticking up in the air, blocking out the sun.*

I giggled to myself, I had an idea where this was going and it was thrilling.

Chris Knight: *On the contrary, I was thinking that those shorts would be easy to move aside, I could easily fuck you from behind while you're exercising.*

I didn't know what it was about the crudeness of his words, but every time he said "fuck" it sent shivers down my spine. I squirmed in my seat.

Olivia Jones: *I imagine that would make it difficult for me to get through all my reps. Some trainer you turned out to be, preventing me from doing my exercises.*

Chris Knight: *Not at all, I'd wait until you're at the end of your reps, and sex is a great calorie burner.*

Olivia Jones: *Sexercise?*

Chris Knight: *LOL.*

Olivia Jones: *It can't burn that many calories; you'd have to be at it for ages, surely?*

Chris Knight: *Oh God, is this one of those times where you offer some kind of revelation of your limited and frankly poor sexual experience?*

Olivia Jones: *Um well, it doesn't exactly take very long does it?*

Chris Knight: *LOL let me guess ... You're in bed in your flannel pyjamas, facing the edge of the bed. He* *cuddles up behind you pressing himself into your lower back, stroking your arm and kissing your hair. You lie there wondering if you can pretend to be asleep. His hand creeps round to squeeze your breast and you realise he's not giving up so you roll onto your back and kiss him. His hand heads south, bypassing any kind of build-up, snakes his hand inside your pants and fumbles about quickly, you gasp because it's uncomfortable but he takes it as a sign of pleasure and speeds up before climbing over you, removing your pants and plunging on in. You lie there waiting for it to be over and he slows down realising you're not that excited and thinking he needs to take it slow so you start moaning enthusiastically so he'll come and get the hell off you ... The whole thing takes two-and-a-half minutes. Or thereabout.*

It was a strange experience because somehow his description of my rather lacklustre sex life was absolutely spot on, and yet it aroused me, because he was describing it. I imagined that if it were Chris Knight, those two-and-a-half minutes would be much more erotic than my paltry experience. Of course, I was as much to blame for the lack of spice in the bedroom, perhaps if I'd actually been interested in sex I'd have been more forthcoming.

Olivia Jones: *Like I said, not many calories getting burned off there.*

Chris Knight: *Oh Liv, what I wouldn't give to show you how it could be.*

Olivia Jones: *Even in two minutes? Because apparently I get bored easily.*

Chris Knight: *You wouldn't get bored if you were enjoying it. Sex doesn't have to be a race, Liv, the aim isn't just to come as quickly as possible then go to sleep.*

Olivia Jones: *OK, so what would you do that would be so great?*

I waited ages for a response. I could see he was writing something but no message came through. I went to the toilet, I grabbed another beer from the fridge and watched the screen. Finally, the message bar flashed and I had an answer. It was well worth the wait.

Chris Knight: *You wouldn't be wearing flannel pyjamas, you would want to look nice for me, you'd be wearing a short, silky nightie with spaghetti straps. Let's assume you got changed while I was in the bathroom or something, because if you changed in front of me you wouldn't get as far as wearing the nightie. I would kiss you, gently at first, trailing kisses along your jawline up to your ear. I'd slide a strap off your shoulder and trail kisses down you neck and across your shoulder. I'd slide the other strap down and then gently pull the nightie to the floor. I'd walk you backwards towards the bed till you were sitting and I'd kneel before you, exploring your body with my hands and mouth. I'd feel your nipples harden against my tongue and trail kisses down past your belly button. My hands would move slowly up your thighs trailing across your panties, already damp with arousal. I'd slide them down your thighs and explore with my tongue, teasing your clitoris with little kisses and licks. I would insert a finger inside you and explore you inside and out moving gently and picking up pace until you are almost ready to explode, then I would pull you off the bed onto me so I can enter you while continuing to explore your body, teasing your nipples with my tongue and my teeth until we both explode.*

I was glad he had logged off after sending, I was flushed, aroused, and slightly embarrassed, unsure what I would even say in response. I felt excited and frustrated at the same time. I still couldn't imagine being so naked and on display in front of someone, the thought of being so exposed was horrifying and thrilling at the same time. I knew I would be desperate to drag the covers over me and hide. Maybe when I lost some weight I'd feel less vulnerable. And oral sex? The thought grossed me out completely but he made it sound so erotic. I wondered what it would feel like to have someone lick me down there. The thought sent a shiver down my spine and I squirmed again in my seat. I could do with another shower! I stared at the screen for a long time willing him to come back online but he didn't. I felt tightly wound like I wanted to explode and went to bed feeling frustrated and disappointed.

Chapter Sixteen

Steven was quiet the following Monday. It had been a few weeks since that kiss, since he promised to stop flirting with me and to stop talking about us being together. I wondered when he would ask me out on a date for the first time. It still hadn't happened and I was beginning to worry it might not happen, perhaps he had, as I expected, changed his mind, met someone else, or just lost interest. I spent most of my day responding to phone calls about the jobs I had advertised. I was still undecided about all the roles so I had only advertised four vacancies. I had also called James to find out if he was still interested in working with me and he was. He was really pleased, still unemployed and willing to start straight away. I told him he could start the following week. I wanted to decide what to do with Steven before anyone else started.

The fact was that Steven was an excellent worker, he had a lot of potential, and would be snapped up by any of the major games developers and I wanted to keep him, not just because of my attraction to him but because I could see him being a major part of the expansion of Inspired. I was worried that the new staff might not respect him if he was an intern, but as I had grown to trust him a lot I imagined he would be the first person I would approach with new projects, and to discuss new ideas. Would that seem odd to other staff? It certainly put him in a much more vital position than an intern.

Besides which, I was sick of writing monitoring reports for his internship coordinators. I thought if I could give him a promotion, it would relieve me of that added annoyance. There was also the fact that he was good with people and would be a great poster boy for the company, representing us at conferences. I tried not to think too much about a poster of Steven on my wall, smiling down at me while I slept.

He'd shown great initiative so far with the project he had taken over from me, his time management was fantastic, always exceeding his goals, the current app was well ahead of schedule, and the client was very pleased with what he had seen so far. I realised that it was going to be my job to bring in the work and to make decisions about the in-house games and apps we worked on. I needed to make sure that I had someone I could trust to oversee production and someone I could trust with my own ideas. Was Steven too young, too inexperienced to be given such responsibility? Could I really trust him or was my judgement clouded by my attraction too him? I've never been very good at sharing my work, getting the opinion of others, I'm always worried it will be dismissed as not good enough. I found it easy to talk to Steven about my ideas. He understood where I was coming from, recognised my vision, and suggested ideas that complemented and developed my original concept. We worked well together, and as this was a huge step for me, taking on staff, handing over my work and my ideas for others to make reality, I needed someone I trusted to work with first. But that almost suggested a management position and I wondered if his age was a problem. But then, I was hardly experienced in management. I had my position purely because I owned the business.

I wondered how other companies operated. They probably had all kinds of departments, lots of different specialists working on their own area. Or they were small like me, working on small apps on their own. I was trying to move us into a larger arena but I still wanted to retain my small-scale operation.

It was an exciting time, I had several ideas in various

stages of development that I was keen to work on but client commissions came first. With more staff, I could delegate that work out and concentrate on both bringing in more clients and developing my own apps and games.

My mind wandered to Chris Knight. I hadn't heard from him since Friday night but I'd certainly thought about him. He was a mystery, I wasn't even sure what he looked like, although I felt fairly sure he was the guy in the photo with Steven, but I felt an attraction towards him. I knew it was unlikely we would ever meet but I had lost several hours imagining us meeting, falling into each other's arms and making love, slowly, passionately. I knew he was fit, I assumed as a fitness instructor working in a gym he had to be and I imagined him being tall, muscular like an Olympic swimmer or gymnast.

A commotion outside my office roused me from my thoughts. I heard the door burst open and I recognised Dave's voice apologising to Steven. I heard a frantic, angry female voice shouting and heard Steven's voice rising, sounding frustrated. I marched to the door and flung it open. 'What the fuck is going on?' I shouted loud enough to drown out all the other raised voices, silencing them, all three faces turned towards me. I surveyed the scene before me, Dave was looking uncomfortable, stood in the doorway of the office. Steven looked tired, his short-sleeved shirt was crumpled and the top buttons were undone revealing a small smattering of chest hair. His hair, normally carefully styled, was flopped across one side of his head obscuring his left eye. His shoulders sagged and he looked deflated and ashamed, his face was already red, angry, but now he was calming and he just seemed embarrassed. Dave looked relieved that someone was taking control of the situation, he was such a nice guy, always supporting everyone, but he found it hard to be assertive and stand up to people. Finally, my eyes fell on the girl – slim, attractive, well dressed. She looked rich, well groomed. She was wearing tight-fitting jeans, high-heeled shoes, and a silk vest. She wore a camel coloured, soft leather jacket and her hair was scooped over on one side and secured with a band, cascading across her right shoulder in a soft curl. Dave had hold of her upper arm, apparently trying to hold her back. Her expression was hard to read. She looked at me and a look of triumph flashed across her eyes. Melissa.

'Well?' I demanded. 'What do you want?'

Her eyes narrowed and she watched me, a small smirk tugging at one corner of her mouth, then her eyes flickered across to Steven and she nodded her head towards him.

'I came to tell him that I'm pregnant.' She announced, her eyes flashed with a challenge to me, daring me to argue with her. I couldn't tell what she was thinking, she didn't look upset, she looked victorious. Was this a trick? Had this been her plan all along; to tie him to her? Was she really so desperate to be with him that she would resort to such measures? I felt sickened by her actions, but I also felt sorry for her, being content to trick a man into being with her, a man who clearly didn't want her. I forced myself to look at Steven. His face was ashen, drained of his earlier rage and numb with shock. He was staring at her, defeated, confused, and sad. He glanced at me, and seeing me looking at him, his face flushed. I gestured to Dave and he nodded, releasing his grip on Melissa and backing out of the room. I followed him, closing the door behind me without a backward glance.

I was drained by the time I got home, and decided to treat myself to a takeaway. I convinced myself it wouldn't hurt for one night and I needed cheering up with comfort food. I didn't care how many calories pizza cost – I was getting one anyway!

I opened up the laptop and saw Chris Knight was online. Good, I needed distracting after the bombshell

Melissa had dropped earlier that day. I still couldn't believe it. Dave had been really kind; he knew how I felt and I was kicking myself for not heeding Steven's words about snapping him up before someone else did. I'd missed my chance like an idiot. Dave had said, 'if someone else is able to snap him up then he wasn't meant to be yours after all and it's best to know now before you're too involved.' I knew he was right but it felt so disappointing. It was just so frustrating. There was no question of him not doing the right thing, he was too good a guy not to, old fashioned to an extent, but how galling to be forced into a marriage with someone he doesn't even like. He had been right when he'd said she would never leave him alone. Now she had exactly what she wanted. It wouldn't have made any difference if I'd snapped him up when he told me to, the damage had already been done. I wondered if he'd have left me to do the right thing by her then and knew deep down he would have to. I wanted him to be that sort of a man, but I didn't want him to be that sort of a man for her. Dave was right, at least I'd saved myself that heartache.

Olivia Jones: *So, you're pretty frustrating yourself. Leaving me dangling like that, I couldn't get to sleep at all last night.*

Chris Knight: *Is that all it takes to excite you Liv? Goodness, you're in for a treat.*

Olivia Jones: *I am? But not all men have your prowess surely? I mean wouldn't I have had some satisfaction by now if it was more common?*

Chris Knight: *Good point, but maybe you've just been unlucky.*

Olivia Jones: *Or maybe it's my fault for being a little prudish.*

Chris Knight: *Well we'll get you over your fears and then you can enjoy some good sex. ;-)*

Olivia Jones: *When was the last time you spoke to*

Steven?

It occurred to me suddenly that Steven might need a friend. It had been difficult when I returned to the office. I watched Melissa leave, looking triumphant in her conquest, happy to be ruining Steven's life, denying him a life filled with love.

Steven was slumped on the sofa in my office, his arm across his eyes. I'd perched on the edge of the sofa and touched his arm to let him know I was there. He didn't say anything for a long time until he eventually asked if he could take the rest of the week off. He said he needed some time to think. I flushed with a warm glow when he said;

'She's turned me into the type of man I never wanted to be; I'm not the sort of guy that has sex in public toilets, and I'm not the sort of man that doesn't face up to my responsibilities and do the right thing. She somehow made me do the first point and right now she's making me want to walk away. I mean fuck her, I hate her. But I don't know if my conscience will let me just abandon her. But I look at you and I want to, I want to just tell her to go to hell. You know how I feel about you, Ols, but I have to work out what to do for the best, what's the right thing to do, and I can't do that around you.'

I had been unsure how he felt, whether he still wanted me and now I knew, now it was too late. I had just nodded and made my way back to my desk, leaving him free to head home.

Chris Knight: *Yeah, he emailed me earlier. Fucking Melissa!*

Olivia Jones: *Did you know her at uni?*

Chris Knight: *Yeah, she made herself known. She was always hanging around the bar when Steven was working. She had something of an obsession with him. But she's not to be trusted. There's more to Melissa than meets the eye. I thought it then and I still think it now.*

Olivia Jones: *What do you mean?*

Chris Knight: *I can't prove anything, it's just a feeling, maybe it's wishful thinking, I just think there's an ulterior motive here. Steven's a good-looking guy, but he's a nerd and he's going to attract a particular type of woman – sure beautiful women might want him until he opens his mouth and starts blinding them with geek speak, then they'll just lose interest thinking 'such a shame that someone so handsome is so dull'. Melissa is pretty but she's after something, her ambitions are much bigger than settling down and playing happy families with Steven.*

Olivia Jones: *But what else could she be doing?*

Chris Knight: *I wish I knew.*

I tried to reply but for some reason my keyboard stopped responding. I couldn't believe it, I was just learning something interesting about this whole mess and I couldn't respond. I restarted the laptop but when I restarted it I got the black screen warning me that the computer hadn't been shut down properly and asking me to choose whether to start up as normal or in safe mode. The keyboard wouldn't respond. Completely dead. I couldn't believe it. I screamed and slammed the lid shut and threw a cushion at it. That'll show it!

I picked up my phone and left a status on Facebook, hoping Chris would see it and understand my sudden disappearance. *Laptop just died, guess I'm going laptop shopping tomorrow.*

Chris replied instantly. *Get one with a webcam.*

Am I finally going to get to see the anonymous Chris Knight? A fizz of excitement jolted through me, followed immediately by butterflies.

Chapter Seventeen

By Wednesday, I was miserable in the office. I stood by the kitchenette waiting for the kettle to boil and stared forlornly at his desk. I missed him. Funny to think only a few weeks ago I was plotting ways to get him out of the office so I could have some peace, and now that he had been away for two days, I was missing him. The office seemed empty and quiet without his usual carefree banter.

As I was stirring my tea, I heard the door open and, turning, I saw Dave pop his head around the door frame.

'Hi, Dave, how are you?' I asked warmly. I'd not spoken to Dave since Monday when we had left Steven and Melissa to talk.

'Hey, Olly, I'm good, just wanted to pass your post in,' he replied handing me a pile of letters and packages. 'Popular this week.' He smiled.

'Yes, job applications. Advert went out last week.' I explained, nodding.

'Any word from Steven?'

I shook my head, my sad smile frozen in place.

'He'll be back in on Monday.'

'Well, what will be, will be. Don't let it get you down.' He smiled reassuringly and patted my arm before leaving.

I took my post and my cup of tea into my office and settled on the sofa. I had twelve job applications and three invoices. I piled them neatly on the coffee table and turned my attention to the package. It was addressed for my attention and, after the last parcel, I was relieved I was opening the post.

Inside the envelope was a blank DVD case with a sticky note attached saying:

'The next lesson of your sex education.'

Inside the case was a blank DVD. There was nothing written on the disc to identify it. I was so curious I contemplated inserting the disc into my computer but I had a feeling it would contain material that should only be viewed in private and although I was alone in the office I didn't want to risk anyone popping in to visit me. I threw the DVD into my bag and returned to my desk.

That evening I followed my new routine; turned the oven on, changed into my exercise clothes and spent twenty minutes working out. Finally, after I'd showered and eaten I opened up my bag and retrieved the disc.

I don't know what I was expecting, but as it was from Chris, I knew it would be in some way highly embarrassing. And yet I was still surprised when I selected the first story and found myself watching porn.

The scene opened on a blue door, sunlight bouncing off the glossy paint. A tanned fist knocked on the door and a man was revealed, his dark hair brushed back off his face and few tendrils falling across his forehead. He wore dungarees, with no shirt underneath, showing off his muscles. The door opened to reveal a young woman, blonde hair piled on top of her head with curls escaping and falling down the back of her neck. She had a bath towel wrapped around her body, held in place by her hand. She was lean and tanned.

'Someone call for a plumber?' The guy asked smiling, revealing a perfect set of pearly white teeth. She stepped aside to let him in as she moved her eyes across the full length of his body. She led him upstairs to the bathroom, and leaned against the door.

'I was taking a shower and the water just went cold.' She explained, her hand still holding the towel fastened at her chest but her fingers idly stroking her breast as she spoke. The plumber glanced at the filled bath.

'The bath water is hot?' He asked surprised.

'No, I boiled some pans of water.' She moved towards the bath and dropped her towel, 'You don't mind if I take a bath while you work do you? I have to get ready.'

He shook his head as she stepped into the bath, moaning as the warm water covered her.

She lathered some soap in her hand and proceeded to wash her breasts. He stopped to watch her for a while, his hand moving to stroke his penis through his clothes. She noticed him watching her and stopped.

'Why don't you join me?' She asked, her voice heavy with longing.

He unclipped his braces, letting his dungarees fall to the floor, and stepped out of them and over to the bath. He sat on the edge, his legs in the water. She turned onto her knees to face him, running her hands up his thighs and her tongue up the length of his considerable erection. She sucked him into her mouth, her lips moving right down to the base and slowly back to the tip, teasing him with her tongue and sucking him back in to the back of her throat. On and on this continued, his hands weaving into her hair, directing the rhythm of her movement.

He pulled out of her mouth, stood up, and lifted her into his arms and carried her out of the bathroom.

The scene changed, she lay on a large bed with black satin sheets, her feet dangling over the edge as he kneeled between her knees, his tongue running slowly up and down her clitoris, she was moaning seductively as he inserted fingers inside her. Fingers – plural!

I couldn't even imagine that much attention being paid to me down there. I watched fascinated as he flipped her over onto her knees pulling her backside towards him and plunging himself inside her, thrusting deeper and deeper as the volume of her moans increased.

I became aware of a sensation building in my lower belly and a tingling in my crotch. I squirmed in my seat, tensing my thigh muscles and gently rotating my pelvis. My hand moved instinctively inside the waistband of my jeans and I felt a flush creep over my face as I realised what I was doing. But I didn't care. I was masturbating to porn and it was hot.

On the screen the blonde girl was on her knees looking up at his huge erection as he moved his hand quickly up and down until his orgasm burst forth across her face. She opened her mouth, catching the drops and licking the juice from the tip of his penis as it gushed out.

My own orgasm shuddered through me as I watched, my hand slowing its pace as I squeezed every last bit of sensation out of my body.

I stared at the menu screen on the television, contemplating whether to watch more. I shook my head, bringing me back to my senses.

I couldn't believe what was happening to me. I'd never been so easily aroused in my life, never so interested in sex, and yet lately it was all I could think about.

Chapter Eighteen

Five p.m. on Friday was welcomed with open arms. I was missing Steven and was worried about him, wondering what he was thinking, how he was feeling, and what he would do. I desperately wanted him to go against his instinct and tell Melissa she was on her own, but part of me wanted to know he was the type of man who did the right thing. I was already convinced he was lost to me, even though a small part of me was still hopeful. One thing I knew for certain was that if by some miracle he was still free when he returned next week I wouldn't waste any more time wondering what I should do about my feelings for him. If he still wanted me, I was his. But sadly, I knew it was unlikely.

I changed into my shorts and vest and made a start on my exercises. Chris had suggested I buy a skipping rope after a conversation we'd had about games we'd played at school. He said skipping was really good exercise. It had been years since I'd skipped but I had been really into it when I was younger, learning different rope swings and tricks. I had a big open space in the hallway with high ceilings which was perfect for skipping so I had started doing it to warm up for twenty minutes before moving onto my strength exercises. I'd even bought some dumbbells to work on my bingo wings!

I had hoped that skipping would distract me from constantly thinking about Steven, but it just gave me more freedom to think. I needed to do something otherwise I'd spend the whole weekend driving myself insane, reproaching myself for my missed opportunity and then feeling guilty for only thinking of myself and not considering the awful situation Steven found himself in.

I was distracted from my thoughts by a ringing noise shrilling loudly from the living room. I stopped skipping, sweat running down my neck and my arms shining with moisture from my exertion. I hadn't even noticed how tired I was. The ringing confused me. It wasn't my telephone or my mobile; it was a noise I'd not heard before. I followed the sound into the living room towards my new laptop. On the screen was a black window with a message 'Chris Knight wants to Face Time with you' and two buttons – green to accept and red to reject.

I remembered his comment on Facebook telling me to get a laptop with webcam and felt a jolt of emotion, a mix of excitement and panic. Was I about to see the anonymous Chris Knight for the first time? I was a little nervous. I liked to imagine he was attractive and sexy but what if he wasn't? An image of an old scruffy man wearing a tea-stained vest crossed my mind and I felt nauseous at the thought of him making sexual comments to me. I shuddered and decide it was time to find out the truth. I clicked accept.

Nothing appeared on the screen except for a small square in the bottom corner of the window which was showing me. I was surprised at first when I saw it and realised that it was the webcam filming me. I guessed that was what Chris could see on his screen. I still had no image though, just a black screen. I waited until eventually I heard a voice.

'Well hello, Liv, nice to finally see you. You look hot.'

His voice surprised me, it was soft but firm and American. I hadn't thought about where Chris might be from but I definitely wasn't expecting that accent. I blushed at his words.

'Thank you.'

'Haha, no I mean you look hot, you have sweat rolling down your face,' he said, amusement in his voice.

I flushed again wiping the back of my hand across my forehead.

'I'm in the middle of my exercises, I was skipping.' I heard him chuckle, I still couldn't see him though, 'Why can't I see you?'

'What do you mean?'

'I can't see you; I just have a blank square on my screen.'

'Really? OK, hang on.' I heard noises, keys tapping, wires moving, him swearing under his breath, 'what about now?'

'Nope nothing.' I sighed, disappointed, 'you didn't think to test it out beforehand?' I teased.

'How can I test it out? I can see myself on my screen, I assumed it worked.'

'You could've called your phone.'

'Ah, I did not think of that,' he chuckled quietly, 'I'm really not a nerd, huh?'

'You're really not.'

'OK so I guess I need to go buy a webcam. You can hear me OK though, right?'

'Perfectly.'

'So, please continue with your exercises, I can check you're doing them right.'

'No!' I exclaimed.

I didn't want him to see me exercising in case I was doing it wrong; I hated being corrected about anything.

'Liv, if you're not doing them right they're not doing you any good. You said last week you weren't sure if you were doing them right. Show me.' His voice had a soft tone of amusement but he spoke firmly, with a commanding authority. I sighed loudly and moved aside to check where the camera was picking up and crawled away from the laptop to the space where I was sure he would see me.

Facing the camera, I got into the position for push-ups.

'I can see straight down your top,' he teased.

I sat back on my heels and glared at the screen. He laughed loudly.

'Sorry. OK Liv, turn sideways, let me check your shape.' I obliged and he continued barking instructions; hands further forwards, knees slightly back, back flat and straight.

'That's good, OK face away.' I turned around and struck the same pose.

'What are you checking for now?' I asked confused

'I'm just checking out your ass in those shorts. Very nice. Definitely easily fuckable.'

I spun round on my knees and stared at the screen, mouth opened wide in shock. Words I'd seen him write many times, they sounded so strange spoken out loud and yet at the same time they sounded so hot. I became increasingly aware that I wanted this man to find me attractive and sexy. He was chuckling again. I crawled over to the laptop and grinned.

'Well hope you made the most of it, I'm going to take a shower!' I said smiling, then I closed the laptop.

Chapter Nineteen

'What's happened?' Ruth asked, seeing right through my wide grin and over-enthusiastic greeting. I had just arrived at All Bar One and joined her at the bar. My face fell and I sighed.

'Melissa.'

My face hardened and I scowled as I said her name. Ruth raised her eyebrows.

'The girl from the toilets?' She asked. I nodded in confirmation, 'what's she done to him now?'

'She burst into the office to tell him she's pregnant.'

I could hear the defeat in my voice. Ruth's mouth fell open and she stared at me for a long time. She turned to the barman,

'We're going to need tequila over here and a couple of raspberry martinis.' She instructed him.

She pushed a shot of tequila towards me and I threw it back gratefully, the pale yellow liquid burning the back of my throat and distracting me momentarily from the misery I was feeling.

We took our cocktails and settled into a booth on the far side of the bar.

'So what's he going to do?' She asked.

I shrugged.

'I don't know. He took a few days off to get his head round it all.' I smiled sadly, 'he said he couldn't think straight around me, I made him want to do the wrong thing.'

Ruth's eyes widened and her mouth dropped open.

'So you think he wants to do the right thing?'

'He's that type of guy I guess, he doesn't want to be

this time, but I think he will all the same.' I shrugged and stuck out my bottom lip, 'I should've snapped him up when I had the chance.'

'So you were cautious, this still might have happened even if you had snapped him up.'

Ruth was trying to reassure me but it didn't make me feel better.

'Maybe I'd have been there that night, or he would've been with me somewhere else.' I pointed out.

'Or maybe you snapped him up after and she still turns up pregnant. At least you don't have the heartache of him leaving you for her.'

I closed my eyes at her words. They were too horrible. 'Of course if he had an actual choice in the matter he would obviously choose you.' She added, supportively.

'It's such a mess. She finds him when he's drunk, fucks him, gets pregnant. It's like she planned it. But why?' I frowned, it didn't make any sense, 'Surely she doesn't just fancy him that much? But what else could it be?'

'Is she mentally ill? Is she convinced she's in love and determined to tie him to her forever? Maybe she's not even pregnant.'

I hadn't considered that. *Could she be making it up?*

'Of course, she might insist they get married before she starts to show so she will look good in the photos, then conveniently she miscarries.' I suggested, hopefully.

'But then he would just divorce her surely? It's not a very good long-term plan if all she wants is to be with him.'

I shook my head, accepting defeat and leant back in my seat.

'I guess I don't know enough about him to know what other reason she would have. I guess it doesn't matter anymore. The one that got away.'

'At least you still have the cyber vampire.' she grinned.

I felt my face flush betraying my embarrassment. I

didn't know what Ruth would make of Chris, I had moments when I felt ashamed to admit to myself that I found his attention erotic and that I looked forward to our communications. I tried to prevent the secret smile pulling at the corner of my mouth but it was too late, Ruth had noticed it before I could stop it.

'Spill, Olly, what's he done now?' I closed my eyes embarrassed.

'OK, you remember I told you he's advising me with losing weight?'

'I do,' she nodded, 'and he seems to be doing a good job, you look fantastic.'

'Thanks, although that's more credit to you and your shopping skills.'

I tried valiantly to change the subject.

'It's a special talent I have. Continue.' *Damn!*

I recounted the conversation we had shared last week, him asking what I wore to exercise and his comments about fucking me from behind. I faltered as I said the words, closing my eyes in shame but feeling a delightful warmth rush through my body at the memory. I had no idea why I found those words so arousing. Ruth leant forward captivated by my tale, dropping her mouth when I told her about the webcam and him openly perving at my backside.

'Please tell me you were not wearing those hideous pyjamas that look like a 1950s American high school basketball kit.' She wrinkled her nose is disgust. I nodded, grinning.

'The very same.' I giggled at her reaction.

'So what does he look like, is he the cute guy who looks like Angel?' she asked, frowning as my face fell.

'Well that's the really annoying part. His webcam broke so although the microphone works the camera does not. I can't see him.'

'Denied. That is annoying'

'He's going to go buy a new one so hopefully I'll get to see him soon. I hope he's the Angel guy, I hope he's not ugly.' I blurted, my inappropriate filter had deteriorated the more cocktails I consumed. I knew I shouldn't care what he looked like, but I did.

'What does he sound like?'

I closed my eyes trying to summon up his voice in my mind.

'Sort of dreamy,' I murmured, while Ruth rolled her eyes and made gagging gestures. 'He sounds gentle, but authoritative, and he has an American accent.'

'No wonder he likes your shorts then!' She giggled. I smiled, relieved that she wasn't outraged by the nature of the conversations we had been having. 'You'll be having cybersex before you know it,' she grinned, waggling her eyebrows suggestively at me.

'Cybersex?'

'Got to keep things alive haven't you? Basically, you talk each other through masturbating, pretending your hands are their hands doing what they tell you they want to do. We used to do it all the time during the college breaks, and sometimes if Andrew is working away.' She trailed off noticing the look of horror on my face. I put my hands over my ears.

'Too much information,' I cried, she laughed at me and rolled her eyes. 'There's no way I'm doing that, I'd feel stupid.'

'I thought that at first, but it's pretty erotic once you get past the embarrassment. And it's safer than one night stands, and you can pretend he's that gorgeous poster pin up, imagine the fun you could have!'

I just couldn't imagine it, I was only just evolving to the point where masturbating didn't fill me with guilt and shame, but that was a very new thing, I doubted I could cope with someone watching me. *Could I?* It had been quite a revelation hearing Ruth describe it; she obviously didn't think it was something to be ashamed of. I remembered the reactions through my body whenever Chris said anything about sex and tried to imagine how I'd react if he was directing me to pleasure myself. I felt a shiver run down my spine, gathering in a pool in my crotch. I squirmed in my seat and exhaled slowly.

I felt drunk suddenly. I couldn't remember how many drinks we'd had, five or six maybe. I had forgotten to eat before coming out to meet Ruth and my stomach was growling at me.

'I think I need to go home.' I mumbled.

'Me too. Your face is all swirly.' She giggled.

I giggled too. If Ruth had double vision there was no hope for me. I'd be lucky to stand up.

'I'm going to ring Andrew and get him to pick us up.' She said as she stumbled out of her seat and made her way outside to use the phone.

I swayed across the room to the toilets and splashed my face over the sink. Feeling slightly refreshed and more awake I wiped the water away with a paper towel. It scratched across my face, the sensation reassuring me that I still had some senses. I looked in the mirror and saw streaks running through my make-up, dark lines from my mascara and water marks cutting through my foundation. I looked a mess, but I didn't really care. I wiped my fingers under my eyes to remove the excess mascara and made my way outside.

Ruth and Andrew were waiting for me at the bar. Andrew handed me a pint glass filled with water and ordered me to drink. His arm was round Ruth protectively, holding her upright. She had her eyes closed, leaning into him. Ruth was capable of falling asleep upright so I downed my pint of water and motioned for us to leave while Ruth was still awake.

I battled feelings of nausea as we drove home. I was so hungry and I could feel the alcohol sloshing around my belly. I knew I would be fine if I ate something. I wondered how many calories I had left. How many calories were there in a raspberry martini?

'Can you just drop me at the top of my road? I want to get some food, I forgot to eat dinner.' I called to Andrew from the back seat. He nodded and pulled up outside City Pizza.

'You sure you'll be OK?'

'Yes of course, I only live there.'

I pointed at my building a couple of houses along from the pizza place. Andrew nodded and after wishing me a good night he drove home. Ruth was fast asleep in the passenger seat.

I concentrated on walking into City Pizza. Antonio, the owner, was sat at the side of the counter. He stood up, grinning, when he saw me.

'Bella, Olivia!' He exclaimed.

I had always found it comforting to have become such a regular that the staff and proprietor knew me, Ruth thought it was a bad thing, showing just how bad my diet was.

'It's been so long, where you been hiding?' He asked.

'Hey, Tony, I've been dieting, trying to lose some weight.'

He took hold of my arms and looked at me.

'So I see, you waste away to nothing, Antonio will feed you up, what would you like?'

'The usual please, Tony.' I said gratefully.

The smell of toasted cheese was driving me insane. I'm certain Antonio could hear my stomach growling.

I watched him while he worked, throwing mushrooms and pepperoni on to the base and sprinkling the grated cheese across the top. If I had to choose one food to eat forever it would be pizza. I rested my head on the counter and became aware I was drooling onto my hand. I was so hungry.

Finally Antonio handed me a pizza box and grinning I made my way the few yards to my flat. I knew I had to be patient to avoid burning my mouth but I was so desperate to eat. I opened the box and left it on the sofa while I filled a pint glass with water.

Sitting down, I let out a loud sigh, happy to be home. I picked up the first slice of pizza and sank my teeth into the melted cheese and tomato. It tasted amazing, all the better for the extreme hunger I was feeling. The first slice was gone in seconds and I was pulling at the next slice, I could feel tomato sauce dripping down my chin and bits of mushroom dropping into my lap and down my top. I didn't care, no one could see me and I was ravenous, compelled only to get rid of the nasty, drunk, empty feeling in my stomach as quickly as possible.

I slowed down after four slices, wiped my chin on the back of my hand and decided to open up the laptop. It was late but then my Knight in shining armour was a night owl.

I found his contact details in the previous callers list and clicked connect. The laptop rang, I didn't know what to expect but after a short time my image dropped to a small rectangle in the bottom of a plain black window.

'Good evening, Liv, did you just pick pepperoni out of your cleavage?' I had forgotten he could see me. I grinned.

'I forgot to eat before I went out so I'm eating pizza. I don't even care how many calories that will cost me.' I said matter of factly.

I heard him laughing.

'Are you a little bit drunk, Liv?'

'No!' I realised I sounded offended and stopped, smiling 'I'm a lot drunk!' I grinned, taking another bite of pizza.

'Did you have a nice time?'

'I did, but I got through an awful lot of alcohol. What did you do tonight?'

'I was working with a client and then I came home to

work on an essay.'

I was surprised by the pang of envy at his reference to a client. I remembered what he'd told me about his rewards.

'Where did you fuck this one then? Changing rooms? Your car?' I heard him chuckle.

'The Jacuzzi actually.'

I snorted loudly and continued eating. I was angry at myself for being jealous, it's not like I could ever do anything about it, I couldn't be with him, being jealous was stupid.

'So where are you going to fuck me?' I heard silence for a moment and realised I'd surprised him, or offended him. I waited to see what he would say and eventually I recognised the sound of his quiet laugh.

'Well that's a little tricky, you'll have to find an excuse to come visit me, and then I'll fuck you anywhere you want, Liv.' His voice had lost his teasing tone; it was soft and gentle, but commanding. It sounded honest and at odds with his words. I realised I loved the way he said "fuck" and clenched my thighs involuntarily.

I let out a slow quiet breath and took a sip of water. I was feeling brave because of all the alcohol.

'I might just take you up on that, Mr Knight.' I said trying to inject as much seduction into my tone as I could muster. I stood up, depositing the pizza box on the kitchen counter and walking towards the hallway, removing my jacket. I heard a whistle from the laptop and I turned round surprised, as I hung up my jacket.

'Walk slowly, I want to look at you.' His voice was commanding again, like when I'd demonstrated my push-ups earlier. I slowed down my pace and crept on tiptoes to the sofa. 'You look beautiful.'

I flushed with pride and happiness.

'Thank you. I need to change though, I'm not overly comfortable in this kind of outfit.'

'Getting ready for bed? Do I get to see some

comfortable flannel pyjamas?' The teasing tone had returned to his voice and I smiled.

'I suppose so, if you're sticking around.' I walked slowly towards the hallway again, swinging my hips from side to side knowing he would be looking at my bottom.

Chapter Twenty

I pulled open the nightwear drawer, gathering all the items into my arms and dumped them on the bed. I had no idea if I had anything in there that was vaguely attractive but I knew I wasn't about to walk back into the living room wearing tatty but comfortable pyjamas.

I rummaged through all the items on the bed until I spotted them. Brian had bought me some kind of sexy nightwear for Christmas, optimistically thinking I'd wear it for him, but of course that would have encouraged him and I certainly didn't want to do that, so the offending items had been shoved to the furthest corner of the nightwear drawer. The set was a matching vest and shorts in black sheer material with lace edging and pink satin ribbon woven through the top edge. They were pretty but they didn't leave anything to the imagination, I would need to wear something underneath or Chris would see everything. I felt a moment of disgust as I pictured Brian shopping for these, I wondered if he picked up the first thing he saw or if he compared a few sets. I shuddered and shook my head, clearing the image from my mind.

I turned my attention to my underwear drawer and retrieved a matching set, black and pink to match the nightwear, the bra was underwired and slightly padded to push up my breasts. I was amazed by the transformation as I examined myself in the mirror. The diet and exercises had paid off and I looked good. I pulled the band out of my hair and let it fall loose around my shoulders; it was thick and messy but it made me feel slightly less exposed.

What was I doing? Was I really going to go back in front of the camera dressed like this? I remembered Ruth's talk of cybersex and I felt a jolt of excitement in my stomach. Could I do that? Would I? No, surely not. I looked at myself in the mirror again and decided to see what happened. If nothing else surely he would compliment me and make me feel sexy and attractive. Maybe that was enough for now.

I walked slowly, purposefully into the living room, trying to look nonchalant. So I'm wearing see through sexy nightwear, I thought. Who's to say I don't wear this all the time? I heard his sharp intake of breath and smiled to myself. I bent down to pick up the pint glass, knowing as I did it that he would get an eyeful of my backside before moving to the kitchen to refill my glass. I placed the glass on the small table behind the sofa and finally settled down in front of the laptop.

'Jeez, Liv, what are you doing to me?'

'What do you mean?' I asked innocently, although on the inside my stomach was doing somersaults.

'Nice pyjamas, you look sexy as hell. You wear them often?' I shrugged.

'I'm wearing them tonight,' I stated simply.

'For someone who's not had sex for five years you sure have some sexy nightwear.' His voice sound full of appreciation. I shrugged again.

'Well truth be told, these were a present from my ex. I guess he hoped to see me in them himself but he didn't.'

'Wow, poor guy, he would've loved this sight. I'm honoured to be the first guy to see it.'

I smiled. There was no point in pretending otherwise, he already knew my lack of experience.

'When I opened this present on Christmas day in front of his whole family, I was mortified.' I giggled at the memory, 'and every time I've found them since I've just felt a bit disgusted. I don't know why I even kept it.'

'Well I'm glad you did, you look hot in it.' I could hear the appreciation in his voice and it made me feel attractive and desirable and sexy. I could feel my temperature rising in anticipation, wondering what would happen next.

'So where did you go tonight?' He asked, abruptly changing the direction of conversation. I blinked, confused by the return to normal conversation. I don't know what I was expecting him to do but I felt a little disappointed, almost like I'd been rejected in some way. I mentally shook myself and answered him.

'We went for cocktails. We were planning to go dancing but we got too drunk!' I giggled at the memory of the swirly patterns Ruth had described on my face, 'pizza sobered me up though. Pizza is like the food of the gods!' I think I believed that. I had missed it so much since I started dieting.

'It's a pity you didn't get to dance. Why don't you dance now?' I giggled.

'I'm not dancing now, I'd feel stupid.'

'Why?'

'Dancing is strictly for the anonymity of crowded dance-floors or the privacy of my bedroom.'

'Well do you see anyone watching you?' He teased.

I frowned. I couldn't see him, but I knew he was watching me, that made it different. I heard movement from his end then I heard music coming though the speakers. It was my favourite song, Erma Franklin's (*Take Another Little) Piece of My Heart*. How did he know?

'I love this song'

'So Facebook told me,' he explained. 'Of course I realise this isn't exactly a song you can dance to.'

I heard the challenge in his voice rather than the acceptance of my refusal and before I gave it a second thought I was on my feet.

I closed my eyes and ignored everything I was feeling and focused on the music. My body started swaying slowly to the rhythm, slow deliberate movements, I crossed my arms around my body, trailing my hands up and down tracing the shape of my hips and back up my sides to my neck, I slowly tilted my head back tickling my neck and trailing my hands down towards my breasts moving back to the sides of my body and dropping my arms to my sides. As the song approached the chorus I arched my back, drawing my hands up my body and throwing my arms into the air, bringing them down slowly, sashaying my body from side to side. I was lost in the music; the webcam, laptop, and Chris all forgotten, I felt the flimsy material beneath my hands and I felt sexy. I enjoyed it, the feeling was thrilling. His voice broke through my trance but didn't stop me dancing.

'If I was there right now I'd be moving those straps off your shoulder and trailing kisses along your neck and arm.'

I heard his sharp intake of breath as I slipped the strap over one shoulder, tracing my fingers up my neck and down my arms. I continued swaying gently as I moved to the other strap and repeated my action. His voice was a whisper when he next spoke.

'Then I'd pull that vest down and let it fall to the floor.'

I crossed my arms over my body, reaching for the straps, and pulled them down my arms, feeling the material strain across my breasts before releasing itself as it moved over and down to my waist. I pulled my arms through the straps and gave my hips a little shake, letting the vest drop to my feet.

'Then I'd lead you to the sofa and sit you down, sitting on the floor in front of you, between your knees.'

I moved to the sofa as the music came to an end. I was relieved, I knew if I'd been stood up when the music stopped I'd have felt silly, exposed, and vulnerable. Instead I was feeling exhilarated, my body was tingling with desire and excitement. His voice had adopted a husky whisper, betraying his own desire. My heart was beating loudly in my ears and my breathing was shallow. I leant right back into the sofa and waited for his next instruction.

'I'd take your face in my hands, stroking your cheek gently, and kissing you long and slow on the lips, teasing your lips apart with my tongue and dancing with yours inside your mouth.'

My stomach somersaulted and I squirmed in my seat. I moved my right hand up to the left side of my face and stroked my cheek, holding my face just below my ear I traced my lips with my thumb slightly parting my lips I touched the tip of my tongue against my thumb, gradually widening my mouth and moving my thumb inside, twirling my tongue around it.

'I'd pull your bra straps down your arms and I'd trail kisses down your neck, past your collar bone and onto your breasts, teasing your nipple with my tongue.'

I shivered at his words. My left hand drew the right strap over my shoulder and I slowly pulled my thumb from my mouth and traced a line from my lips, across my chin, down my neck to my breast, pulling aside the bra to expose the nipple and tracing a circular pattern with my wet thumb.

My nerves felt like currants of electricity coursing through my body, little pulses of ecstasy jolted through me and I tensed my thighs together, rolling my hips to gain some friction against my public bone. I could feel a dampness spreading through my pants. I felt my nipple harden and pinched it between my thumb and forefinger, rolling it gently. I opened my eyes and glanced at the laptop. I saw myself, just my head and my breasts were caught on camera. I wondered how far Chris would take this, would he just concentrate on what he could see? I moaned involuntarily with frustration and I heard him gasp.

'I'd turn my attention to your other breast.' I obliged, pulling down the strap on my right side, I slowly licked my thumb and traced the outline of my body down to the left breast, moving aside the bra and tracing a circle around my nipple, as I felt it harden beneath my touch I pinched and rolled it between my thumb and forefinger. I was feeling braver as this dance went on and I wanted him to see me. I crossed my arms over my body and pulled the bra straps, forcing the bra to fold over itself onto my stomach and out of view of the webcam. I crossed my hands over my chest and concentrated on my breasts, squeezing them in my hands and tracing my thumbs across my nipples. I heard his breathing turn shallow and smiled to myself, satisfied that this was turning him on as much as it was me. I looked directly into the camera and smiled slowly, and, I hoped, seductively.

'What would you do now, Chris?'

'I would trail kisses across your stomach, all the way down your thighs, parting your legs and trailing kisses back up your inner thigh.' I trailed my hands across my stomach and up and down my thighs, slowly tickling my inner thigh. I tensed my thigh muscles but kept my legs apart. The overload of sensation was gathering at the apex of my inner thighs, frustrated and ready to explode. I trailed my fingers across my pants and felt their dampness. A flush of shame washed over me but I shook it off. I needed this.

'Then I would tease your clitoris with my tongue, licking up and down, slowly, driving you wild until you release yourself to me.'

My fingers moved across my pants rubbing gently, all the sensations finally feeling relief that they were being seen to. I moved my hand inside my pants and felt the dampness pooling in the smattering of hair. My fingers found my clitoris and rubbed gently back and forth, building up pace. My hips rolled, meeting my hand and causing a build-up of friction; my hand moved faster.

'Come on Liv, come to me,' his voice was my undoing

and I moaned loudly as my orgasm crashed around me, my hips gyrating against my hand, squeezing out every last drop of sensation. I removed my hand from my pants and slumped exhausted against the sofa. I became aware of my surroundings again and what I'd just done and wrapped my arms across my body protectively.

I heard him groan and guessed he'd just had his own orgasm. Satisfaction welled up inside me, knowing that watching me had turned him on.

'Then I'd wrap my arms around you, kissing your hair, and we'd both fall asleep.' He sighed.

I giggled and heard him chuckle.

'Are you OK?' his voice was gentle, he knew I had a lot of hang ups about this type of thing, he knew I was drunk and he knew I was likely to realise what I'd just done at any minute and freak out. But I knew what I'd done. I knew I'd feel ashamed in the morning but right at that moment I felt amazing, satisfied, and liberated. I nodded, smiling shyly.

'I can't believe I just did that.' My mind was full of wonder, but not embarrassment.

'You looked so sexy, Liv, you are so sexy. I wish I was there with you right now.'

I smiled. Suddenly thirsty, I remembered about the pint glass of water behind the sofa and turning onto my knees I leant over to retrieve the glass. I heard him chuckle.

'Man, now I really wish I was there, what I wouldn't want to do to you in that position.'

I closed my eyes smiling to myself and tried to ignore the feeling of desire welling up in my stomach at his words. I'd never done anything so intimate before, even the few times I'd had sex never felt this special. I felt connected to Chris in a way I'd never experienced.

I realised I no longer cared what he looked like, I just cared that he liked the look of me.

I stood up and bent down to retrieve my vest, keeping

my legs straight and bending all the way down, I waited for his reaction grinning to myself. I heard him whistle.

'Damn, Liv, you got to stop doing that to me.' I pulled the vest over my head and returned to the sofa grinning. I knew he could still see my breasts through the top and it excited me.

'You're right about one thing, Chris, you sure do know how to make a girl feel good about herself'

'You should feel good about yourself Liv, you're a beautiful, sexy, smart woman.'

I felt my face flush and a shrugged.

'Thanks.'

'Seriously Liv, I'm in awe of you tonight. I wasn't expecting this. I didn't think you would ever consider something like this.' I didn't like the way he was speaking, I was beginning to feel uneasy about the last thirty minutes, shame was beginning to creep in and I closed my eyes, trying to block out the images in my mind. He saw my body stiffen.

'Liv,' his voice was gentle, 'you're human, a sexy, desirable woman. There's no shame in exploring your body and there's no shame in sharing yourself with someone else. Please don't freak out about this.' I nodded. He was right. I'd gone without sex for five years, without having even the slightest desire for sex, and now suddenly I felt alive again. It was weird, but it's not as if I was the first person to do it. I thought back to the conversation I'd had with Ruth that evening. OK maybe the only weird thing about this was that Chris was a complete stranger to me, but I felt like I knew him after all this time, and he was a friend of Steven. It was OK. And more than anything else, I realised I'd not thought about Steven at all since I switched on the laptop. If this could stop me thinking about Steven, stop me wanting him, stop me regretting my missed opportunity, then that could only be a good thing.

'OK. But only on one condition.' I said suddenly.
'Anything you want, Liv.'
'I want to do this again.'

Chapter Twenty-one

It wasn't the banging in my head that woke me the next morning; it was the ringing. An alarm going off in my dream gradually brought me into consciousness as I realised the phone was ringing. I wanted to ignore it, I thought that if I made the effort to get out of bed, by the time I had crossed the hallway into the kitchen the phone would stop ringing. Or it would be some annoying cold caller trying to sell me something. They don't even have the decency to be people anymore, just automated recorded messages.

The ringing wasn't stopping and I knew only one person this persistent. Why couldn't she just call my mobile which was right by my bed?

'Hello?' My voice crackled into the phone, my throat was dry and I was beginning to feel the sensation of too much alcohol despite a lack of headache.

'Hey, sorry, did I wake you? What time do you call this to still be in bed?' I swallowed, moistening my throat.

'Erm, I call it Saturday morning.' Ruth was not usually known for her love of mornings, I guessed it was quite late if she was up before me, 'some of us didn't go to sleep during their night out!'

She giggled.

'Sorry, I fell asleep in the car.'

'In the car? You fell asleep standing up at the bar!' I cried.

She laughed again.

'So why are you in bed so late anyway?' A note of suspicion crept into her voice. I frowned, it hadn't all come back to me yet. I glanced around the room and spotted the empty pizza box on the floor by the sofa.

'Well I got pizza on the way home, and,' I trailed off noticing the bra on the arm of the sofa. I glanced down at myself and realised I was in the sheer nightwear Brian had bought me, 'I think I was chatting to Chris.' I whispered. *Oh no.* The memory of the night before came flooding back, slapping me in the face. Ruth heard the change in my voice.

'You did it, didn't you? I knew you would, how was it?' Her voice was excited. I frowned.

'Seeing right through me is one thing but how do you hear through me too? I couldn't ever keep anything from you, could I?' I asked in disbelief.

'Nope.' her voice was smug, 'So? How did it happen?'

'He asked me to dance.' I gave her an abridged version of the night before, pausing to cringe as I tried to describe it without going into too much detail. She laughed at my awkward account and obvious discomfort. Sex wasn't something that embarrassed Ruth; she'd probably get on well with Chris.

It was good talking to her about it though, it helped keep the shame at bay. I hadn't imagined I would ever admit to what I'd done last night but Ruth wasn't the slightest bit fazed, she was encouraging and helped me see the fun side to it. I waited for guilt to rear its ugly head, but it didn't. My devil was sitting on my struggling angel, grinning widely.

I ended our call and filled the kettle to make a cup of tea. I popped some bread into the toaster and idly opened up the laptop. Chris wasn't online but he had sent me a message, just one line simply saying,

'Hope you're feeling OK about last night.'

I smiled and hugged myself. He wasn't just some old perv after all, he actually cared how I felt too.

I was dozing on the sofa that evening, ignoring whichever

mindless talent show was on TV, when my laptop started ringing. I jumped up quickly, smoothed the wrinkles out of my sweater, and ran my fingers through my hair before accepting the video call.

'Hey there,' he said.

His voice had that warm teasing sound but it was mixed with a tinge of uncertainty. I remembered suddenly that I hadn't replied to his message.

'Hi,' I replied, brightly, 'I was hoping you would call.'

He chuckled, relieved.

'So you're not mad at me for taking advantage of you while under the influence?'

I felt a warmth spread through me, tingling the back of my neck and face.

'No, I sort of felt a bit ashamed, but only because I enjoyed it.'

'Oh, Liv no, you shouldn't ever feel ashamed about enjoying the pleasure your body can experience.'

His voice was soft and gentle. I smiled.

'Well I guess the more I do it the less it'll bother me.' I raised one eyebrow and smiled slowly, looking straight into the camera. I hoped I was coming across as seductive but feared I may have just looked slightly menacing. He laughed.

'Not quite so innocent any more, huh, Liv?'

'No, you're a terrible influence!' I grinned. I sat back into the sofa and curled my legs under me.

'So what have you done today, after sleeping off your hangover and overcoming your shame?'

The hint of teasing returned to his voice. I sighed.

'Work. I've been drawing up contracts for new staff and working out what to do about Steven.'

'What's the problem with Steven?'

I realised he must be concerned for his friend and perhaps talking about him wasn't such a good idea.

'Oh nothing,' I assured him, 'he's brilliant, but with

bringing in new staff I've been reconsidering his role. He's so much more than an intern, I don't want the other staff to undervalue him.'

'I'm sure he'd be over the moon to hear you think that. Can't you just give him a permanent job and cancel the internship?'

'Oh absolutely, that's the plan. But I'm new to this employer role, handing over parts of my business to other people to manage, it's scary and I need to know there's someone there I can trust, someone who understands my vision, the way I want Inspired to be perceived. Steven gets that. His work has been fantastic and his ideas are brilliant. I've never felt comfortable telling people my ideas before because I'm just too scared of negative feedback. But for some reason I shared them with Steven and I didn't even flinch at his criticism, just recognised his suggestions were constructive and made sense. Made my ideas stronger. So how do I sum that up as a job title?'

'Sounds like he'd be your right-hand man, your go-to guy.'

'Is he too young to have a management position? He's straight out of uni, only a few months into an internship? I'm worried I'm a bit biased too.' I admitted.

'You have feelings for him?' Chris sounded surprised, I didn't blame him after my behaviour last night. I wasn't entirely sure what I felt at the moment but I knew I still had a fondness for Steven. I was just more realistic about our chances as a couple since Melissa's revelation.

'It's funny but I found him really irritating when he first started.'

Chris laughed.

'Yeah I get that, he's so charming and likeable, there has to be something wrong with him right?'

'Right, too confident and cocky for one so young.' I smiled remembering the way I'd described him to Ruth that first night, 'I didn't want to go to work on his second day!' I laughed.

'Surely you had already seen that from his interview?'

'Well it was between him and James, James is starting with us on Monday. James is much more like me, quiet, methodical, unsociable, I knew James would come in do his work and go home, I'd barely know he was there and he was my choice. But something nagged at me, I wanted to expand Inspired, I wanted to get new business, I wanted to move into new developments. Something told me I had to go with Steven, he was confident, his skills were completely up to date, and he would be great at representing us at conferences and events, having that easy ability to talk to people and sell himself.'

'Does he know any of this?'

'God no! I'm not going to tell a staff member I didn't really want to hire him! Especially when it turned out to be the best decision I made.'

'So what changed?' Chris sounded amused, maybe he was proud of his friend for changing my opinion of him.

'I realised I was just jealous of his easy confidence. And once I got to know him a bit, I realised he was more similar to me than I'd first thought. Then there was his work, it just blew me away. I found it quite arousing actually.' I giggled.

'Hey whatever turns you on, babe,' his teasing voice had returned and it made me blush.

'When he first told me he liked me, I immediately went on the defensive, thought it was a joke. Then I became suspicious that it was some kind of ruse to ruin me.'

'How? Like sexual harassment or something?'

'Yes, that's exactly what I thought. I just couldn't see why he would like me. But I realised that I did like him so it was really distracting in the office, so much so I had to get my own office to put some distance between us.' I heard Chris chuckling and I grinned at the ridiculousness of the situation.

'It doesn't surprise me that you like him, Steven sort of reminds me of The Doctor in way, not to look at, but he's like an undercover nerd. Looks all normal and trendy, but beneath the cool threads and big hair he's hiding this humungous brain.'

'Yeah well, the thing I realised is that my attraction to The Doctor isn't actually about David Tennant, I didn't fancy him at all in *Casanova* or *Secret Smile* or even *Blackpool*.'

'Sideburns.'

'What?' I asked puzzled.

'He has sideburns in *Doctor Who*.' I thought about that for a moment and realised he might be on to something.

'I only fancy Colin Firth as Mr Darcy too. Wow, that's a revelation. I've got a thing for sideburns.'

'So it would seem.'

'But that's beside the point. I realised that while I was trying to get to know Steven to be sure I could trust him, I was trusting him already. I was booking places for him to represent Inspired at conferences and I was running all my ideas past him. I was just worried about the moral question over dating my young intern.'

'He knows his own mind, Liv. He's a nerd but he's also a romantic. He's always been quite certain about finding The One. He's stayed single because he believed he would know when he met The One and he would only be with her, no wasted time, no heartbreak. I'm not saying he didn't break some hearts along the way. He worked behind the bar in the student union; he brought a different girl home every weekend. I stopped asking their names in the end, he never saw them twice.'

Part of me didn't want to believe that, it didn't fit with my impression of Steven, the good guy I trusted. But then, I reminded myself, he did fuck Melissa in a public toilet and get her pregnant, there was a side to him I didn't know.

'But now it's all irrelevant. He's going to be a dad. Melissa won. Maybe it's a good thing, no distractions. Just a good working relationship.' I concluded.

'Such a shame that after five years being single you finally find someone you could be with just as it's too late.'

His voice sounded full of regret and sympathy.

'But on the other hand it awakened something in me that had been missing for five years. And he also led me to you.' I added.

Chris had done more for my sexual awakening than anyone had. I heard him sigh.

'Well I sure am glad about that last part and if he's with Melissa I can feel less guilty about seeing you naked.'

I felt a flush creep across my face and hugged my arms around my body, hiding it. He chuckled, his teasing laugh and I decided it was time to change the subject. Talking about Steven was making me sad, but I felt as though this last conversation had finally closed the door on that chapter of our relationship and I could move forward next week with a good working relationship.

'So it's Saturday night, aren't you taking one of your clients out?' I asked innocently.

'I don't take my clients out, Liv, I fuck them once when they throw themselves at me.'

His voice was warm, chiding almost, I could hear amusement there. I thought he was laughing at me, perhaps he thought I was jealous. Am I jealous? I shook my head mentally, how could I be jealous of them fucking a man I'd never met?

'How does that even happen? I couldn't imagine doing that.'

'That's because you fear rejection Liv, which you shouldn't, you're very, very fuckable, who could say no to you?'

I blushed but inside I was singing.

Chapter Twenty-two

'So tell me how it happens.' I was genuinely interested in how women made the first move and wondered if they were always successful or if it was just because Chris had this desire to make them feel good about themselves. Did he ever regret it? Did he even fancy them?

'OK, well, usually I've been working with them a few months and we will agree mutually that they no longer need one to one training sessions and we will book in for a final session.

'Generally they turn up to that session in the skimpiest gym outfit they have, no longer in sweat pants and a T-shirt, they arrive in tight leggings or short shorts like your skimpy things, they wear a sports bra with no padding so their nipples are visibly straining against the material of their tight, figure-hugging vest. Instead of facing me while they exercise they turn away to make sure I get a full view of their ass as they bend and squat. They look back at me batting their eyelashes as they do their push-ups so I can get an idea of how they'll look if I'm fucking them from behind. You get the idea. They find excuses to giggle girlishly and touch me on the arm or shoulder. They admire my muscles, lingering a little too long as they trail their fingers along the length of my biceps. They press up against me as they squeeze past me. And I know what they're doing, I know even before the session starts how it'll be and I comply, I stand in the way so they can touch me, I look at their ass, I make eye contact with them in the mirror, and I pretend to be surprised and excited by their attention.' He paused and I heard a laugh snorting through his nose. I was on the edge of my seat, the way he described things, building up this picture, was so hot. I remembered how it felt knowing he was checking out my shorts yesterday and I felt a rush of warmth pooling in my stomach. I waited for him to continue, biting my lip in anticipation.

'So picture the scene: the session comes to an end and we make our way to the changing rooms. Our gym has three sets of changing rooms; male, female, and a unisex one. They all have a spa area, showers, and changing cubicles. Hardly anyone uses the unisex one, usually just couples who come to work out together but it's nearly always empty.

'We wander in to the room, the first time she's ever used the unisex changing room, but then she's already planned this out in advance and I'm just innocently going along with it. She starts removing her clothes in front of her locker and then she'll step out wearing a towel and tell me she's using the spa. She'll take me by the hand and lead me towards the Jacuzzi. She asks me something about how she should relax her muscles after working out and whether I recommend massage. I'll demonstrate, massaging her shoulders and arms and she'll drop her towel pressing herself against me before moving into the Jacuzzi. She'll tell me to join her and I'll remove my clothes and follow her in to the warm bubbly water.'

My breath caught as I tried to picture what Chris might look like naked. Probably not my usual type, all bulging muscles, I preferred a skinny body but still I found myself feeling aroused by his story.

'She'll sit between my legs and ask me to massage her again and I will, she'll moan quietly and lean back against my chest tilting her head back against my shoulder. My hands will move round her massaging the front of her arms and moving towards her breasts, cupping them in both hands and squeezing them, kneading them together, rubbing my thumbs across the nipples in circular motions feeling them harden at my touch despite the heat of the water.'

He stopped suddenly and gasped, I opened my eyes and realised I was holding my breasts in my hands, my thumbs echoing his description, rubbing across my nipples. I gasped and dropped my hands and I heard Chris laugh.

'You're becoming insatiable, Liv.'

I blushed, I felt truly embarrassed. But so turned on at the same time and slightly frustrated. I could feel my pants were damp and I wanted to touch myself, relieve the frustration.

'Do you want me to continue?' he asked, teasing me with his warm soft voice. I nodded.

'OK then. I'll lift her hands up to her body and guide them to massage her own breasts, beneath my hands, I'll then watch for a little while as she pinches her own nipples between her perfectly manicured finger and thumb. I'll move my hands down her body, along her thighs and around the outside, cupping her ass, and I'll lift her body, slightly repositioning her over the air jets of the Jacuzzi. She'll start moaning again as the air blows against her sex and I'll move one hand round to cup her, gently teasing one of my fingers back and forth along the length of her clitoris. She'll arch her back and moan into my ear as I kiss her exposed neck, nipping the skin with my teeth and tugging at her earlobe.

'The bubbles stop and the engines quiet and the silence distracts her, she'll open her eyes as I gently push her away from me. She'll float to the opposite side of the Jacuzzi and face me as I rise standing in the water before her. She'll look up at me and move towards me, moving her hands up my thighs, cupping my ass, and pulling me towards her mouth, she'll press her tongue against the tip of my cock and slowly lick a path from the tip along my full length, watching it harden before her eyes, she'll return to the tip and pull it into her mouth, sucking gently and moving her lips up and down against my erection, weaving her tongue along the length. My legs stiffen and I'll knit my fingers into her hair, wrapping the tresses around my wrists and pulling tightly, holding her head in place as I begin to buck my hips, forcing myself deeper into her mouth. She'll wrap one hand delicately around the base of my cock and slow me, moving away she'll stand up to join me and press her mouth against mine, our tongues dancing together. I'll pick her up, wrapping her legs around my waist, and carry her out of the Jacuzzi and into the steam room. The steam room has tiled walls and a large marble bench in the centre of the room. I'll place her down on the centre slab on her back, looming over her, her legs still wrapped around my body. I move my body, slightly teasing her clitoris with my stiff cock, rubbing it up and down as her hips buck against me, trying to maintain a constant pressure against her. I'll back off, pulling her body to the edge of the slab as I sink to my knees, holding her legs up and tracing a path along her inner thigh with my tongue. I'll press my lips against her clitoris, darting my tongue along its length and circling the entrance to her sex, lapping up the evidence of her arousal and entering her with my tongue. As she moans and writhes against the hard marble stone I'll trace a circle with my tongue against her clitoris and insert a finger inside her, moving in and out and building up a rhythm as she comes closer to the brink of orgasm. Then I'll stop.'

He paused and I felt frustrated, I hadn't even realised I was doing it but I removed my finger from inside me and wiped the moisture on the inside of my pants, embarrassed. He laughed gently.

'Please do continue, you look unbelievably sexy fingering yourself to my story Liv, it distracted me momentarily.'

I flushed with shame. I couldn't believe what was happening to me, it was as if I'd lost all sense of reality and some carnal lust took over. His words were hypnotic and I followed his story, playing it all out on my own body. I remained silent, my breath coming in shallow gasps and waited for him to continue.

'As she moans in frustration I'll lean over her, wrapping her legs around my body and picking her up off the bench. I'll carry her towards the door and into a shower cubicle, turning on the warm shower I'll push her against the wall and enter her, holding her in place against the wall and pushing myself deeper into her with each slow, deliberate thrust. I'll take one of her nipples into my mouth, holding it between my teeth as it lengthens and hardens and tease it with the tip of my tongue. She'll moan, trying to control the tempo of our thrusts but unable to move under my grasp, I can hear the frustration in her groans but I know when I finally let her come it will be worth it. I'll turn the water to cold, cooling our bodies and slowing our rhythm, she'll open her eyes and blink at me, confusion evident in her eyes. I'll pull out of her and release her legs from around my waist till she is standing and I'll drop to my knees, massaging her legs, tense from being wrapped around me for so long. I push my face against her, my nose teasing against the apex of her frustration and delight in her flinching with pleasure as she moans quietly, almost sadly. I'll rise, taking her hand and leading her to the Jacuzzi again, turning on the jets as I sink into the water, pulling her against me as before, my hands following the contours of her body and lifting her onto my still throbbing cock – filling her, pushing her forward, and holding her body in my hands, squeezing her breasts together as I thrust into her. I'll pick her up, pushing her to the opposite edge of the Jacuzzi onto her knees and I'll drive her home, thrusting hard into her until she screams, her orgasm shattering around me, undoing her. Her climax tips me over the edge and I'll come, slowing my thrusts to squeeze every last drop of my orgasm into her.'

I gasped as I reached my own orgasm, moving my hand against my clitoris slowly, trying to extend the duration of my climax. I opened my eyes and sighed.

'Sorry, you were saying?'

I heard Chris chuckle again before finishing off his story.

'Well that's pretty much it. The cycle ends, the jets slow down, and the spa is silent except for the sound of our heavy, gasping breath. I pull out of her and take her in my arms, turning on the Jacuzzi again. I hold her against me, kissing her long and deep until the bubbles finish. Then I get out, wrap the towel around her, and kiss her goodbye. She doesn't ask for my number and she doesn't come to the gym again. I go get changed and wait for my next appointment.'

'Wow, now I'm disappointed I won't get your workout reward.' I smiled shyly.

'Yes you did appear to enjoy that story quite a lot, Miss Jones.' His voice was full of longing.

'Is it like that every time?' I asked, amused by the thought of these women thinking they were doing something special when Chris has a predetermined plan for them.

'No, they make it happen, sometimes they just ask me to carry something to their car and then pounce on me in the parking lot.'

'You can tell me that story next time.' I grinned, excited that there would be more stories.

'I look forward to it, Liv. You're very receptive to my story telling and I like that a lot.'

'Good. Well I'm going to go take a shower and try not to imagine you fucking me in there. Have a good night whatever it is you're doing.'

'Well, I've done it, my plan was to spend the evening with you and that's what I did. I'm going to do some coursework and then go to bed.'

I felt a glow of happiness spread through me, this sexy man would rather stay in and talk to me than go out and potentially meet someone. I felt like a very lucky girl indeed.

Chapter Twenty-three

Steven arrived early to work on Monday morning and I was relived. I made a cup of tea and invited him into my office, gesturing towards the sofa. He sat down warily. He looked tired and I was itching to ask him about Melissa, about his decision, but thought it best not to pry. I didn't really want it confirmed, couldn't bear to hear him say it out loud. I think he could see the question lined up in my mind, and was tensed in preparation for it. I relieved him of his fear.

'Hey, good to have you back.'

I touched his shoulder lightly and he looked at my hand and back at my face, his eyes registered surprise, and a glint of humour appeared.

'Did you miss me?' He teased.

'I did.' I nodded genuinely and I saw a tiny hint of pink touch his cheeks and he looked down at his hands. I continued.

'I wanted to talk to you about your job description.' His eyes flickered up to meet mine, his forehead crumpled in confusion.

'James is starting today, and I'm interviewing a few more candidates next week. I don't want them coming in above you. You're much more important to Inspired than just an intern.' I paused, waiting for my words to sink in and watched his face soften. His eyes sparkled.

'You just hate filling out those weekly monitoring forms.' He grinned.

'That is true,' I grinned back, 'but it's also true that I trust you with project work, and with my own personal ideas and designs. I trust your judgement and I value your opinion.' I stopped and met his eyes, 'I've never sought anyone's opinion before, Steven, and the fact that I seek yours is a huge thing for me.'

He nodded, blushing.

'Well I'm glad, glad you trust me.' He looked away sadly and I closed my eyes as his words hit me.

'I wish I'd realised it sooner.' I said quietly, smiling sadly.

He nodded imperceptibly, the slight movement of his cheek was the only indication of his emotion as he tensed his jaw.

'So what's my new job title?'

'"Projects Manager"; I've drawn up a new employment contract.'

I handed him a pile of papers that included his job description and contract.

'I'm sure the pay rise will come in handy too under the circumstances.'

He shrugged slightly and looked at me, his eyes shining with amusement.

'Thank you, Ols. This means a lot to me. I know I'm young and inexperienced but I won't let you down, I promise.'

My smile grew into a grin and I threw my arm around his shoulder.

'I know you won't –' I squeezed him '– and no bossing the staff around either, they report to me, not you, you just get to allocate the work and oversee the production.'

He nodded, grinning. 'I'd make a terrible boss, Ols, but time management, programming, and ideas? I can do all that in my sleep.'

'Good, well go do some work – you're three days behind schedule.' I chided but my eyes were smiling.

He nodded, rising to his feet, and moving towards the door. He paused in the doorway.

'I haven't made any kind of decision yet, Ols, except

that until I work out what to do about Melissa I can't be chasing after you. The only decision I made is to forget about you and me. Whatever I decide to do, we've been ruined by this situation.'

His words made sense to me and I knew he was right. I'd already made the same decision about it, but hearing his words, the finality of it, cut through me. I stood up, my eyes locking onto his, so full of regret and sadness. I moved forward and kissed him lightly on the lips. He didn't move, didn't respond, he just closed his eyes.

'I know.' I whispered and moved away to my desk. By the time I turned around he had gone, the door slowly clicking shut behind him.

James arrived promptly at 10 a.m. He looked every inch the stereotypical nerd: brown corduroy flares, comic book T-shirt, and thick-framed glasses. His hair was a mass of uncontrolled curls. He was the complete opposite of Steven who was sporting his well-styled floppy hair, distressed-looking jeans, and a paisley shirt over a T-shirt, the sleeves rolled up revealing his slightly sun-kissed forearms. James peered round the door of the office cautiously, relief flooding his features when he saw me smiling at him.

'Hi, James, come on in. This is your desk. Can I get you a drink?' I asked, standing up from his chair and moving aside to let him sit down.

'Coffee would be great thanks, Olivia.'

It struck me as odd to hear someone call me Olivia, it sounded so formal. I shook my head remembering my irritation at Steven's familiar use of Olly on his first day.

'You can just call me Olly,' I said over my shoulder as I filled the kettle. I saw him nod in understanding.

'James, this is Steven, he's the projects manager, so you'll be liaising with him a lot on your assignments.'

I watched as he leaped out of his seat, thrusting his

hand towards Steven to shake it. Steven looked bemused, still getting used to his new job title and responsibility.

'So shall we all hang out on the sofa for a bit and we can fill James in on what we are working on?' I suggested, setting down the three hot drinks on the coffee table and settling into the larger of the sofas.

Steven joined me and James sat on the opposite sofa. We discussed the new projects, on-going projects, and potential clients we were meeting with. Steven updated us on his progress to date and his projected time scales and how the work would be split between him and James.

An hour later we were all back at our desks working. James settled in immediately, happy just to have a computer in front of him and a project to programme. I spent my afternoon sorting through HMRC documents, registering James as an employee, changing Steven's salary, and sorting out our monthly BACS payments. I hated doing the accounts and was relieved I'd advertised for a finance and admin worker. I couldn't wait to hand those bits of work over to someone else.

Steven knocked on my door as he was on his way out at 5 p.m.

'Hey, Ols, I've left a few sections of programming for James to do tomorrow, you remember I'm in Birmingham for a conference, right? He answered my puzzled expression before I could ask. I nodded.

'Of course, you all set for it?' I asked, I'd actually completely forgotten about the conference.

'I think so, not really sure what to expect but I'll just charm the pants off everyone and hope for the best.' He grinned, his eyes sparkling.

'OK, well, have fun. Are you taking Wednesday morning off to make up for travelling tonight?'

'I can do that?' His eyes widened in surprise. I nodded, frowning.

'Of course, I'm eating into your free time. In fact take it

whenever you want, doesn't have to be Wednesday morning, take Friday afternoon if you want. Whenever, just let me know in advance.'

'Cheers, Ols.' He lingered at my door, wanting to say more but not really knowing what to say, and eventually smiling to himself he left the office.

I sighed, I had known the first day would be difficult, but we had survived it. I felt almost guilty at times that I'd turned my thoughts towards Chris whenever I was feeling distracted by Steven and it helped me put him out of my mind. Once again he was my Knight in shining armour. I closed down my computer and made my way out to the main office.

'Oh hey, James, we finish at five.' I said startled that I wasn't alone.

'Steven said it would be OK if I just finished up this section of code, I just finished it anyway so I'm good to go now.'

'Great, I'll wait for you and lock up.'

'Did you get your parcel? Some guy dropped it in earlier.'

I frowned, shaking my head and looking around I spotted the parcel on the edge of Steven's desk. It was addressed to me, I guessed Steven had known better than to open parcels addressed to me after the unfortunate incident with the vibrator. Once again I hadn't ordered anything and my stomach flip-flopped as I wondered if it was another inappropriate gift from Chris. I stuffed the parcel into my bag and followed James through the door.

When I arrived home, I pulled the parcel from my bag and ripped it open. Inside the wrapping was an Agent Provocateur box. My heart started beating loudly. This was serious lingerie. I lifted out the underwear neatly folded inside the tissue paper and held it up for inspection; it was a cream coloured lace basque, the material heavy

171

and stiff, with a delicate lace covering. It fastened at the front and had satin ribbon threaded through the front for tightening. I glanced back in the box and saw a sheer lace thong to match the basque and cream stockings and suspenders. My body flushed with wanting, I was so excited to try this outfit on. There was a card inside the box that simply said, *Hope to see you wearing this later*. My heart skipped a beat. I wondered if he was online and decided to wait until later. I needed to exercise, shower, and eat. Then I could slip into something sexy and make myself available online. God, I sound like an adult chat line or something, perhaps I should start charging!

Chapter Twenty-four

I stared at my reflection in disbelief, partly because I couldn't believe I was wearing this outfit and partly because I looked pretty good in it. I'd always imagined I'd look and feel stupid in something like this but I didn't. I felt sexy, beautiful even.

The basque hugged the contours of my body, flattening and smoothing as it went. The underwiring lifted my breasts, displaying enticingly soft, mounds above the top of the material. The basque sat on the top of my hips and dipped toward the centre, skimming the top of my pubic bone and displaying a glimpse of the lace thong.

It had taken me ages to work out how to use the suspenders, eventually finding the loops on the bottom of the basque to hook them in. The stockings were pure silk and felt luxurious against my skin. Clipping the suspenders to hold them in place felt like I was strapping myself in. My outfit was connected from top to toe.

I let out a long breath and made my way to the living room and flipped open the laptop.

I decided to call him first so that I could get into a position while he was answering the call so he would get a full view of his present when the camera connected. I stood waiting in the middle of the room.

'Wow!' I heard his voice loud and clear though the speakers, 'you look amazing.'

I grinned, I couldn't help it, I'd been aiming for seductive and aloof but I was just so pleased by his compliment. I took a step towards the sofa.

'Wait! Give me a twirl first. Slowly,' he added with that quietly demanding voice, full of authority.

I slowly turned a circle, pausing as I faced away from him and bending one knee slightly, forcing me to lean forward, showing my mostly naked bottom. I smiled as I heard his sharp intake of breath. He's definitely an ass man!

'Thank you for my present,' I said as I took a seat on the sofa, 'although I think it's more a present for you than it is for me.' I raised an eyebrow in question and waited for his confirmation.

'I like to think of it as a learning resource. But I certainly can't complain about the view. I have good taste I think.' His voice was teasing again.

'Impeccable taste. I'm amazed it's the right size.'

'Oh, but Liv, it's my job to recognise weight and body shape. Of course I knew the right size.' He sounded almost offended that I didn't recognise his skill.

'I thought I would feel a bit slutty in something like this, but I don't.'

'Why should you? It covers up almost all of your body, and yet looks far sexier than just a bra and panties set. The imagination is a very powerful thing, Liv, it's always good to leave something for us to think about.'

'So what are you thinking about now?' I asked, smiling slowly.

'I'm imagining ripping that thong off you and fucking you hard against the back of the sofa.' There was no embarrassment or teasing note to his voice, he sounded soft but firm and completely honest. My muscles clenched, sending waves of excitement through my stomach.

'I was hoping you might imagine something more realistic.'

'But then it wouldn't be a fantasy.'

I felt a prickle of disappointment at the back of my neck and realised I'd secretly hoped that somehow we would meet in person and have some mind-blowing sex. I heard him chuckle quietly.

'Don't look so disappointed, Liv. You'll find your dream man soon enough I'm sure and you'll be ready to fuck him all over the place.'

My smile was resigned, but I knew he was right. After all I still didn't know for sure what Chris looked like, and what if I met him and just didn't fancy him? His voice might be my undoing but I doubted I would want to let him touch me if I didn't find him physically attractive.

'So when are you replacing your webcam?'

He laughed, 'It's ordered, don't you worry, you'll see me soon enough.'

'So what are you going to teach me next?' I asked, happy with his news.

'Well I believe we've completed stage one of your training, you seem to be quite confident about your body now. You even seem a little more confident about sex judging by your response to my story the other night.'

'But you said there was still a lot to learn.' I cringed at the whine in my voice, I didn't want this to stop, but he sounded as if he had already helped me as much as I needed.

'Oh there is, Liv, you need to get to know your body, what it wants, what arouses it, what it takes to make you come.' His words were vibrating through me sending ripples of pure lust to the centre of my sex. I shifted my body, forcing myself against the sofa, trying to rub some of the frustration away. I heard him chuckle again, he knew what I was doing, he knew what he was doing to me. I felt a flush of shame.

'Where is your vibrator?'

My eyes widened. Surely he didn't want me to use that?

'It's in my bedroom.'

'Go get it,' he demanded, 'and walk slowly,' the softer teasing tone returning to his voice. I felt a rush of excitement wash over me as I made my way slowly to the bedroom, rushing as soon as I was out of sight of the webcam. I returned to the sofa and held up the vibrator. It felt heavy in my hand and I regarded it with interest. Except for that first time I'd used it, I hadn't really looked at it. There was still something about it that just felt dirty, I didn't like to think about it, although I realised feeling uneasy about a vibrator was ridiculous compared to the way I'd been behaving lately.

Chris instructed me to lie back on the sofa, my head resting on the arm, my left knee raised, lying along the back of the sofa, and my right foot bent, placed on the floor. I felt exposed, but immediately turned on. This felt different, he was commanding, directing me, I shivered with anticipation.

'OK, I'm going to tell you another story, you feel free to join in anytime you like.' He paused and I nodded to show I understood. He went on, 'I had a final session with a client today. This particular client wanted to get into shape to join a boxing club. So we had been doing a lot of skipping to improve her agility and stamina. Anyway, she works unusual shifts and this morning she had to be in work for 7 a.m., which meant that we had to meet at the gym at 5 a.m. Luckily, I have keys for the gym and my boss trusts me to be in there outside normal opening hours. It also meant, of course, that we were completely alone and would be right up until she had to leave at 6.30 a.m.'

'So you rewarded her for all her hard work?'

I felt a ridiculous stab of envy at the thought of Chris with someone else. I wanted him to only want me, but I knew that was stupid, I doubted for a moment if he even wanted me at all. I heard him chuckle quietly.

'I didn't plan for anything to happen if that's what you mean, Liv, but I was aware of the possibility that something might happen. You see, we entered into a professional relationship which would end at the same time as this final session, no more restrictions.' I rolled my eyes and I heard him chuckle again. 'Don't be jealous, Liv, I can assure you I thought only of you.'

Despite the teasing in his voice, I smiled and nodded.

'I should think so too.'

'When she joined me in the gym she was dressed differently to her usual gym outfit. She was wearing a black spaghetti strap vest, not tight and figure-hugging, but quite loose, and tiny shorts.. As soon as I saw her, I thought of you demonstrating your push-ups last week and I confess I felt myself harden. I think she noticed because her smile changed from shy to confident and I realised she had planned for exactly that effect. Although she couldn't have possibly known why short shorts would have such an effect on me.'

I could feel my pulse quicken, I no longer cared that he was talking about another woman, I only focused on his desire for me, that he was about to pretend he was with me. I was thrilled, happy to know he did want me after all. I shifted my attention back to his voice.

'We ran through the usual workout, warming up on the bike and treadmill, strength exercises, punch bag, and skipping. She faced the mirror during her floor exercises, her eyes catching mine as she performed her push-ups, I followed her eyes as she looked at herself in the mirror, her loose vest falling forward to reveal her breasts, her eyes then moving to her rear forcing me to look at her tight ass encased in those tiny shorts. I could see the material hanging loose and knew they would be easy to move aside. I started the countdown bringing her to the end of her reps and she leant back on her heels watching me in the mirror. Slowly she eased herself up into a downward dog, walking her hands up the mirror until she unfurled herself up slowly stopping halfway she caught my eye in the mirror again smiling slowly, seductively, almost inviting me to press myself against her. But not yet, not until our contract was over. I tore my eyes away and moved across to the treadmill setting it for a five-minute cool down.

'She had brought her own skipping rope, asking me to check it was suitable for her own practice. It had smooth thick plastic handles rounded at the end and the rope could be retracted to vary the length. I was adjusting the length when she finished her cool down and joined me, taking it from my hands.

'She said, "I guess that means an end to our beautiful relationship then."

'I nodded and replied, "Yes, we are all done here, you've done brilliantly."

'She hooked the skipping rope around my neck and pulled me towards her. As her lips approached mine, she whispered, "Good," and kissed me. I was momentarily stunned, but not surprised. I held her head in my hands and returned her kiss, my tongue dancing around hers, exploring her mouth.'

I recognised my cue to join in, holding my left cheek in my right hand and inserting my thumb into my mouth. I closed my eyes, concentrating on his story to keep up with his directions.

'Her hands released the rope and snaked under my shirt, tracing a pattern across my lower back and cupping my ass, squeezing and pulling me towards her. I picked her up wrapping her legs around my body and pulled her vest down, revealing her breasts, I slowly licked my tongue along the valley between her breasts up to her neck, sucking her chin and returning to her mouth.'

I ran my wet thumb over my chin to my chest, tracing a damp line down to the valley between my breasts and back up to my mouth, listening intently.

'I lay her down on the bench press and stood over her. She looked frustrated and reached out for me. I took her hand and kissed it. "Do you trust me?" I asked her. She nodded. "Do you like playing with this rope?" I asked suggestively. She nodded again, her breath catching in her throat. "Do you want me to play with the rope?" She nodded again, closing her eyes as I kissed her once more; she wrapped her arms around my body, trying to mould me against her. I pulled away, sitting on the end of the bench, and unhooked her right leg from around my waist, I placed her right hand around her ankle, weaving the skipping rope around them, binding them together.

'Her eyes widened and I searched her face for consent. She nodded and closed her eyes. I passed the rope beneath the bench to the other side and bound her left hand to her ankle. Her knees were raised, her legs open, and she was restrained, unable to touch me. I lengthened the rope further and took the handle, running it along her body, tracing the contours of her legs, her inner thighs, skimming her shorts and up over her navel, between her breasts, and up to her lips. Her tongue darted out to lick the plastic handle, watching me as she did so. I pushed the handle into her mouth, dancing with her tongue as she sucked on it. I moved it gently in and out of her mouth as she groaned.'

He stopped and I sensed him watching me as I trailed my fingers across my body, moaning as I skimmed the thin fabric of my thong and up the front of my body to my lips.

'You're using fingers, Liv. Isn't there something more similar to the handle of the skipping rope you could be using?'

I frowned. I felt a rush of shame flood over me; acknowledging my actions and feeling embarrassed at doing it wrong. I didn't know what he meant, I spied my skipping rope hanging from the door hook but the handles were wooden and the thought of splinters down there made me shudder. Then it hit me, the vibrator. I held up the vibrator and heard him sigh happily. I closed my eyes and ran the cool plastic up my inner thigh, skimming across the lace of the thong and following my body up towards my face. I licked the tip of the vibrator, and sucked it into my mouth, feeling it move in and out slowly. I imagined it was him and moaned gently, waiting for him to continue. I recognised the lust in his voice when he continued and sighed, content that he was enjoying my performance.

'I gently pulled the handle from her mouth and teased it over her body, using it to unhook the vest straps from her shoulders to expose her breasts. I ran the handle across her breasts, teasing her nipples. I leant across her and took a nipple into my mouth, teasing it with my tongue.'

I tugged at the cups on the basque, freeing my breasts and forcing them above the material. I moved the vibrator across my nipple and switched it on, the soft vibrations sending ripples of pleasure from my breast down my spine. I licked my thumb and circled it around my other nipple, squeezing it between my thumb and forefinger.

'I drew the handle down past her belly button and pressed it against her clitoris, rubbing it gently up and down its length, her thighs tightened and her hips bucked as she moaned in frustration, forcing herself against the plastic. I lightened the touch, merely skimming her, cooling her sensation while I moved the crotch of her shorts aside exposing her soft flesh. I held the end of the handle against her opening and gently pushed it in.'

I felt my cheeks flush as I followed his direction, enjoying the familiar sensation of the vibrator rubbing against my clitoris, rolling my hips gently against the vibrating plastic, tensing my thigh muscles. As I moved the tip towards my opening, I felt my muscles tense in frustration as the sensation was taken away when I felt so close to climaxing. I slowed the rolling of my hips and gently pushed the vibrator inside myself, gasping as it filled me. My body was perfectly still taking in this new sensation.

'I rubbed my thumb gently against her clitoris and I moved the handle in and out of her, filling her and then removing it almost to the tip, then plunging it back in. Her hips met my thrusts, gradually speeding up until she climaxed noisily, gasping for breath.'

My own orgasm broke at his words, a combination of the soft vibrations and movement inside and the assault on my clitoris, every nerve in my body was concentrated on the pleasure at one point of my body and it was sensational. My orgasm lasted for so long I wanted to cry with the overwhelming intensity of it.

'I brought her down slowly, removing the handle of the rope and untying her ankles and wrists, before kneeling at the end of the bench and pulling her onto my knees holding her and rubbing her aching arms and legs.'

I smiled, sitting up and leant towards the laptop.

'So you really did reward her for her hard work? I assumed you just fucked them and sent them on their way. So selfless, Mr Knight.' He laughed in surprise.

'You give me too much credit, Liv, I haven't finished yet.'

I felt a faint stirring in my lower body at his words, knowing there was more to come. Could I go again?

'I carried her to the changing rooms and into the shower, her clothes moulding to her body, I peeled of her vest and shorts and she removed my pants and shirt. The jets stopped and I pulled her naked out of the cubicle and into the Jacuzzi, switching on the bubbles and sinking under the water. I sat on the edge of the pool and pulled her between my knees, holding her over the jets as she squirmed against the sensation of warm water being pumped against her clitoris. She took my cock in her hand and tugged it gently as it lengthened and stiffened under her touch, then took it in her mouth, sucking gently, darting her tongue along its length.'

He stopped and I'd heard the smile in his voice as he'd been talking. I knew what he wanted me to do, the thought made me feel quite sick, but I sensed that he expected me to wuss out and I wanted to surprise him, prove him wrong. I still had the vibrator in my hand and I sat in front of the laptop, my face and breasts filling the camera view and brought the plastic up to my lips. I could see my juices glistening in the light and closed my eyes as I pulled it into my mouth, tasting the saltiness of my climax. I smiled at his gasp and opened my eyes, staring into the camera as I waited for him to continue his story.

'I lifted her out of the Jacuzzi and led her into the locker room and stood her in front of the mirror. I pressed my body against her, moving her against the cold mirror and stepped away from her pulling her hips towards me as she walked her hands down the mirror. I watched her reflection as she brought one hand to cup her own breast, twisting her nipple. Her eyes never leaving mine.'

As he was talking, I had stood up, pushed the sofa back slightly and bent over the seat to hold onto the back of the chair. I kept my legs straight and my back flat. I heard his voice croak slightly as his next words came out.

'I parted her legs and thrust myself inside her quickly, pulling her hips towards me as I thrust deeper into her.'

I brought vibrator up from beneath me and pushed it deep inside me as I imagined him fucking me from behind. I tensed my muscles around the shaft and rolled my hips as I moved it in and out, picking up speed. I couldn't move it quickly enough and pressed the button twice, crying out as the strong vibrations caused my body to convulse in orgasm. I pulled the vibrator out of me and rubbed it against my clitoris enjoying every wave of my climax. Exhausted, I collapsed on the sofa, catching my breath. I heard Chris gasp as he achieved his own orgasm.

'Fuck, Liv, that was amazing. I didn't expect you to do any of that.'

I smiled, feeling the warmth of his words flood through me. If only he could be here, if only it was me he was fucking.

Chapter Twenty-five

Steven was much happier when he burst into the office on Wednesday afternoon. He appeared in my doorway, knocking on the wood of the doorframe, grinning. His hair was styled in its trademark forward quiff and he was clean shaven, his chequered shirt was ironed, and his blazer was smart. He looked relaxed, confident, and devastatingly handsome.

'Hello, how was Birmingham?' I asked smiling in amusement at his return to good humour.

'It was brilliant.' My eyebrows shot up in surprise, 'Seriously, it was so interesting, I learned the future of programming!' He grinned again. Then he seemed to remember something, 'Oh and I think I got us a couple of new customers.'

'Now that is interesting, go get yourself a brew and come and tell me all about it.'

I watched him bounce out of the room and heard him chatting to James as he filled the kettle. I smiled to myself, it was the happiest I'd seen Steven in a long time. I wondered if he had made a decision about Melissa, whatever it was it had certainly relaxed him.

I heard the door open and Steph's voice rang out through the office, 'Lunch is here.' I leant against the doorframe waiting for my sandwich. Steph eyed Steven suspiciously. 'I thought you weren't in today, I don't have anything for you.'

'That's OK, I only just had breakfast, this one works me so hard I had to sleep in this morning.' He nodded his head at me grinning. Steph frowned slightly but smiled.

'I always suspected she'd be a tyrant!' She smiled at

me, 'Where do you hide the whip?'

I shivered imperceptibly. What was wrong with me? I couldn't hear the word whip without feeling slightly aroused. I felt a flush creep over my cheeks as I heard the word in his voice and shook my head to clear the thought, focussing again on Steph's voice.

'How's your crazy stalker? Haven't seen her prowling around the pub for a few weeks.' Steven's smile flickered slightly and he glanced across at me. I narrowed my eyes, sensing I was going to dislike what I was about to hear. He cleared his throat.

'Well now that's no way to talk about the mother of my unborn child now is it?' He smiled.

Steph's eyes widened and her mouth dropped open.

'Shit, sorry, I mean, congratulations.' She rushed over to hug him and he caught my eye across the top of her head, his eyes full of apology. I nodded and returned to my office, leaving the door open so I could listen in.

'It's OK, it was hardly planned,' I heard him explain. Steph snorted.

'Wasn't planned, my ass!' Steph exclaimed. I smiled to myself, Steph had a way of saying what everyone else was thinking.

'But that's not the kid's fault is it? So I just want to be a good dad to my kid, whatever.' I closed my eyes and accepted it was over, before it had even had a chance to begin. I watched my Mr Right framed in my doorway laughing with Steph and my heart felt heavy with sadness and regret. I'd been stupid resisting him, I should've taken the chance, allowed myself to just enjoy the ride instead of being suspicious and cautious. Now the only man I'd ever felt myself with, felt I could really be with, was lost to me forever.

I vowed to myself in that moment to say yes to any opportunity that came my way. To fill my void with adventure and new experiences in the hope of one day finding something or someone that could be half as right for me as Steven.

I wasn't in the mood for Chris that evening, normally it would be just what I needed to distract me but I had decided on my walk home that pizza was also what I needed to distract me and I knew Chris wouldn't approve. Nevertheless I accepted his call when it came through but I didn't care about my sweat pants, slippers, and oversized *Doctor Who* hoodie.

'You seem troubled tonight, Liv,' he remarked immediately. I shrugged.

'Why do you call me Liv?' It had never really occurred to me before that he used his own name for me; he'd never asked me what I preferred to be called. I'd grown accustomed to being Olly from an early age but I liked Liv, it made me feel grown up.

'It's just short for Olivia.' The confusion was evident in his voice.

I laughed.

'Well yes, I get that, but everyone else calls me Olly.'

'Olly? That's a horrible name!' He exclaimed, horrified. I smiled. 'Olivia is a beautiful name, but it has way too many syllables, Liv seemed an obvious short term. But Olly? Sounds like a boy's name. I couldn't call you Olly. You wouldn't prefer me to call you Olly, would you?'

'No, I like Liv, it's just that no one has ever called me that before. It makes me feel more feminine and grown up. I like it.'

'I quite like that I'm the only one that uses it.' I heard the smile in his voice, 'it's like my pet name for you.' I giggled. Just like that he'd cheered me up. My Knight in shining armour.

'I wish I could meet you.' I blurted out, frowning. I paused, I hadn't intended to say it out loud. I heard his sharp intake of breath.

'I know, Liv, I do too. Sometimes it's all I can do to stop myself jumping in the car and driving to London.' I felt the familiar sensation of heat creeping across the back of my head, my heart pounding at his words.

'Why don't you then?' I heard him chuckle.

'Because it would take so long that by the time I got there you'd be leaving for work.'

'Why can't you just come and visit me? Or I could visit you?' I frowned, biting my bottom lip.

'OK. When? I have classes so I can't really leave Edinburgh, but I'd be happy to book a flight for you.'

My eyes widened in surprise, I wasn't expecting that. I thought he'd give me some excuse.

'Next weekend? Is that too soon?' I asked hopefully, but not wanting to sound desperate. My pulse quickened as I imagined all the things he would do to me in person.

'Next weekend is difficult for me, I have exams on the Monday and I know you'll distract me all weekend. Let me check my exam schedule and get back to you, OK?'

I nodded grinning. I was so excited suddenly.

'I can't believe I'll finally get to meet you. I feel like I've known you forever already.'

He chuckled.

'Well you'll get to know a whole lot more of me.'

'Will I get to see your gym?' I asked innocently.

'Do you want to see my gym, Liv?'

I nodded.

'I especially want to see the Jacuzzi in the mixed changing room.' I grinned.

'I think you should remove those hideous clothes, Olivia, and make yourself comfortable.'

I closed my eyes and inhaled slowly, shaking my head. 'I'm sorry, Chris, I'm just not in the mood. I just want to curl up and watch TV.'

'What's on your mind? You can talk to me, you know,

Liv.'

I wasn't sure what to tell him, could I explain that I was sad about Steven? Would it seem strange after my recent behaviour with Chris to be so upset about someone else? I'd just arranged to go visit him! I really was the queen of mixed messages.

'I'm just tired I think, a little bit achy, nothing a good sleep won't fix.'

'OK babe, I wish I was there to rub your back or something.'

'I imagine my back is the last thing you want to rub, you big perv,' I grinned, rolling my eyes. I heard him chuckle as I closed the laptop.

The following morning Steven was back in his distracted mood. He barely acknowledged me when he arrived and he settled into his work immediately. I called him in for our weekly catch-up meeting to check progress against deadlines and I could tell I only had half of his attention. I put down my pen and looked at him. He looked tired, his hair was flopped to one side, and his chin was sporting stubble.

'What's going on?'

He looked at me in surprise and shrugged.

'Nothing, it's all good.'

I frowned.

'Come on, Steven, if nothing else we're friends and I care about you. But I'm also your boss and I'm not getting your full attention, so what is it?'

His face flushed and he looked at me with sorry eyes.

'Melissa, I called her last night, told her I would stand by her and the baby.' He frowned, puzzlement flooding his face, 'She didn't react the way I expected.' He sighed, slumping back in his chair, looking at me thoughtfully.

'What did she say?'

'She just asked me if I'd told my father yet.'

My eyes narrowed, and he nodded in agreement at my expression, 'I know, that's weird right?'

'Oh well, you've told her where you stand on the situation, I guess it's up to her what happens next.' I suggested.

'Maybe she wants me to prove my commitment by telling my parents, but I just can't tell them yet, it'll destroy them.'

'Are they too young to be grandparents yet?' I teased trying to lighten his mood, He smiled briefly.

'They have dreams for me, they met Melissa already at uni, she's not who they would want me to spend my life with. I mean I don't want to spend my life with her, but that's irrelevant.'

'Maybe that's why then, she wants the satisfaction of knowing she's got you despite what your parents think.'

He shrugged and picked up his pile of papers, signalling the end of our conversation. He paused in the doorway and turned back.

'Ols, it's Friday tomorrow, we should take James to the pub.'

I hadn't thought about the pub, I wondered if I could just leave that to Steven to sort out but his expression didn't fill me with much confidence. I nodded.

'OK, but first sign of girl trouble and he's on his own!' I grumbled.

Despite himself Steven grinned and left the room.

Chapter Twenty-six

Ruth was far more excited about Friday night drinks than was necessary. I had to remind her that meeting Steven was a wasted effort now that he was no longer available to me but she didn't care, she was curious enough to want to see him in the flesh.

'What reason am I going to give for you being there other than wanting to check out my staff?'

'I'm taking you out. I have two free tickets from work for this gig at The Garage, I have to write a review for it, so that's our excuse.'

I groaned loudly down the phone, emphasising each note.

'Oh, Olly, shut up, it'll do you good to come out with me. I could fix you up with one of the band backstage, road test some of your new confidence.' she teased. I blushed to my roots.

'Shut up.' I scolded as she giggled girlishly.

'Oh come on, Olly, you can't save it all for Mr Vampire online, get out there and tango with a real man.' I sighed.

I didn't need to answer, she knew I would go, if only to keep up the pretence.

That was how I found myself propping up the bar in The Garage on Friday night, watching a strange couple have sex on the sofa in the dark corner. I was trying really hard to divert my eyes but I was just drunk enough that my curiosity got the better of me and my brain function prevented me from behaving appropriately and looking away.

Ruth had met us at 6 p.m. in The World's End. She was

quite mesmerised by Steven, and she kept glancing at me sadly every time he told her something about himself, which inevitably made his likability shoot though the roof. I knew what she was thinking: how could you have let this one slip through your fingers, you idiot! I'd thought it enough times myself in the past few weeks, although not as much lately, my sessions with Chris had given me something new to focus on and I was enjoying my strange romance with him. I was still waiting for a date to go visit him and I couldn't wait.

'Seriously, how do you concentrate?' She hissed at me as we left the pub.

'I shut my office door and pretend he's not there.' She nodded, 'and I have lots of cybersex with the vampire,' I grinned. Her eyes widened and she burst out laughing.

'Now the repressed Olly that I know and love would never have said that. You've changed,' she said accusingly. I grinned and nodded. Ruth linked her arm through mine and we made our way to the tube station.

So far I hadn't heard anything I liked out of the support bands and hoped the main act would be better, so I was relieved to have something else to entertain me when I spotted the openly amorous couple in the corner. It was hard to see them in the dark corner but I could just make out her movement as she writhed on top of him, their hands tangled in each other's hair. The pair stopped suddenly as a group of giggling girls stomped up the steps towards the bar. I glanced back at the couple as the girl pulled him up from his seat and wrapped her arms around him.

He sat himself down on a stool, straddling her onto his knee as he stroked her back, reaching into her hair and kissing her. I was mesmerised as she began to gyrate her body against him, reaching down with her hands to undo his jeans. He hitched up her skirt, exposing the flesh of her bottom and yanked at the material. She gasped as the thong broke, digging into her flesh as the material stretched and ripped apart. He lifted her easily as she positioned him beneath her, sinking onto him. The music was loud, and drowned out her moans as she bucked her hips against him. He threw his head back, his mouth wide open as he came, thrusting once more into her and then pushing her off him. He stood up, reaching into his pocket and handed her a note, nodding his head towards the bar. She touched his face affectionately and skipped to the bar. I turned away, not wanting to risk her seeing my shocked expression. Two things had occurred to me; first, that was nowhere near as erotic as the scenarios Chris had described to me and second, if no one has sex like Chris does, I'm going to be sorely disappointed.

I glanced up and caught sight of the girl's face in the mirror behind the bar and my mouth dropped open. It was Melissa.

I needed to go home, should I tell Steven? I wanted to talk to Chris, he would know what to do. I searched for Ruth to tell her I was leaving.

'Hey did you see that couple shagging in the corner?' She giggled when I found her. I nodded.

'That was Melissa,' I shouted into her ear. She stared into my face looking for the joke, her eyes wide.

'Melissa from the toilet? Mother of his child?' I nodded.

'Or is she the mother of someone else's child? I need to get home, I want to speak to Chris about it and see what he thinks I should do.'

'You should tell Steven, straight away.' she shouted in surprise.

'What if he doesn't believe me? What if he thinks I'm making it up?' she frowned shaking her head.

'He knows you wouldn't do that, Olly.' I shrugged.

'I'm going to talk to Chris. He knows them both. He'll know what to do.'

I hugged her goodbye and left.

I was out of breath by the time I got home and opened up my laptop, waiting for my online contacts to appear and willing him to be there. He was, of course. I clicked his link and requested a call.

'Come on come on,' I whispered impatiently until the screen went black and I heard is calming voice through my speakers.

'Hey, Liv, where have you been all night?'

'Did you miss me?' I teased, distracted momentarily by his words.

'Of course. I've been lonely all evening.'

'Listen I need to talk to you.' I said abruptly. I heard him shift in his seat, alerted by my tone, 'It's about Steven and Melissa.'

'What about them?' His voice was cautious.

'I saw her tonight at a gig, she was, well let's just say for now that she wasn't behaving much like a mum to be.' Chris snorted.

'Was she drinking? I knew she wouldn't give a crap about anything like that.'

'That's not all. She was fucking some guy in the dark corner of the venue near the bar.'

'What?' He hissed.

'Yeah you heard, which kinda makes me wonder how she's so certain the baby is Steven's.'

'That little bitch. You haven't told Steven yet?'

'No, not yet.'

'Why haven't you told him this, Liv? This changes everything. Isn't this what you wanted?' I held out my hands helplessly.

'I was scared he might think I was making it up. It's too late for us now anyway, too much has changed. I'm not the same person I was when we met.'

'It's funny, but I knew how Steven felt about you. I was trying to help you for him as well as for you.' His voice was quiet.

'I guess you were to start with but then all this shit happened and our conversations evolved. Could you imagine how he would feel if we were together and he ever found out what you had seen me do.'

I held my face in my hands, the old repressed guilt and shame washing over me. I felt sick. I heard him shushing me gently.

'Liv, you've done nothing wrong, please stop this.' His voice was commanding and I stopped wallowing in my guilt and looked up at the camera, 'Whatever happens in your future don't you ever feel guilty about this. And certainly not because of how Steven might feel. Christ Liv, why shouldn't you enjoy yourself? There is no shame whatsoever in you enjoying your body.'

I nodded, wiping my face.

'Will you tell Steven about Melissa for me? I asked quietly, 'I won't see him until Monday.'

'Sure, I'll call him now.' I waited for him to say something else but he remained silent. I closed the laptop and went to bed.

I was so confused. Was Steven available again? I expected to be thrilled at the thought of getting a second chance, but I just felt disappointed that I would have to say goodbye to Chris. I had spent all this time using Chris as a distraction from my heartbreak over Steven and as a result, I'd practically fallen in love with him. I didn't even know what he looked like! But it didn't matter, I'd developed so much through my video calls with Chris and I trusted him. I wanted to meet him, see if there was something between us in reality. I felt uneasy that our conversation had ended talking about Steven, something about it felt final, as if he was saying goodbye.

I knew I was being silly. He was all the way in Edinburgh and was due to return to America in the summer; it was hopeless. Or maybe I could move to

America. I could certainly set up Inspired over there. Nothing was impossible.

I drifted asleep with images of tall buildings and cherry pie floating around my mind.

Chapter Twenty-seven

Ruth had been ringing my doorbell for ten minutes before the sound filtered through to my subconscious and woke me up. I shuffled to the intercom and buzzed her up, and stood in the doorway waiting for her to reach the top of the stairs.

I stared at her through narrow eyes, yawning as she bound past me. She had stayed out later than I had and was still bright and perky. It was a phenomenon I imagined would never happen to me. I struggled to wake up after an early night as it was.

I followed Ruth into my flat and filled the kettle.

'So what happened? Did you tell him yet?' I yawned again shaking my head.

'I told Chris last night, he's going to pass the message on for me.'

'It certainly casts doubt about the baby, doesn't it?'

I nodded as I carried our tea into the living room and curled up on the sofa. I took in Ruth's outfit; light camel-coloured jacket over a long pale pink vest, black jeans, and flat shoes. The shoes raised my suspicions.

'Why are you wearing flat shoes?'

'I'm taking you shopping. You need a smaller wardrobe and that disgustingly handsome employee of yours is back on the market.' I closed my eyes and frowned. I hated shopping. Ruth threw a cushion at me.

'I hate shopping,' I moaned.

'I know, that's why you need me to take you. Go take a shower.' I made a production out of dragging myself off the sofa and shuffling reluctantly to the bathroom. I paused in the doorway and turned round thoughtfully.

'Actually I do need something. You can help me pick out some sexy underwear. I'm planning a trip to Edinburgh.' Ruth's mouth dropped open.

'What? What about Steven?' She frowned, confused. I didn't blame her, I was confused myself.

'We talked about it last week, haven't set a date yet but we decided I'd go visit.'

'You've had more cybersex, haven't you?' She accused, amusement seeping into her voice. My face flushed in response.

'Are you going to Edinburgh for a booty call, Olly?' She giggled and I closed my eyes, trying to suppress the laugh I had bubbling inside me. I nodded and Ruth squealed. She eventually calmed down and her tone turned serious, 'What about Steven?' I shrugged.

'I think that ship has sailed. I'm not even sure how I feel about him, I think I got over him around about the time Chris started talking me through the most amazing orgasms I've ever had!'

'Are you sure you want to meet him though? What if he's really horrible? I don't know, Olly, I think this could be a really bad idea.' I felt doubt creeping in.

'Well, we haven't confirmed anything yet.'

'Just think it through carefully.' She saw my crestfallen expression, 'but some sexy underwear for your next web chat we can definitely arrange.' I grinned, eyeing my laptop and wondering if he'd be online tonight.

I stood in front of the mirror and examined the outfit I was wearing. It wasn't quite as impressive as the Agent Provocateur lingerie from Chris, but it was pretty sexy all the same. Ruth had a good eye for clothing. I was surprised by the size of some of the clothes she was passing me but everything I tried on fitted perfectly. I was finally happy with my figure. But for what reason? Who was going to see it? I wondered briefly about Steven. I wasn't sure how I felt. I knew I had felt disappointed when he chose Melissa, although I understood why and I'd certainly thrown myself wholeheartedly into my emerging romance with Chris. Now that it appeared as though Steven might be available again I wasn't sure how I felt; I had thought I would throw myself into his arms and never let go if I was given a second chance, but now that it seemed possible I wasn't sure I wanted it. Perhaps all this happened for a good reason, perhaps Steven and I were never meant to be – I was his boss after all and that had always felt awkward to me. We had been getting on well since the obvious sexual tension was removed and I really valued his work for Inspired.

I barely even noticed how attractive he looked this week. It no longer set my pulse racing. I felt affectionate towards him of course but thanks to Chris I was over the worst of my infatuation.

Chris made me feel something entirely different. I felt liberated and even when I occasionally felt dirty about what we did, that feeling generally aroused me too.

I smiled at myself in the mirror, the deep red of the satin vest highlighted the slight mahogany tones in my dark hair. The hem of the vest skimmed my thighs, displaying only the bottom edge of the matching satin shorts. It was a prettier version of my workout clothes, equally short and equally loose. I heard the laptop ringing and feeling a flutter of excitement I ran to the living room to answer the call.

'Hey beautiful,' he greeted me.

I flushed with warmth at his words and smiled. 'Hey yourself, how's your day been?'

'It would've been better if you'd been here, but I got lots of revision done for my exam on Monday.' He paused. 'I guess seeing you like this is reward enough for now.'

'I can't wait to visit you, Mr Knight.' I smiled seductively into the camera. He chuckled.

'You are incorrigible, Miss Jones, why are you so impatient to see me?'

'I think you know why.'

'Is it my Jacuzzi?'

I giggled, 'Maybe.'

He sighed suddenly and I felt a prickling sensation crawl up my neck, something wasn't right.

'Have you really thought this through though, Liv?' He asked seriously.

'What do you mean?'

'I just don't know if this is such a good idea. You know I'm going back to the States next year. I don't want to lead you on or anything.'

I understood what he was saying, but I knew I needed to meet him, I needed to experience what he had to offer, just once.

'When I saw Melissa last night, before I knew it was her I watched her fucking that guy and two things ran through my mind. First of all it was quick, passionless, I noticed that it was the complete opposite of all the things you've described to me. Secondly, I realised that if no one else fucks like you do then I am always going to be disappointed.' I heard him laughing and smiled. 'Don't you think I deserve to be completely satisfied at least once in my life?' I wheedled.

'Of course you do, Liv. But then again, if you don't know any different you won't be quite as disappointed in future.'

'Well I'm certainly feeling disappointed now.' I grumbled.

'You'll be fine, maybe you just need to find the right man that sets your pulse racing and you can take the lead,' he reassured me.

'What? I couldn't do that!' I gasped.

'Sure you could, in fact that would be sexy as hell. Try it now; tell me what you would have me do to you if I was there right now.'

I heard the challenge in his voice, the teasing tone, and I knew he expected me to refuse. I felt stupid but I wanted to do as he asked at the same time. I tried to imagine the way he spoke to me and to think what I wanted. I snorted as I realised all I could think about was his Jacuzzi stories. Well that couldn't happen here. My mind drifted to the DVD he had sent me, I could have him in the bath. A tingle ran down my spine and my cheeks flushed. I heard him chuckle.

'You're imagining it, aren't you, Liv? Don't shut me out, tell me what you're thinking.' His voice was soft and gentle. It lulled me into a sense of calm and a desire to share my innermost feelings and desires.

'OK, picture the scene,' I began. 'I'm in the bath, the water is hot, the bubble bath has formed a thick layer of foam on the top of the water covering my body. I'm relaxing. You are on your way to visit me and I'm expecting you to arrive in a couple of hours. I'm a little nervous because it's the first time we will meet in person, the first time I will see you, see if you look like I imagine.' I pause, allowing this fact to sink in, wondering why he doesn't have any tagged photos on Facebook.

'Go on.' Chris encouraged, giving nothing away.

'OK, so the doorbell rings and I'm trying to ignore it, but it's persistent so I climb out of the bath and grab a bathrobe which I put on as I'm making my way down the stairs to the front door. When I open it there's a handsome man grinning at me with a sports bag slung over his shoulder.

'"Hey, Liv," you say to me, "I'm a bit early."

'You shrug apologetically and walk past me through the door and up the stairs. I follow you and make my way to the kitchen to fill the kettle.

'"I was hoping to be a little bit more presentable than this." I laugh. "I was just in the bath," I explain.

'"You look as beautiful as ever, Liv," you say in response.

'I turn to the counter to plug the kettle in when I feel you behind me, your hands on my hips pressing yourself into the small of my back.

'"Does this prove how attractive I find you?" you whisper in my ear, I lean back against you as your hand unties the belt on my robe and sneaks inside, tracing a path across my stomach and up to my breast, your lips trailing kisses along my cheek and down my neck. You turn me to face you, your mouth covering mine as you lift me onto the counter, opening up my robe and exploring my body with your tongue, teasing my nipples with your teeth as they harden and leaving a tingling path down my body to my clitoris. Your tongue flickers against me as your finger enters my body, moving in and out, picking up pace as I tense my thighs around you and explode as the overload of sensations reach their peak and my orgasm is released.

'You pick me up in your arms and carry me to the bathroom, placing me in the water. You then remove your clothes and present yourself to me. My tongue traces a path from its base up to the tip of your erection before I take you fully into my mouth, moving my lips and tongue slowly along the shaft, all the way to the tip then all the way to the base, my tongue dances around you as my lips move up and down, picking up speed until you release yourself into my mouth.

'Then you climb into the bath pulling me against you. You dribble shower gel along my body and slowly rub it into my arms, my stomach, and my breasts. I feel arousal building again as you move down to my crotch and suddenly you're pushing me forward onto my knees and entering me from behind, slowly, stretching me, moving in and out as you pick up pace until we both reach our climax.' I shrugged. 'I mean, it's no Jacuzzi story, but something like that would be good.'

Chris chuckled.

'It was a little rushed, Liv, I would want to take a lot more time than that, but I do realise that perhaps the first time might be a little frantic.'

I blushed. Since these conversations with Chris, my desire for sex was becoming almost desperate. I found myself thinking about it all the time. I'd waited a long time and I wasn't sure I would be able to take my time when the opportunity finally presented itself.

'What do I look like?' he asked suddenly. I giggled.

'I think it's you that should be telling me that!'

'I mean how do you picture me?' He laughed.

'Well, you're tall, slim, muscular, like a swimmer or a runner rather than a bodybuilder. I imagine you have thick dark hair – sideburns, of course. Your eyes are brown, and they sparkle with amusement and mischief.' I smiled as I said this, knowing he was always teasing me. 'Your face is slim and angular, a narrow nose and jaw, perhaps a little stubble.'

'Interesting.' His voice was amused.

'Am I warm?' I asked, intrigued. It occurred to me that I was basing my description on the guy in the photo with Steven without knowing for certain if that was actually Chris.

'Quite warm, yes. I have green eyes and sadly no sideburns but I'm sure I could grow some if we were to meet so as not to disappoint you.'

'I don't think sideburns are a deal breaker.' I laughed. 'They would take too long to grow, and we don't have that much time before you leave for good.'

He sighed again.

'Just promise me you'll think about it carefully before we decide.'

I grinned, I could promise that, and then I would book a train. I nodded eagerly.

'I promise I will think about nothing else.'

Chapter Twenty-eight

I didn't know whether to say anything to Steven about Melissa on Monday. I watched him carefully when he arrived, made him a cup of tea, and lingered near his desk to see if he would mention anything. I had forgotten to ask Chris about it on Saturday and was beginning to worry he hadn't told him about Friday night. The morning passed by slowly while I waited for him to come in to my office and talk to me, but he didn't. I don't know what I had expected, really – the old flirty Steven to come back, looking at me with that twinkle of suggestion in his eye? I felt a stab of guilt, I shouldn't want him to want me when I have Chris occupying my thoughts. I flicked through my diary to find a suitable weekend to suggest visiting Edinburgh and occupied myself with emailing Chris.

From: Olivia Jones
To: Chris Knight
Subject: Jacuzzi

Dear Mr Knight,
I have thought about it and I am impatient to become acquainted with your Jacuzzi.
When can I come visit?

O
X

I watched the screen, hoping for an immediate reply, but I was distracted by the front door bursting open, I looked up and saw Steven's face darken with anger and I knew it had to be Melissa. I couldn't understand why she was so keen to make such a public exhibition of her private life, but then I reasoned, this was a girl who seemed to have no private boundary if her penchant for public sex was any kind of indicator.

I made my way to the doorway of my office to observe. Melissa was standing in the entrance to the office, hands on hips. She wore a hideous fake fur jacket, tight fitting jeans, and high-heeled knee-high boots. Steven was watching her warily.

'Well? Here I am. What did you want to see me for?' She demanded, her perfectly plucked eyebrows were raised in question and her ruby red lips rested into a natural pout. She looked like a doll. She was beautiful under the heavy make-up, which made her look cheap. Her scowl betrayed her outer beauty, showing her true nature.

Steven nodded, smiling. He moved away from his desk towards her pausing a meter away from her.

'Did you have a good night on Friday?' He asked politely. 'You and your friend seemed pretty intimate at The Garage.'

The colour drained from her face as she stared at him. I watched the thoughts bounce around her vacuous head as she tried to think of an explanation and I almost laughed out loud when she turned to leave. Steven grabbed her arm tightly and pulled her away from the door. She stared at his hand and then looked up into his face. His happy smile had been replaced with a hard expression, his jaw was tense and his mouth a thin line.

'What's going on? You spent all that time relentlessly pursuing me and as soon as you get me, you're off fucking other men in public.'

Melissa stared back at him silently.

'I was prepared to stand by you, but how can I be sure the baby's mine?' He paused, 'and you were drinking alcohol, you can't be drinking alcohol while you're pregnant.'

Her face flushed crimson and she avoided his gaze. His eyes narrowed.

'You are still pregnant, right?'

She raised her face slowly to look at him and shook her head. Steven took a step back and stared at her.

'Was there ever a baby, Melissa?'

'No,' she whispered miserably. 'I just wanted the money.'

Steven paused, confusion replacing his irritation He clearly hadn't expected her explanation.

'Money? What money?'

'You were supposed to give me £500 for an abortion.'

I felt my mouth drop open, mirroring Steven's reaction. I knew it was none of my business but I found myself moving closer to speak.

'But abortions are free on the NHS,' I said.

Melissa turned to me and shrugged. 'They don't know that,' she replied.

'So the guy on Friday night? Will you be asking him for £500 too?' I asked incredulously.

Melissa glanced over at me, she looked ashamed but then something in her brain switched and she pulled herself up, stared at me defiantly and nodded.

'It's a new take on prostitution I suppose. So how many men do you fuck each week to trick them into believing you're pregnant?' I asked, shocked at this new development. Melissa shrugged.

'Two, sometimes three.' She looked up at Steven, 'of course some of them insist on using condoms so it doesn't always work, but then when they're cute I don't mind trying again.'

Steven reached into his back pocket and handed her an envelope. 'Take it,' he hissed. I could see he was losing patience with her.

Confusion filled her eyes as she took the envelope, she

searched his face questioningly. I sensed she was hoping it was money.

'That's an injunction. Come within ten metres of me again and you're going to prison.' He looked at his watch as he released her arm. 'Starting in five, four, three ...' Melissa rushed to the door, her face crimson with shame and disappointment.

I jumped as the door slammed, and let out the breath I'd been holding. Steven stood by the door, collecting himself, before turning back to his desk. He didn't look at me. I glanced at James who was concentrating on his screen, his headphones still in place. I doubted he'd even been aware of Melissa's presence. A natural-born nerd. The thought made me smile.

When I returned to my desk, I had a reply from Chris.

From Chris Knight
To Olivia Jones
Subject Jacuzzi

Hey, Miss Jones,
   I have spent a significant proportion of my free time imagining you naked in my Jacuzzi, but I'm afraid I'm heading back to America for Christmas this weekend, so we will have to wait until next year. I may struggle to talk to you while I'm at home, I don't have the same luxury of living on my own as I do in Edinburgh and my nieces and nephews don't leave me alone much.
   But you can be assured that I will definitely be thinking about you and your gym shorts.

Chris
X

I was so disappointed. It hadn't even occurred to me that

he might go home for Christmas or that he wouldn't be able to communicate with me in the same way from his home. I had always thought of him as being online, his physical location was irrelevant. I flushed with shame as I imagined his mum walking in on us, seeing me on the computer screen half-naked. I was relieved he had warned me otherwise I might have called him and who knows who would have seen me. January felt far away.

I thought about what Ruth had said to me on our shopping trip. She'd gently reminded me that in reality Chris wasn't a real person, he was a name on a computer terminal. I should think about spending my time with someone real. Perhaps a bit of space from Chris would be good for me, give me a chance to return to the real world a bit more. But I still had a few days before he left.

Steven appeared in my doorway. His red and black shirt hung over the top of his loose-fitting jeans, his sleeves were rolled up just below his elbow exposing the olive skin of his forearms. His hair was spiked and he wore a lazy smile on his face. He knocked lightly on the wood of the door frame.

'Hey. I'm just getting myself together for this conference in Manchester tomorrow. Just wanted to check you had everything sorted for the testers coming in on Wednesday.'

We had interviewed several testers last week and had hired three. I also had a part-time assistant hired. I was planning to wait until after Christmas before anyone started, but they were all keen to work right away, I guessed they needed the Christmas cash. I nodded.

'I have your notes plus James is up to speed.'

'I can't believe you used to do all this yourself,' he grinned at me, I smiled.

'Never was very good at sharing my toys, but this way is much more productive. I can't believe how quickly all this has come together.'

'Well it has to now; we've had jobs lining up since Birmingham.' Steven looked pleased with himself as he said it. 'Hopefully more to come after tomorrow too.' He looked at me thoughtfully. 'You should come next time; you'd enjoy it, you know.' I shrugged and promised I'd think about it.

Steven turned to leave and then, remembering something, he turned back. 'By the way, Ols, are we doing something for Christmas?'

I looked at him in horror, I hadn't even thought about Christmas, it was going to be way too late to book somewhere for a staff night out.

'What can we do?' I asked helplessly. Steven smiled indulgently.

'Leave it with me, I'll sort something. Next Friday, yeah?

I returned Steven's smile gratefully and nodded.

When is our last day?' he asked, still smiling.

'December 23rd?' I cringed at the question in my voice. He must think I was an idiot. The truth was that I hadn't really thought about that either, I was so used to just working all the time it hadn't occurred to me that my staff needed to know what their Christmas holiday period was. Being an employer was much more complicated than I had realised.

Steven nodded smiling.

'Cool, we get Christmas Eve off? I was going to book it off anyway to drive up to my folks.'

I grinned back at his smiling face, relieved I had got something right. Then I remembered Melissa.

'Are you OK? About Melissa?' I watched as he sighed and moved into the office, closing the door behind him. He smiled sadly.

'I was sort of hoping to just brush that whole chapter under the carpet and forget it happened.'

'You seemed quite content to become a dad.' I said,

remembering his conversation with Steph last week. He had seemed almost proud that he was going to be a father. I expected him to be relieved that this episode was behind him but I couldn't help wondering if he might also feel a little bit sad too.

Steven began to fidget under my gaze.

'Ols, you're doing that thing again, you know, where you stare at me.' His face cracked with a mocking smile. 'I know I look particularly handsome today but really, you're embarrassing me,' he teased.

I shook my head to clear it and smiled.

'You've had a rough couple of weeks, I just wanted to know you were OK and if you wanted to talk about it, you know I'm here, right?'

Steven smiled, but his expression was bemused. He stood up to leave.

'Cheers, Ols, I'm fine. I'm free! I'm going to head off to Manchester. See you Wednesday afternoon.'

Chapter Twenty-nine

The following evening I was playing *Wii Fit* when my laptop started ringing, I turned down the volume of the TV and made my way to the sofa and I stopped in my tracks. The familiar black square had been replaced by a living room. I saw movement as the bright room was obscured and a figure sat down in front of the camera. He was difficult to see with the light behind him, the faint glow from his computer monitor not really casting much light on his face but I could see him well enough. My heart beat loudly in my chest. This was Chris Knight. He looked different to his photos; he was wearing a baseball cap and dark-framed glasses, and his stubble was almost long enough to be classed as a beard. He looked mature but handsome. Distinguished.

'Notice anything different about me?' he asked, smiling.

'You're actually human?' I grinned.

'The camera finally arrived, just as I'm getting ready to leave. Typical.'

'Oh well, better late than never. It's nice to see you finally.'

'So how do I compare to your imagination?' His voice had that teasing tone but sounded slightly uncertain.

'Different, you look much nerdier than I expected. I know you're not a nerd.' He laughed. 'So you must be quite fashionable then, the nerdy look is in at the moment.' I concluded.

'Not really, although I am in the business of making people look and feel good, it makes sense for me to follow fashion, but not when I'm sat at home on my computer.'

'I wasn't expecting a beard.'

'Ah that's because for the last few weeks I've done nothing but write my dissertation and hang out with you. Don't even ask to see my hair, it's disgusting.'

'I like it, it suits you.'

'Really?'

'Yeah, I mean I wouldn't want it on my face so feel free to shave before I visit, but it looks good on you.'

He chuckled. 'You still want to visit me?' He sounded surprised, 'this is probably our last chance to chat this year, I've got end-of-term parties to go to and packing to do.'

I closed my eyes and sighed sadly. I was going to miss him. 'Best make the most of it then.' I smiled, running my finger across my bottom lip. I saw him smile and stopped, frowning.

'What is it?'

'I don't know. I think I feel strange now that I can see you watching me.'

'Are you having performance anxieties, Liv?' He teased.

'I feel self-conscious, it was different when you weren't visible, I could hear your voice but it didn't feel as though you were watching me, you were more like a self-help recording or something.'

'Would you prefer it if I turned my camera off?' He seemed amused when I nodded shyly, but in an instant my screen went black and he was gone. 'How will you cope if you come visit me and see me in the flesh, Liv?' His voice sounded stronger somehow without the visual.

'That'll be different. You won't be watching me, you'll be pleasuring me.' I grinned.

Steven was true to his word and sorted out a fabulous Christmas meal for the team on the last Friday before the holiday. We closed Inspired at noon on the 18th and made our way to a restaurant his friend Callum had recently opened in Kentish Town. We had a private room to ourselves and had the chance to get to know each other over a full turkey dinner. The new staff were working out brilliantly. Maria was a godsend; she had spent the first three days creating a logical filing system and had installed a finance package to keep track of the accounts. I'd felt a bit guilty handing all the invoices and receipts over to her but she took them all and handed me a report of the month's finances an hour later. Far more efficient than I ever was and worth every penny.

Colin, Mike, and Chloe had spent the first morning getting to know their way around, filling out personnel paper work, sorting out their salaries, and choosing their desk space in the testing room. In the afternoon Steven arrived, took them through the app they would be testing, and got them straight into work. I was proud of Steven, he had proven to be an efficient projects manager, with great people skills – he got the best out of the staff.

The restaurant was modern and clean, there was a decorated Christmas tree in the corner of our room and Steven and I had been out and bought presents for all the staff, which were now wrapped and waiting under the tree until after dinner. Steven had even convinced Callum to dress up as Santa to give out the presents. I'd really struggled with what to buy for Steven but had managed to get an advanced copy of *Dark Void* for the PlayStation 3, which wasn't due for release until January.

While we were waiting for dessert, I ordered a bottle of champagne and after everyone had been given a flute I made a toast.

'I'm not really into speeches or anything but I just wanted to say that this year has been a really big year for Inspired expanding from just one member of staff –' I paused and pointed at myself '– to a team of seven.' I opened my hands, indicating everyone sitting around the table.

'And to be completely honest with you all, I never imagined I would ever have a team working with me, but it's been a blast, I'm really glad you all joined me.'

I noticed big grins breaking out across everyone's face and feeling a boost of confidence I continued, 'but I also have to say that I had completely forgotten about things like Christmas break and Christmas parties, so the fact we are all here right now is down to Steven, so I want you all to raise your glass to Steven because actually, it's not just the Christmas meal he's sorted, Steven is actually the reason you all work for Inspired.'

Steven stood up, his eyes never leaving mine as he took a mock bow.

'What she isn't telling you is that she found me so annoying she had to bring more people in so she wouldn't have to deal with me!' He raised his eyebrows inviting me to deny the statement.

Everyone laughed loudly, watching me for a response as they gradually quietened down. I smiled and nodded.

'That's completely true, he's also the reason I have my own office now!'

I caught Steven winking at me, the corners of his mouth twitching with amusement, 'but regardless of how annoying he is, he has had an absolutely amazing impact on Inspired and I am truly thankful to him for choosing to join me.' I raised my glass, 'So to Steven and to you guys, I couldn't wish for a better team of people to work with. Merry Christmas!'

'Merry Christmas,' the whole team chorused. I sat down as the table cheered loudly. I looked round and saw Santa burst into the room.

Callum was a great Santa; he waddled into the room under a ton of padding and danced around the room to Slade, dragging Chloe up as he waltzed her around the room before returning her to her seat and pulling me up, I dragged my heels but there was no denying him, he was strong and quick on his feet and he spun me around until I was dizzy, and holding me in his arms he lowered me towards the floor until my head fell back and I saw my team upside down clapping along to the music and grinning at us. He set me back upright and walked me to the Christmas tree as the music came to an end.

'Ho ho ho!' he bellowed, his voice was filled with laughter and I could tell he was having fun in his role. I looked round at Steven who was laughing hard at his friend. He caught my eye and grinned, it was the happiest I'd seen him since the Melissa debacle, and it was great to see him back to his old self.

'Right, I have presents here, but only for all the people who have worked hard and been good for Mother Inspired here.' He reached for a present. 'Mike,' he said loudly handing the gift to me to deliver. He called each name out one by one until everyone had a present.

'Steven ...' As I handed over his gift, Steven frowned, confused. Apparently, he hadn't been expecting anything. I gave him a kiss on the cheek, pulling away as I felt his arm snake around my waist. I'd had just enough to drink to get carried away and at that moment, I was reminded of our earlier days together. I returned to my seat as Callum walked over to me holding out a gift, I glanced around the table frowning, certain that everyone had a present.

'Olivia,' he said kindly, I looked at the present in surprise but, sure enough, there was my name written on the tag. I caught Steven's eye and he smiled nodding imperceptibly. He'd done the same for me as I had for him.

We both opened our presents at the same time. I gasped when I saw mine. It was perfect; a Tardis USB hub. Steven grinned at my reaction before gasping when he glanced down at his gift.

'How did you get this? It's not out until next month.' I

shrugged nonchalantly, closing my eyes.

'I know people.' I squealed as he picked me up and spun me around hugging me tightly.

'Well I know what I'm doing over Christmas!'

'Thank you for my gift, it's brilliant.'

Steven clapped his hands together.

'Right everyone, I don't know what you guys want to do, and there's no pressure to stay out if you have places to be, but I'm going to The World's End to catch up with the other guys from our building, who's with me?'

Everyone in the room raised their hand. Steven looked at me imploring me to say yes. I nodded, grinning.

The World's End was heaving with Christmas drinkers. We fought our way through the crowd and found Steph and Dave and the rest of the tenants around a large table in the back of the pub. I pressed some money into Steven's hand and asked him to buy drinks for everyone. James joined him at the bar to help him.

I introduced everyone as Mike, Colin, Chloe, and Maria squeezed around the table. Dave slid along the bench to join me.

'So here it is then, a full staff team at Inspired.' He nudged me. 'You did it, kid.' I grinned at him. I still couldn't quite believe I employed six people.

'They're all great, Dave. Thank you for all your advice this year. I wouldn't have known where to start.'

'I hear the baby situation was resolved?' he whispered, nodding towards Steven at the bar. I nodded.

'Yes it's an interesting career choice. She's lucky he hasn't reported her.'

'And what about you? How do you feel about him now?'

'I think that ship has sailed for both of us.' I shrugged. 'We make a brilliant team, though. Chloe just told me she thinks of us as the mum and dad of Inspired!' Dave laughed.

'Well, I've always thought that you looked great together; there's something about you both that just seems right. But what do I know?' He smiled kindly, moving to make room for Steven and James as they returned with drinks for everyone.

'Hey, Ols, James was just asking how you could've forgotten about Christmas?' I noticed a hint of red flush across James' cheeks. Dave looked amused.

'You forgot about Christmas?' He asked confusion filling his face.

I pursed my lips together while Steven explained.

'Ols forgot about planning a Christmas do for everyone.'

'Luckily Steven was on hand to save the day, but apparently not my embarrassment.' I looked at him pointedly and he stuck his tongue out at me.

'Well then, Ol, it's a fair question, how could you have forgotten about Christmas?' Dave asked.

'I don't celebrate Christmas.' I shrugged, I took in the horrified expression on everyone's face and shrugged, 'I'm not saying I don't like it, I do. I love Christmas. It's great, but I don't celebrate it any more.'

'Is that a religious thing?' James asked frowning.

'Oh God, no!' I shook my head. 'My folks died in a car accident six years ago. I have one brother, but he lives in Australia. I don't have any other family, and apart from Ruth, I don't really have any friends either.'

Dave nudged me.

'Hey, you have us, we're your friends.'

I smiled up at him gratefully. 'Oh, I know that, but you know what I mean. I don't have a Christmas Day. I mean, I have no one to pull a cracker with. No one to swap presents with. Christmas Day is just any other bank holiday to me.' I realised I had completely destroyed the mood around our table and tried to lighten it, 'but you know what? One day I'll be married with kids and Christmas will be the best day of the year again.' I raised my pint glass, 'here's to two weeks off work!' All of my staff cheered and the mood was restored. Dave made his way around the table, stopping to chat to various people and introducing himself to my new team members. Steven slid closer to me and took hold of my hand.

'Spend Christmas with me, Ols?'

I shook my head, I didn't want him to feel sorry for me and under any obligation to invite me to his family Christmas.

'I'm fine, Steven, I haven't spent Christmas with anyone since my brother moved to Australia three years ago. It's really no big deal at all, I'll watch loads of TV and play video games. I'm still only halfway through *Lego Batman*.'

'I can't stand the thought of you being on your own on Christmas Day, Ols.'

'Even after I just told you how I'll spend it? You wish you were spending it the same way, go on admit it.'

He grinned, despite the concern on his face.

'Well sure, sometimes the family thing gets a bit intense after a few hours but I wouldn't miss it, Ols. Please will you join me, my folks would love to meet you.'

'Can I think about it?' I asked, trying to change the subject.

He smiled nodding enthusiastically.

'Of course, I'll be driving up there on Christmas Eve so let me know by Wednesday.'

I wished I could speak to Chris. I wasn't sure what to do. I guessed there was no harm in spending the holiday with Steven. It would be nice to be a part of a family Christmas again, but I wasn't sure if it meant something more. Today had felt so much like those first few weeks with Steven, I was confused about how I was feeling towards him and unsure about his feelings towards me. I didn't want to get drawn into feeling something for him again, especially given my situation with Chris. I knew it was silly to even compare the two men, Steven was right here, right now, I knew him, trusted him, cared for him. Chris was far away, a voice on a computer, seeing him had been strange, I almost wished he hadn't got the camera, he was right about the imagination being powerful, I had preferred the fantasy to the reality. Not that Chris wasn't attractive, he was, but would I really choose him over Steven? Or did I just want to experience amazing sex, just once, before I embarked on a real relationship?

'Do you know what I really want right now?' I heard the slight slur in my voice as I spoke. Steven's eyes lit up with amusement as he shook his head. 'I want to go dancing.'

I stood up addressing the rest of the table, 'I'm going downstairs to dance, who's with me?' Maria, Chloe, and Steph all stood up. The boys looked at each other. Steven stood up, followed by Colin.

'OK, then. Mike, James, Dave, have a great weekend, see you on Monday.'

I hugged each of them in turn and lead the way downstairs to The Underworld.

Chapter Thirty

The club hadn't been open long but was already heaving with office Christmas party revellers. Steven found a table by the bar and set up camp while Colin was at the bar.

I followed Chloe to the dance-floor as Madonna filled the air. Chloe was in the middle of a group of dancers when I caught up with her, she seemed to know some of them and they welcomed me into the circle, I felt a hand on my waist and a body pressed up against mine. I guessed it was Steven and turned around. It wasn't Steven. I was staring into a set of the most piercing blue eyes I'd ever seen. Long curled eyelashes made his eyes sparkle. They were breath-taking. His hair was long, tied back in a ponytail. His hand was still on my waist and he pulled me closer to him, pushing his knee between my legs and rotating his hips. He lifted my arm and placed it around his neck, smiling seductively at me. He had a perfect set of teeth; his smile was as dazzling as his eyes. Before I knew what was happening he was spinning me away from him. My hand slipped from his and I crashed into someone, I felt strong arms around me, steadying me. I looked up into Steven's eyes, smiling at me, and felt the familiar rush of affection for him. He released me and I beckoned him to follow me to our group. Blue Eyes tapped me on the shoulder as the song came to an end, and offered to buy me a drink. I shrugged and nodded. He motioned for me to follow him.

Steven caught my arm as I was following him off the dance-floor, he looked uncomfortable.

'Where are you going?' He handed me a bottle of lager.

'I think I've pulled.' I giggled.

'Stay away from that guy, Olly, he's no good.'

I shrugged him off, my sober self telling me I should listen to him, but my inebriated self was enjoying the attention I'd been getting on the dance-floor and didn't see the harm in allowing this mildly attractive man to keep me company.

'I'm fine, Steven don't you worry about me, I can take care of myself.' I turned towards the bar but he stopped me again, insistent,

'Please, Olly, it's late, it's time to make a move, I'll walk you home.'

I shook my head, shrugged his arm off me, and made my way to the bar.

Just as I reached the bar and located Blue Eyes, my phone started vibrating in my pocket. I shot him an apologetic look and dug my phone out. I didn't recognise the number and usually I would ignore unknown numbers but because I'd had a few drinks I decided to answer it.

'Hello?' I shouted down the phone.

'Hey.'

His voice caught me by surprise and I shivered. I would recognise that voice anywhere, soft but strong. I closed my eyes; it felt like a long time since I'd heard that voice. 'Are you there?' he asked.

'Yes.' My voice cracked as I spoke and I cleared my throat. 'Yes, why are you ringing me?' I strained to hear his response but the music was overpowering. The guy at the bar was watching me impatiently and I debated whether to just hang up and pretend the phone got cut off but I was curious and excited at the sound of his voice.

'I'm going to head outside, I can't hear what you're saying.' I said. The guy at the bar tuned his back on me, ignoring me, and I felt a stab of disappointment – that was the most attention I'd had for years. I weaved my way through the crowd to the entrance and stepped outside into the cool air and the relative quiet.

'Hi,' I said into the phone.

'Hi yourself.' There was a slight teasing tone to his soft voice.

'What were you saying?'

'I was saying maybe you should go outside so you can hear me.' I laughed.

'So why are you ringing me? Did Steven tell you to call?' I groaned.

'Steven? No, why would he? Have you got yourself into some kind of trouble? Liv, are you OK?' I could hear the concern in his voice.

'Why do you care?' I asked, a scornful note creeping into my words.

'Liv, of course I care.' I felt my heart beat a touch faster. He cared about me? 'So why was Steven worried about you?' I gave a small laugh and sighed.

'Some guy started dancing and flirting with me, he offered to buy me a drink and I followed him off the dance-floor. Steven tried to stop me, don't know why, but I ignored him.'

Chris was silent. I looked at my phone to check we were still connected and listened again.

'Are you still there?' I asked quietly. He cleared this throat.

'Yes.' He paused. 'I was just surprised, I guess, but I shouldn't be, we worked hard to improve your self-confidence, to understand your body and your sexuality, it's only natural you would want to go get laid,' he teased. 'It would seem I've gotten quite used to the idea that you're mine, I was disappointed that someone else would get to fuck you.' He laughed again.

I felt the familiar tingle through my body. What was it about the way he said "fuck" that sounded so erotic? And he thinks of me as his ... My stomach did a somersault and I whispered, 'But why can't it be you?' I cringed at the childish whine that had entered my voice. 'When I come to

Edinburgh,' I reminded him about our vague plan. Chris sighed.

'We can't, babe, I don't think visiting is a good idea. It couldn't go any further and that wouldn't be fair on either of us,' he said gently, his voice sounding kind and firm at the same time. I felt a stab of disappointment.

'Sure, I understand,' I hissed 'you're happy to watch me pleasure myself but you don't want to touch me.'

'Oh, Liv, of course I want to touch you.' His voice changed, taking on the commanding voice I had come to love. 'Don't you think I want it to be me? When I tell you to imagine my hands, don't you know I want it to be my hands running up your thigh, my fingers trailing across that paltry amount of material that make up those lacy thongs you wear?'

I smiled to myself glad that he would never see the pants I was wearing tonight. He saw my costume, I wasn't myself for him, I was playing the role of a more vibrant, sexually confident, and carefree woman. I would never have imagined wearing sexy underwear but as soon as I pulled the skimpy lace over my hips I felt transformed. I bit my lip and remained silent as he continued speaking softly, almost sadly.

'I want to feel you, I want to taste your tongue in my mouth, feel your lip being tugged gently between my teeth, to graze soft kisses along your jawline, and feel the soft flesh of your ear between my lips. I want to feel your nipples harden against my teeth and feel the flat hard end against my tongue.'

I realised I was holding my breath and slowly, quietly exhaled. I glanced around, suddenly embarrassed that people might be able to hear his words and know the changes happening in my body. I gripped the kerbside railing for support and resisted the urge to brush my hand across my breast. He continued his aural torture.

'I want to rip the strings on your thong and tear the

pointless material away from your body, I want to feel you quiver as I tease your clitoris and I want to feel your juice on my fingers, I want you to taste yourself on them and want to feel your whole body as it tenses around my cock, pushing in and out, filling you and releasing you. I want to feel your orgasm shudder through your body, around me and in my arms.' He paused and I sensed him smiling. 'Are you blushing?' he teased. I swallowed and inhaled slowly.

'Yes,' I whispered, 'and I wish I wasn't stood on the corner of Camden High Street next to a taxi rank and a pair of burly bouncers.'

Chris chuckled. It was a sound I had grown to love.

'Maybe you should get in a taxi and make your way home?' He suggested.

'Or maybe I should go back inside and find someone to fuck me?' I murmured.

Chris was silent, and when he spoke, his voice was strained. 'Well, if that's what you want, of course.'

'No that's not what I want. I want what you just described.' I cringed at the pleading sound of my voice. He sighed again.

'Liv, my love, it can't be. Be realistic, it wouldn't work. Suppose you come to visit me and we have the most amazing sex, it would be a one-time thing. And what if once wasn't be enough? We both have very separate lives, it's not possible to have more than what we have and it's not fair on either of us to try.'

'Well in that case, what we have now isn't fair either.' I shot back angrily. I was feeling frustrated, physically and emotionally, mixed with a drunken sense of outrage.

'Perhaps you're right, love. I will leave that up to you to decide. You know where I am if you want to play.'

I was speechless. Just like that? He just said he thought of me as his and yet he's releasing me so easily?

'OK, if that's what you want.' I tried to inject as much

indifference into my statement as I could. He chuckled.

'So quick to be offended, Liv. I will be online every night hoping you will be there too. But I don't want to prevent you from going out there and meeting someone. You are still the same person, Liv, you still have the same needs. You still want to meet someone special, find love, find Mr Right, get your little house in the country. I can't give you any of that. As much as it pains me to say it, if it's best for your happiness, I will end our communication. But if you need it, for your confidence then I'm always there to help you.'

I snorted. 'Ironic that when you called me I had met someone. If you hadn't interfered someone might actually be fulfilling my needs right now.'

'I'm sorry, Liv, I was missing you and I just wanted to hear your voice,' he said quietly. 'I'm sorry if I've upset you, it's late, get in a cab and go home.'

'It's a five-minute walk, I'll be fine.' I snapped.

'I'd be happier if you got a cab anyway. Please be safe, Liv.'

'I'm not sure I care right now about keeping you happy, Chris.'

'At least promise you'll let me know when you get home?' I sighed and ended the call, he was so confusing; he cares about me, but he doesn't want me, he does want me but he wants to leave me alone.

I looked at the entrance to the bar and debated whether to head back in. I was fed up and I wondered if another drink would help, maybe that guy would still be there, it might not be too late and I was feeling pretty horny. But I was tired and Chris was right; I still wanted something more, I hadn't learned to love my body so I could go fuck my way around Camden, I had wanted to feel confident enough to try and meet someone more meaningful, In fact, this had all started because I had simply wanted to look good for Steven, until Melissa came along and ruined everything.

I turned away from the entrance of the bar and clattered into someone, dropping my bag onto the pavement.

'I'm so sorry,' I gasped raising my hand to my head and kneeling to retrieve my bag. I felt a hand around my arm helping me up and looked into familiar eyes, smiling at me in amusement. 'Steven?'

'Catching you is becoming a habit this evening.' His arms were still holding me steady and I realised I was more drunk than I had initially thought, another drink was definitely not a good idea. I swayed slightly on the spot despite his support.

'Come on, Ols, I'll walk you home.' He put his arm across my shoulder and started walking. It felt strangely nice, he smelled familiar and his body was warm. I shivered suddenly, the cool air bringing me back to reality and Steven tightened his arm around me hugging me closer in response.

'I can't decide whether or not I find it insulting, that my young employee is looking after me, shouldn't it be the other way around?'

He squeezed me.

'It doesn't matter how old you are, Ols. Friends look out for each other. What happened to that guy anyway? Did you come to your senses? He was pretty ugly.'

I swatted him on the arm.

'He wasn't that bad, was he?'

'He looked like he needed a week-long soak in a bath.' He laughed at my shocked face. 'Yeah, and he needs to drink some Listerine, I could smell his breath from across the dance-floor.'

'Well it's a good job Chris rang and interrupted me.'

'Chris? Knight? Why was he ringing you?' Steven laughed in puzzlement.

'I actually thought you had put him up to it.'

'Why would I do that? I didn't realise you two were

that friendly.'

'Really? He makes it seem like he tells you everything.' Well, perhaps not *everything*, I hoped. Steven should never be aware that I occasionally pleasured myself on camera for the entertainment of his friend. Was that really all it was?

'Well, sure, I know he was giving you fitness advice and that you guys chatted, but why was he ringing at 11 p.m. on a Friday night, from America?'

I shrugged.

'Anyway, I couldn't hear him so I stepped outside. To be honest, he kept me talking so long that by the time I hung up I had forgotten all about the guy in the bar and had decided to head home.'

'Wow! Chris Knight in shining armour.' He chuckled. 'That's a first; he's usually more like a dark knight than a white knight.'

I stiffened. That definitely wasn't how I saw Chris and I hated the reminder that I really didn't know him at all. How could I have such a strong attachment to someone I'd never met? Perhaps he was right; I should forget about him and stop our communication. But his voice drifted through my mind, his soft, commanding voice that mesmerized me, sending a shiver through my lower body. I was so confused. Was that all I was to Chris – interactive porn? I should be charging him. What if other people were there with him; watching me, judging me? I felt sick. I'd been such a fool, what was I thinking?

Steven's voice broke through my thoughts as we stopped at the side door entrance to my flat.

'Ols, are you OK?' I blinked up at him and shook my head to clear my thoughts. 'You were miles away, what were you thinking about?'

I stared at him, my eyes full of misery, and he pulled me close to him, wrapping his arms around me and burying his face in my hair. He couldn't possibly guess what I was thinking about. I closed my eyes and let the moment wash over me, enjoying the close contact of his body against mine, the feeling of protection his arms offered me. I buried my face against his chest, knowing that if I moved even slightly to look at him I would be in danger of overstepping the mark. Chris had left me feeling embarrassed and rejected and I wanted to feel some connection to someone, to feel attractive, to be wanted. Would Steven reject me if I kissed him right now? In that moment it didn't feel likely, but I was just his boss, Melissa ruined everything for us. Even if he responded it would be so awkward, and if he didn't respond, awkward would be the best I could hope for instead of a sexual harassment suit.

I pulled away from Steven, keeping my eyes fixed on the floor as I rummaged through my bag looking for my keys. My hands were shaking and I was starting to feel light headed. Too much to drink. I fumbled with the keys, trying to find the right fit. I needed to be in bed, or near a toilet. I wanted the feeling to go away, to clear my head and stop me feeling confused. Steven took the keys out of my hand and unlocked the door, pushing it open, and stepping aside to let me past. I stumbled through the doorway, bouncing off the door frame and the wall in my hallway. I heard the door close quietly behind me and turned to look. Steven was gone – he had pulled the door shut.

I heard the key turn in the lock and then a thud as the keys landed on the doormat through the letterbox. I sniffed, offended. I climbed the narrow staircase and made my way to the sink to fill a pint glass with water. I glugged it down in one and filled the glass again. Panting, I wiped my mouth and made my way to the bathroom to brush my teeth, discarding items of clothing as I walked, kicking off my shoes in the kitchen, throwing my blouse across the back of the sofa, and undoing my jeans. I sat heavily on the toilet with my toothbrush in my mouth and sighed. I knew I was going to end up opening up the laptop to see if Chris was online. I wanted to hear his voice again. I knew I shouldn't, but it was like an addiction, I felt powerful when I was with him, he was right about the imagination, but his words and encouragement stirred a feeling in me that no one else had ever touched no matter how much I thought I was in love with them or how attractive I thought they were. But Chris was right, this situation could get in the way of my dream of finding Mr Right and living in the country. What if I became too scared to express myself with a real man in the flesh? What if I were only capable of it alone? Did I even need Chris, the faceless voice crackling through the speakers of my laptop directing my pleasure, imagining him there with me? Did I need him to imagine that? Couldn't I imagine it by myself?

Leaving my jeans in a heap by the toilet, I made my way to the bedroom and threw myself onto the bed in my faded white T-shirt bra and high-waist control pants. I caught my reflection in the mirror and immediately felt my arousal subsiding. I closed my eyes and curled up, tucking my knees up to my stomach. I wrapped my arms around my body and trailed my fingers back and forth along my side. I imagined myself sat at a dressing table wearing a silk dressing gown, covering a lacy set of underwear. I imagined soft, warm hands pulling the silk off the edge of my shoulder and kissing my neck softly, pulling at the silk on the other shoulder, I pulled the straps of my bra onto my arms as I imagined his hands pushing the cups down to free my breasts. I rolled my nipples between my fingers, and pictured myself watching in the mirror in fascination as his hands moved across my body. I can't see his face but his body is toned, lean, and warm. I watch his hands move down my body, stroking my thighs up and down slowly and circling from side to side, gently parting my legs. I squeezed my bottom as I imagined him lifting me easily, straddling the stool below me and sitting me on him, pulling my legs apart to sit either side of his knees. I rolled onto my back as I imagined his hand trailing up my thigh, teasing me through my pants.

My hand moved faster, more insistent, and I imagined him sinking his fingers into me; swirling around in small circular motions back and forth. My free hand squeezed my breast desperately as I pictured him twisting my nipple between his fingers, all the while continuing his exploration down below. I increased my pace, rubbing back and forth, side to side, circular motions, bucking my hips to create friction against my hand as I imagined moving my body against his fingers before watching him lift me and place me onto his stiff cock, entering me, filling me, fucking me, his arms wrapped around my body teasing my nipples and pushing his wet fingers into my mouth. I moaned loudly as my body reached its peak and my orgasm forced my body to tremble against my hand and I imagined him holding me tight, his soft voice whispering in my ear telling me I'm beautiful and sexy. My breathing was hard and laboured as my body came down from its exertion. I felt relief flood through me and a small, satisfied smile broke over my face. I did it. Without him.

I opened my eyes, blinking as the sight of my small bedroom broke the illusion. I felt a stab of guilt as I pulled my hand from out of my pants and felt a flush of shame creep over my cheeks. Why? Surely it was more acceptable, more natural to masturbate like this, in the privacy of my room, my imagination, than it was to do it on camera under Chris' direction? So why did I feel ashamed? I closed my eyes and drifted towards unconsciousness as a thought hit me: I didn't feel guilty, I felt lonely.

Chapter Thirty-one

I burst into the office on Monday afternoon with a huge grin on my face.

'We did it!' I announced.

I was expecting cheers, or words of congratulation. Excitement at least. I got tumbleweed.

The office was empty. I shut the door and dumped my coat on the sofa in my office. I heard Christmas songs coming from the testers' room and grinned to myself. I pushed the door open and stepped in. Six expectant face turned to greet me.

'Well?' Steven asked, there was a small flicker of uncertainty across his eyes as he implored me to tell him.

'We did it.' I grinned. 'Jack loves it. Signed off on it and wants it live so they can start promoting it in the New Year.' I turned my attention to James. 'James, can you get the files ready for uploading to all the app stores on Wednesday?' James nodded and wandered past me towards the main office.

Steven was grinning from ear to ear. I remembered it was his first job, his first successful contract. I punched him on the arm.

'Well done, you.' I smiled up at him. He threw his arms around my shoulders and hugged me.

'I can't believe it. I've been so nervous about it.' He sighed with relief.

'Why? You did a brilliant job.'

'I know.' He grinned. 'But surely even you never feel truly confident until they agree it's brilliant, right?'

I considered his words and nodded.

'I guess so. OK, someone get some glasses.' I held up a

bottle of champagne. 'Here's to our first successful team effort.' I handed the bottle to Steven and made my way over to Maria.

'Can you do something with this?' I asked, handing her a cheque. Her eyes widened when she saw the amount.

'Wow.' She laughed. I nodded.

'I know. That's the best bit about signing off on a job. The final balance.'

'That's our salaries for the next six months,' she whispered, quickly calculating in her head. I nodded again, amused. It was nice seeing my business through others' eyes, especially those that weren't used to it. This was not a surprising amount of money to me, but it was the first of many for my team. Steven had brought in so many new clients that we were going to be kept busy for a long time.

The sound of the cork popping distracted me and I went to find James to re-join the rest of the group as the champagne was poured.

'OK, listen up, everyone, this was the first big contract that I passed over to Steven, and I think he has managed it perfectly. You all played a part of it and we've delivered far earlier than expected and we have a very happy and hopefully very loyal client. So well done all of you.' I raised my glass.

'Also well done to you, Ols, for sharing this with us and letting us be a part of Inspired.' Steven added. I smiled back at him.

'It's true I've never much liked sharing my toys, but I'm glad you're all here and I look forward to working with you all next year. It's going to be a very busy year with all the work Steven keeps getting for us.' I smiled warmly at him.

Maria laughed. 'It's that effortless charm of his, could sell snow to the Eskimos.'

'So with all that in mind,' I said, 'I think we can call today our last day. Have a nice few days off before

Christmas and we'll all reconvene back here on the 4th of January.'

They all cheered.

'Merry Christmas,' everyone said as they clinked their glasses and drank their champagne.

I made my way to my office to check my emails when James and Steven appeared in the doorway.

'The files for Wednesday?' James started. I held up my hand to stop him.

'It's OK, James, I'll do it. You all deserve a few days off. I'll make sure the files are ready and uploaded this week.'

'I really don't mind,' he said half-heartedly. I laughed.

'Seriously, enjoy your break.'

He smiled and made his way back to the rest of the group. The Christmas songs got louder and I could hear them all laughing and relaxing.

I looked at Steven expectantly.

'So do I get a few days' holiday too?' he asked, smiling. I nodded.

'Of course.'

'But you don't?' he asked, his eyebrow raised in concern.

'I never get a holiday, Steven, this company is my life, my responsibility 24/7.' I shrugged, smiling.

'But you also deserve a holiday, Ols.' He looked at me thoughtfully. 'Will you consider my invitation, please? I spoke to my family and they would love to meet you, you're more than welcome.'

A huge part of me wanted to say yes. The thought of spending Christmas with people again, a real family Christmas, appealed to me so much. I looked at Steven, his eyes pleading with me to agree. I couldn't understand why it mattered to him so much. Then there was the thought of meeting new people and making all that effort when all I really wanted to do was have a few days to relax. But if I was alone at home, I knew I would be brooding about Chris; maybe a few days away would take my mind off him.

'Maybe, if I manage to get this app uploaded,' I said uncertainly.

Steven's eyes widened.

'OK I'll do you a deal; I'll get the app uploaded if you promise you'll come for Christmas?' He grinned.

I realised he had me cornered and shaking my head slowly, I shrugged and smiled.

'OK, you win. I'll spend Christmas with you.'

Chapter Thirty-two

There was a car horn beeping below my window and I looked out, whistling as I took in the sleek, black Mercedes Benz stopped in the street. I looked across the road to see who was getting in the car and noticed other faces pressed against the window. Movement caught my eye as the window opened and the familiar mess of hair popped out. My mouth dropped open. This was my ride.

Steven tapped his watch impatiently but I detected a grin on his face.

I grabbed my bags and made my way to the door, glancing around the room one last time to make sure everything was switched off.

I still couldn't believe I'd agreed to this.

Steven's persistence in wanting me to spend Christmas with his family had made me realise that I liked the feeling of being wanted. After Friday night, my conversation with Chris and my final realisation that I was lonely, Steven's family might be just what I needed to cheer me up. Chris had been right. I wanted someone, physically, but I also wanted that someone to be him and his confirmation that it could never be him had emphasised my loneliness.

Part of me wanted to wallow in self-pity, spend all of the Christmas period alone, knowing that no one would be bothering me, trying to encourage me to do anything, but I decided being around people would distract me and put a dent into my attempt to forget about Chris.

Steven met me at the door as I was locking up, took my bag, and walked me to the car. It was cold out, I noticed ice on the path, and the wind was cold. I pulled my coat tight around my neck and my hat further over my ears.

'I must be paying you too much, why don't I have one of these?' I asked, eyeing the car appreciatively. Steven grinned.

'You don't need one,' he reminded me, opening the passenger door for me and throwing my bag onto the back seat. He closed the door for me after I slid into the soft leather seat. It was warm, the heat radiating out of the air blowers and from the heated seats. The car smelled expensive and luxurious. Steven slid into the driver seat grinning at me.

'I'm so glad you decided to join us, Ols, I really couldn't bear the thought of you spending Christmas alone.'

I smiled gratefully back at him, my cheeks threatening to blush.

'Well I'm used to it, but I do miss the old family Christmas,' I admitted. 'I would have been OK though, I hope you didn't feel under any obligation to invite me.'

A look of horror crossed his face and he shook his head.

'No absolutely not, you were quite clear about that, Ols, but you're doing me a favour, I love going back to the old house but after a few days it gets a bit stuffy, it'll be nice to have some company.'

I smiled. 'So where are we headed?' I was slightly embarrassed that I'd paid so little attention to his background. 'Are you sure your folks have room for me? I don't want to be in the way.'

'The Peak District, my family home is called Thornton Manor.' He paused, glancing at me. 'It's quite a big house, there's plenty of room.' He smiled awkwardly. 'The house will pass to me when my father dies. Plus the business.'

'Your father's business?'

'Yes, well technically, it's a family business now. My father made me a director when I turned 18, so I earn dividends on the profits each year. He had hoped I would follow him into the business and run the company when he retires but he also encouraged me to find my own path and be whatever I wanted to be. I went into programming because I loved video games, but I always knew I had a fall-back option, I never really took it seriously until the second year of uni when I discovered I was actually pretty good at it.'

I nodded in agreement with his last statement. 'Ain't that the truth! So why come and work for me? Why not just set up your own business?'

'I could've done that, I have enough in savings to set up in business, but I wanted some real experience. And now, I wouldn't want to set up in competition with you, Ols, I enjoy working with you way too much.'

I felt a surge of gratitude towards him and laughed quietly. Steven frowned, questioningly.

'And there was me thinking you wanted to do me for sexual harassment, take all my money, and set up a rival business.'

He laughed, remembering my accusation.

'Yeah, I had to bite my tongue to stop myself just telling you everything.' His voice dropped, losing its humour momentarily. 'I wished I had, when all that stuff with Melissa happened, I berated myself for not being honest with you from the beginning.'

'Well, you did tell me I should snap you up before someone else did,' I reminded him.

He laughed. 'I guess things happen for a reason.'

It was a long drive but the time passed comfortably as we chatted and I was surprised at how late it was, when I realised we had left the motorway and turned off onto a narrow country lane, the roads getting narrower until we were surrounded by fields. Finally we approached a large set of ornate gates attached to stone pillars topped with carvings of lions sat guarding the property.

'Here we are,' Steven announced. We passed through

the gates and drove slowly up the drive.

'Well it's not that big,' I said, 'I can't even see it.'

'That's because it's far away,' he laughed.

To the left was a dense gathering of tall trees, looking empty and bare, their branches glistening with frost in the fading light. To the right were empty fields, in the distance I noticed a small smattering of buildings.

'That's the farm,' Steven explained following my eyes. 'We have a farmer who manages it, he lives in the building to the right. Over on the left are the barns and stables.'

I managed to make a sound with my voice that resembled something like 'Oh'.

I wasn't expecting all this land. I knew he had a big house but I was thinking big as in a four-bedroom detached house in the country. I realised we had been driving for ten minutes since we entered the gate and turned to Steven.

'Seriously, this is the driveway? Your family business must do pretty well.'

'It does, but we already had the house, it's been in the Teller family for centuries,' he paused, glancing at me. 'My father is an earl.'

'Really? OK, how do I address him?' A look of panic crossed my face and Steven relaxed grinning.

'However you like, most people call him John.' He glanced at me again.

'John?'

'Because that's his name.' He grinned again, 'I usually just call him Dad.'

'So you'll be the next earl then?' I said, surprised. Steven nodded.

'I will, yes, I'll take over the business and all this.' He nodded his head as the house came into view and I gasped. It was something out of a BBC costume drama.

'Oh my,' I gasped, 'turn the car around, you're going to have to take me home.'

'We've been driving for five hours. You're stuck here till I leave.' He laughed.

'Seriously, Steven, I didn't pack for this kind of holiday, I packed for lazing on the sofa playing video games and watching zombie films.'

The house was huge. We drove around a small lake and passed gardens on either side of the driveway as I watched the house get bigger and bigger until we were finally in front of the enormous building. Steven moved the car past the house and into a set of garages to the right of the entrance.

'I think I'm about to come over all Jane Austen.' I murmured. I heard him chuckle as he got the bags out of the car.

'Do I get to be your Mr Darcy?' He grinned at me.

'No, you'd be more like Casanova.'

'Ha ha, I'm going to take that as a compliment.' He laughed. 'You know we have period costumes if you want to dress up at any point.'

'Well, I imagine they'll be more appropriate than the clothes I've got packed. Seriously, it's a good job I'm just your boss because I am not going to make a good impression on your parents.'

The side door led into the main hall near a staircase and facing the main entrance. A second staircase was at the opposite side of the hall, sweeping up to meet the first case in the middle, leading to the second floor of the great house. An open log fire was roaring at either end of the immense hall and a huge Christmas tree was in the centre, between the two staircases. Comfortable leather sofas were positioned around each fireplace with a heavy oak coffee table. Huge wreaths of fresh holly leaves and berries adorned the doors and chimneybreast. The room was breath-taking.

Steven dumped all the bags at the bottom of the first staircase.

'Hey, Rose.' I turned at the sound of his voice and saw him hugging a small woman. She looked surprised and embarrassed, patting her hair as he released her and blushing.

'Steven, welcome home.' She spoke with a soft voice and I imagined she'd been in this house since Steven was a child. He turned to me.

'Ols, this is Rose, our housekeeper, anything you need while you're here, just ask her.' Rose smiled warmly at me. It hadn't occurred to me that Steven's family had help. This was just too strange to be real. I longed to be back on my sofa. It was Christmas Eve, the last episode of *Merlin* was on, and I should be there, in my pyjamas with a takeaway.

'Nice to meet you, Rose.' I returned her smile holding out my hand. She clasped mine with both her hands nodding. She looked up at Steven and back at me, smiling.

'Your parents are in the drawing room, I'll make sure some tea is brought through.'

Steven took my hand and led me through one of the doors off the main hall. The room was large by most people's standards but small in the context of the house. Another open log fire dominated the room, surrounded by leather sofas. It was a miracle there were any trees left, the amount of wood they must get through, I thought. Near the large window was a round table with six chairs and at the other end of the room stood another Christmas tree, smaller than the one in the main hall but beautifully decorated in reds and golds. A sea of presents spilled out from under the branches, all tastefully wrapped in matching red and gold paper and ribbons.

Pine branches decorated the mantelpiece above the fire and a wreath of holly adorned the chimneybreast. Two large stockings were pinned either side of the fire.

Steven's parents stood to greet us, his father shaking his hand while his mother introduced herself to me and kissed my cheek. His mother was short and slender with white shoulder-length hair. Her cheeks glowed from the warmth of the fire and her eyes sparkled with joy at seeing her son. His father was tall, his dark hair flopped to one side, shorter than Steven's but with the same unruly thickness. It was sprinkled with grey. I estimated his parents were in their mid fifties.

Rose followed behind us, placing a tray of tea on the table before drawing the curtains. The last of the light had disappeared and the sprawling lands outside the window appeared black in the darkness.

Steven's mother handed me a cup of tea as I sat down. I heard the china cup rattling against the saucer as I took it. I glanced up to see how everyone else was holding theirs so quietly and felt myself blush with embarrassment. It's just a cup and saucer, for God's sake, I chided myself, get a grip.

'Don't get used to this, Ols, this is just the show china, we'll all be drinking out of mugs tomorrow.'

Steven's mother laughed, she had a melodic laugh and I relaxed immediately. 'We are usually less formal around here,' she explained kindly.

His father shook my hand, 'Unfortunately you join us at Christmas when we have to be a little more formal. But next visit I assure you we will break out the cracked ceramics and return the music posters to the walls.' He laughed loudly. I couldn't imagine music posters anywhere in this house.

'It's a beautiful house,' I told them, 'thank you for inviting me.'

'You should take Olivia on a tour of the house, Steven, or at least the main rooms anyway, the full tour could take a while and the guests are due at 7 p.m.' Mrs Teller told him.

I caught Steven's eye, panic filling my face. He hadn't mentioned anything about other guests. He smiled reassuringly at me.

'Come on, Ols, I'll show you around.' He held his hand out to help me up and lead me out of the drawing room.

'Guests?' I hissed.

'Oh that? It's just a party we throw every year.'

'Every year? So any reason you forgot to mention it?'

'Honestly? I thought it would put you off coming.'

I stared at him in disbelief. Sometimes his honesty stunned me, but right now, it just irritated me that he was openly acknowledging he'd kept it from me on purpose.

'OK, well, you'll have to give my apologies to your parents but I'm staying in my room tonight.'

We made our way upwards as we talked. I paused to peer over the balcony where the staircases met, before ascending the single staircase to the second floor. I took in the long narrow hallway with ten doors on either side. The wooden floor was covered with a burgundy coloured carpet running along the centre of the hall.

'Don't be like that, Ols, it'll be fun.'

'What are you wearing to this party, Steven?' I asked innocently.

'Well it's black tie,' he started, glancing at my face as it filled with annoyance.

'So what should I wear? My *Batman* T-shirt or my Lego Stormtrooper hoody?' I punched him on the arm. 'You should've warned me.' I grumbled.

'What would you have done? Gone shopping?' He teased me.

'I might have,' I said defensively, 'or I might at least have given some thought to what I was packing instead of just taking the first things I grabbed out of the dryer and shoving them into my bag.'

Steven stopped outside the fourth door on the right and turned the doorknob.

'This room is yours. It's opposite mine so you'll know where to find me if you need anything in the night.' We walked into the room and I gasped. It was beautiful. Original oak beams ran across the length of the ceiling. The room contained a large four-poster bed, a heavy oak wardrobe and chest of drawers, a free-standing ornate full length mirror stood next to the wardrobe, and a day bed was positioned under the large window, providing a view across the gardens. In the far corner stood a dressing table and large mirror with an array of lotions and perfumes.

A long red cocktail dress was hanging up in plastic on the front of the wardrobe.

'I forgot to tell you about the Christmas Eve party on purpose because you wouldn't have come if I'd told you and I didn't want you to be alone,' he explained apologetically, 'but I did sort out a suitable dress for you. I hope it fits.'

I shrugged. 'How well do you know me?' I laughed. 'A party with a bunch of strangers or a quiet night in?'

'I know, I know, I'm sorry –' he held up his hands and grimaced, '– but we're here now and I promise you'll have a good time.'

'Will there be many people here tonight?' I asked cautiously. I really hated social occasions, especially when I didn't know anyone.

'We hold this party every year; it's for the residents on our estate, the farmer and his family, the steward, and all the tenants, and our staff. There'll be about a hundred people here.' He paused as my eyes widened in horror. 'It's OK, I promise I won't leave your side for a second.' He smiled reassuringly. 'Come on, I'll show you the rest of the house.'

He pointed out the bathroom next door to my room. 'This side is mainly guest rooms, my grandma, my auntie and uncle, and two cousins will join us tomorrow and stay over, they'll be in the these rooms,' he indicated the doors closer to the staircase as we made our way back downstairs, 'I'll just quickly show you the kitchen, so you know where to come if you get peckish.' He grinned, ushering me towards a door to the right of the staircase. 'Help yourself to anything you want in here, feel free to come in anytime.'

He threw his arms around a plump, middle-aged woman. 'Ols, this is Mrs Reynolds, our cook. She makes the best trifle in the whole world.'

I smiled happily at Mrs Reynolds who beamed at Steven indulgently.

'Can I get you both something to eat? The family ate earlier but I have some chicken still warm and I can rustle you up something nice.'

'We stopped off on the way here and had a late lunch. You go and get ready for the party.'

'Are you sure, Steven?' she asked, surprised but grateful. We both nodded in agreement and she left us alone in the kitchen.

'OK, we need to be down in the entrance hall for 6.45, so we should go get ready. Do you need anything?'

'A hairdresser and a make-up artist would be good,' I said, rolling my eyes as I followed him back up the stairs to the bedrooms. I paused outside my room and looked at him.

'Thanks for this, Steven, I'm sorry I'm being so ungrateful, it's really nice.'

'No worries, Ols, I'm sorry I didn't tell you. I'll see you down there.' He winked at me and disappeared into his room.

I was nervous about the dress, it looked expensive and I was scared to touch it. Men had a way of underestimating women's bodies, I had no doubt this dress would be too small. I sat down in front of the mirror and started working on my make-up. I looked at my unruly mass of frizz in the mirror and grimaced. I had no idea what I should do with it.

There was a knock at the door and I frowned in the

mirror as the door opened and Steven popped his head into the room.

'Are you trying to catch me naked or something?'

He blushed and grinned. 'Sorry, Mum asked if you needed any of this stuff.' He walked into the room and dumped a box on the bed. It contained a hair dryer, straighteners, curling tongs, a variety of products, jewellery, and make-up. 'She told me off for not warning you.'

'Good!' I smirked, 'and thanks, I will do my best to look presentable.' I pulled out an implement and regarded it with interest. I didn't even know what it was!

I gathered up my hair on top of my head and examined it in the mirror. I liked how it looked but I didn't know how to keep it up. I rummaged in the box for hairgrips, and tried to open one with my teeth, it pinged out of my fingers and down the back of the dressing table. 'Shit,' I hissed, reaching for another. I managed to wedge this one into my hair and tentatively loosened my hand. Keeping my head perfectly still, I reached for another grip and the pile of hair tumbled down the back of my neck.

I growled and breathed heavily out of my nose, my nostrils flaring angrily. I hated doing this stuff. I checked my phone and saw there was no reception. Brilliant. I couldn't even call Ruth for some advice. I stared angrily at the box and picked up the hair straighteners. How hard could it be to make my hair look presentable?

Chapter Thirty-three

At 6.45, after much swearing, trapped hairs, and near-burn experiences, I made my way down the staircase. I peered over the banister to see the hall below; the lights were twinkling on the huge Christmas tree and carols were playing quietly in the background. Cloth-covered tables had been set up to the left of the hall with beautiful red and gold chairs. There was no one to be seen. I paused at the top of the right-hand staircase. Steven had definitely said to be in the hall for 6.45 but there was no one else there. I started walking slowly down the stairs when I saw the door to the drawing room open and Steven appeared. I stopped as I saw him. He looked so handsome in black tie, somehow making it look comfortable and trendy rather than stiff and formal. His thick hair was spiked forward and he was cleanshaven. My stomach did a somersault when I saw him. Careful, I warned myself. You're just his boss now, remember?

Steven looked up at me and his mouth dropped open as he stared up at me with open appreciation. My hair was tamed straight, framing my face and falling across my shoulders and down to my chest. The dress was beautiful, I was amazed that it fitted me perfectly, hugging my curves and floating to the floor, the deep red colour complemented my dark hair and pale complexion. The sleeves were wide like butterfly wings that hung from my elbow to my wrist. The dress skimmed the floor, hiding my boots. I was thankful he'd forgotten to get shoes. Ruth would be horrified if she saw these boots with this dress but at least I was in no danger of breaking my neck.

I had also found some jewellery in the box; an ornate necklace and bracelet set with red gemstones. I had barely recognised myself when I finally looked in the mirror. I looked the part but I felt like an idiot.

I continued walking down the stairs, conscious of the length of the dress and paranoid about tripping and landing in a heap at his feet. Steven stood with his hands in his pockets, grinning up at me, the picture of cool.

'Will I do?' I grinned as I joined him, looking down at my dress and swishing the fabric from side to side.

'You look beautiful, Ols.' He draped an arm across my shoulder turning me toward the fireplace. I felt him kiss the top of my head, pausing to hold me a little longer than necessary before we made our way towards the drawing room to join his family. I felt goosebumps creep up my neck and shivered. He tightened his arm around me interpreting my shiver as cold. I wasn't cold. I was overwhelmed. I was starting to enjoy being here, feeling like a part of his family, I was enjoying his attention, his familiar touch, his scent. From out of nowhere, the old feelings were resurfacing and I was in danger of being right back where I was before Melissa.

Mr and Mrs Teller met us in the doorway as they were making their way to the hall. They took up a position either side of the main entrance. Steven and I stood next to his father while Rose and Mrs Reynolds both appeared from the side of the stairs and joined Mrs Teller.

'Seven p.m. Let's open the doors.' Steven helped his dad pull open the heavy doors and I gasped when I saw the stone steps leading up to us. Old-fashioned gas lamps lit the edge of the gardens and drive way as far as the eye could see. The lights reflected off the lake in the distance. I sighed. It was a million miles away from my real life – old fashioned, traditional, and romantic, but I had to admit it was beautiful. I felt Steven squeeze me, laughing at my reaction.

'It's nice seeing this through your eyes, reminds me how lucky I am.' He smiled. 'I'm really glad you like it.'

The party was a lot more fun than I had anticipated. I quickly overcame my nerves and found myself chatting with everyone, drifting from table to table, introducing myself, and hearing stories about Steven as a child. I collected plates of food from the buffet for older guests and fetched drinks from the bar that had been set up at the edge of the hall.

I was scanning the room for any sign of Steven when I noticed Mrs Reynolds beckoning me. I weaved through the tables and sat down next to her.

'Miss Jones, this is my niece, Caroline, she grew up in the village,' she said, introducing the girl who sat next to her. I reached out to shake Caroline's hand and noticed the weak response. I smiled at her, encouragingly but she looked straight past me. Mrs Reynolds smiled apologetically at me.

'Are you enjoying the party, Mrs Reynolds?' I asked trying to make light of the situation.

'Oh yes, Miss Jones, it's always such a lovely evening.'

'Please call me Olly. Have you had any food?' It occurred to me that Mrs Reynolds hadn't cooked the food for the evening and I wondered how she felt about that.

'Thank you, Olly, I haven't eaten yet, but I've heard good things about it so far.'

'I bet it's not up to the standard Mr and Mrs Teller are used to though, eh, Mrs Reynolds?'

She chuckled and a huge grin spread across her face. I noticed Caroline roll her eyes and scowl. Cheeky bitch, what's her problem, I wondered.

'Have you seen Steven? I've not seen him since the guests started arriving.' I asked, glancing around the room again.

'He has his duties to perform on Christmas Eve. Especially since he left the Manor, catching up with the tenants and villagers. I'm sure he will seek you out for the dance though.' She explained. My heart fell as I realised I wasn't going to spend any time with him. Suddenly being in his company was the only thing I wanted in the whole world.

'The dance?'

'The last dance of the evening. It's a Teller family tradition dating back several generations, the whole family take to the dance-floor. Mr and Mrs Teller dance together and their children each honour a guest with a dance, until they are spoken for of course. It's one of the most talked about things in the village, who will they dance with, could it lead to something more?' She smiled at me again and I realised why Caroline was so cold towards me.

'So I guess I'm not the most popular person here among the young ladies?'

'You have certainly broken a few hearts this evening.' She agreed.

The whole thing just felt so silly to me. I felt like I was in a time warp. It was 2009, for goodness' sake; we could send people into space and yet all these girls were breaking their hearts over the young man from the big house. I decided to get some air and slipped away towards the side entrance of the house. The cold air hit me as I stepped outside. In the distance, I could see the lights reflected off the lake and the sky was clear, the moon bright and full, and the stars twinkling against the dark canvas.

I jumped as the door opened. Mrs Teller was grinning at me.

'Here.' She held out a champagne flute. 'You look like you could use this.'

'Thanks.' I laughed, taking a sip of the sparkling liquid.

'Overwhelming, isn't it?' She lit a cigarette and took a long drag. I nodded and she continued, 'I met John at university so I didn't grow up around here, I still remember my first Christmas, I thought it was so silly.'

'I just heard about the dance tradition,'

She looked at me thoughtfully. 'You're currently the most hated girl in the room. I remember that feeling well.'

'Brilliant, just the reaction I was going for.' I laughed.

'Every girl in there thinks that she will dance with Steven and he'll suddenly notice her and realise she's the one for him. If they could just be alone with him for three minutes, in his arms, they would almost certainly become the next Lady Teller of Thornton Manor.' She giggled at the thought.

'Do they want him or the title?'

'Well I would say they want him, but I'm biased, of course, he is my only child, after all. Who wouldn't want to snap him up?' She smiled. 'What do you want?'

'I just want a nice, relaxing Christmas.' I laughed.

'I think you came to the wrong place!'

Steven caught up with me as I was making my way from the bar to an elderly couple called Mr and Mrs Bates.

'Mrs Bates, Mr Bates, how are you both?' He shook hands with Mr Bates and bent to kiss Mrs Bates on the cheek. 'Well, it's that time already so if you don't mind I'd like to take this beautiful lady to dance.' He held out his hand to me, smiling. Mrs Bates clapped her hands together and shooed him away.

'I am so sorry,' he said as soon as we were out of earshot of anyone.

'It's no problem. I realise you're the man of the hour. Besides, I've been getting all the gossip on young Steven.' I grinned at his horrified expression and he rolled his eyes.

'So what have you heard then?' he asked. His eyes sparkled with amusement but his voice betrayed his vague concern.

'Well by all accounts there is a fear that there will be no more Tellers at Thornton Manor, what with your lack of interest in girls and all that.'

His eyes widened in shock. 'Everyone thinks I'm gay?' He laughed.

'When was the last time you brought a girl home to meet your mum?' I teased.

'I've never brought a girl home to meet my mum.' He shrugged, looking around the room. 'Look at this place, would you bring just anyone home to meet your family if they lived like this?'

I felt a glow creep into my cheeks. It was quite nice that he'd been willing to bring me, not that I really counted. I indicated my agreement with him and leaning closer I whispered, 'I think there are a few young ladies that rather hoped it explained your lack of interest in them.' I noticed his face redden.

He moved me on to the dance-floor. A couple of young children were sliding around near the DJ, while a group of young ladies hovered around the edge of the room, hoping to be asked to dance. I was both disappointed and relieved that the music was modern, I wouldn't have had a clue how to dance any of those old dances, but it seemed at odds with all the old-fashioned traditions and decor to hear Take That blaring from the speakers.

Steven moved naturally to the music. I shouldn't have been surprised; he seemed to be naturally gifted at everything. He took my hand and spun me round, pulling me to him as the song changed and the tempo slowed right down, signalling the party was drawing to a close. Mr and Mrs Teller appeared next to us and the guests all formed a circle around us. I allowed my head to rest on his chest as we swayed back and forth to the music. I felt people watching us and I didn't care. I felt comfortable in his arms and for a moment, I wished it didn't have to end.

After the last guest had gone home, we gathered on the sofa and watched the last of the flames die out, leaving the red embers slowly fading in the fireplace. Mr Teller poured us all a glass of brandy.

'Well, Olivia, you were quite a hit tonight, hope it

wasn't too traumatic for you.' Mrs Teller smiled warmly at me. I smiled sleepily back at her.

'I had a lovely time, thank you,' I mumbled. I heard her tinkling laugh, and smiled again.

'Steven, I think you should take Olivia up to her room.'

I didn't hear anything else. I was vaguely aware of being lifted to my feet but I was aware of nothing more until I woke up the next morning.

Chapter Thirty-four

A gentle tap on my door woke me the next morning as Rose made her way into my room with a small tray. She placed a cup of tea on the bedside table and opened the curtains. The crisp cool daylight flooded the room.

'Merry Christmas, Miss Jones.' Rose smiled warmly at me.

'Merry Christmas, Rose, please call me Olly,' I insisted. 'Did you enjoy the party last night?'

'Oh yes, I think it was the best one yet.' She smiled again and looked at me thoughtfully. 'Did you enjoy it, Olivia?'

I smiled at the concession; perhaps Olly was a bit too informal. I nodded.

'I did yes, I was a bit nervous at first but everyone was really friendly.'

I sipped my tea, smiling at the heavy mug. I was relieved it wasn't a dainty china cup as it had been the day before. Who could function on such a small amount of tea? I usually needed two mugs before I got started – it would probably take me six of those cups to get me firing on all cylinders!

I retrieved the clothes I'd been wearing to travel and pulled them on. Until I'd showered I didn't want to wear anything else. I was still worried I'd not packed anything vaguely appropriate for this place but was hopeful there might be a smart jumper or cardigan in amongst the comic book T-shirts. I didn't remember going to bed and figured I hadn't removed my make-up. No doubt there would be mascara all over my face. I checked in the mirror for Alice Cooper eyes then, satisfied I didn't look too scruffy, I slipped out of my room into the hall.

'Morning sleepyhead.' I heard his teasing voice behind me. I stopped and waited for him to catch up to me. 'Merry Christmas.' He planted a kiss on my cheek. 'Did you sleep OK?'

'I did yes. Merry Christmas.'

He nudged me playfully. 'I had to carry you to bed last night, you fell asleep in my arms.'

'Oh really? And you didn't drop me?' I squeezed his upper arm. 'Have you been working out?' I laughed.

'You drooled on my shirt.' He grinned back at me.

'A thought occurred to me. 'Did you undress me?'

'No, my mum did.'

I sighed with relief, then blushed again. 'I was exhausted, you all must think I'm a lightweight.'

'Not at all, it was a long night. No one thought anything of it, I assure you,' he said shaking his head.

Steven led me to the dining room, another door off the main hall that I hadn't noticed. His parents were seated at the large table, which was covered with hot plates and dishes containing bacon, sausages, scrambled egg, beans, mushrooms, and toast.

'Ah, Steven, Olivia, come on in, help yourself while it's hot,' Mrs Teller instructed us. We took our seats and tucked in.

I glanced at the clock and my eyes widened. It was only 8 a.m. I couldn't believe it was so early. I was surprised I wasn't still tired, but I'd slept really well and felt rested and relaxed.

'Merry Christmas, everyone,' Mr Teller said, raising a glass of orange juice. We all responded and clinked glasses. 'So the usual drill, we'll leave here at 9.15 for the chapel, sit through the morning service with our tenants and then be back here by 10.30. Dinner will be at three, followed by presents, so you can occupy yourselves until then.'

'Your Aunt Maud will be arriving at 2 p.m. with Grandma and your cousins,' Mrs Teller added.

The air was crisp and cool as we made our way to the chapel. Patches of frost glistened off the trimmed lawn. We followed the path at the side of the house towards the farm and took a turn to the left, which lead to a small patch of trees. Beyond the trees stood the chapel, a quaint, low brick building which maintained its original style on the outside but was more modern and comfortable inside.

I followed behind the family as they greeted each member of the congregation. I recognised a few faces from the party and wished them a happy Christmas.

We made our way to an empty pew at the front of the church. The vicar was a jolly looking man in his late forties, his greyish hair curled around his head and his open, friendly face was smiling. The service was nice, delivered in an entertaining fashion. It felt Christmassy and traditional and I enjoyed it. I was glad when it was over however; I was looking forward to having some free time alone before more family arrived and Christmas dinner would be served.

'Hey, Ols, do you want the grand tour of the house?' Steven asked as we approached the side door. So much for my alone time. I followed him into the house and up the stairs. 'You've seen most of the downstairs, the ballroom, the dining room, the drawing room, we don't use the drawing room that much, just for when we have guests and visitors and of course it's a traditional room so it gets used a lot when the building is open to the public and for TV and stuff like that. The only room we really use downstairs is the dining room.'

We reached the top of the stairs but moved past them to the left. I hadn't noticed the door immediately to the side of the staircase. I glance across the hall and saw an identical door on the other side. Steven held the door open for me and I found myself in another corridor which opened out to a large hallway with several doors.

'Now this is our living quarter.' He grinned. He opened the first door, which revealed a comfortable living room. The first thing I noticed was the 48-inch flat-screen television mounted to the wall. Below the TV was a media case containing all manner of DVDs and CDs. In the corner of the room stood an iMac. My phone vibrated in my pocket as it connected to the wireless network and several iMessages came through. The mobile phone reception was non-existent but at least I had some contact with the outside world again. Steven smiled apologetically.

'Reception is a bit poor out here, but feel free to come in here anytime and connect to the internet. If you want to use the computer, feel free.' He turned back out into the hallway.

'In this room, we have the library,' he announced, holding open the door for me to walk past him. I took in a sharp breath. The room was huge. Every wall was lined from floor to ceiling with shelves and every shelf was full of books.

'There are books in this room dating back several hundred years,' Steven told me proudly.

'Wow,' was all I could think of to say. The room took my breath away.

'In fact, this section here might interest you,' he said, walking towards the centre of the wall and stopping. He scanned a couple of shelves and pulled out an original first edition of *Pride and Prejudice*. 'I think we've got all of hers, actually. Generations of the Teller family have kept everything. This whole house is a family history.'

He led me out of the room back into the hallway and across to the opposite door.

'The games room,' he announced. I stepped in to find a large snooker table dominating the room. Further past the table was an old battered sofa, a large flat-screen TV, and a collection of games consoles; PS3, Wii, Xbox, and a full shelf of games. Behind the sofa was a square table with four chairs and a shelf filled with board games and playing cards.

'This is where I usually hang out,' he explained unnecessarily as we left the room. 'That last door leads to my dad's study. He has offices all over the world but he works from here mostly.'

'What does the business do?' I asked, intrigued by the world in which Steven would one day be working.

'Packaging. He had a partner called Samuel and they set up the business together. Sam was the practical guy. He set up the machines and made sacks while my dad was the sales guy, going out and selling them to all the local farmers. My dad had his sights set higher – he wanted to sell across the UK, maybe even the world, but Sam was too cautious, didn't think he could make enough, and was worried about bringing other people in to help them. My dad had argued that with more orders they could afford staff, but Sam was scared to take the risk. So my dad bought him out. His father gave him a small loan to pay Sam and my father took sole ownership of the business. Within a year, he had repaid my grandfather his loan and within another two years, my father was a millionaire, selling packaging to manufacturing companies across the world. Now they make all kinds of stuff: sacks, cardboard boxes, bespoke packaging.' There was a hint of pride in his voice.

'What happened to Sam?' I asked, fascinated by the story.

'He drank himself to death. Never got over the chance he'd missed.'

'Did you know him?'

'I vaguely remember him; he was my godfather. His wife and daughter moved to Yorkshire, I think, not long after he died. I think my dad feels guilty sometimes.' He shrugged helplessly.

'Well your dad saw an opportunity to expand and took it.' I reasoned. 'You Teller men seem to have a good head for business. I must remember if you suggest something I should take the chance rather than selling to you and losing out.' I nudged him playfully and he grinned.

We made our way back along the narrow passage to the top of the stairs and towards our rooms. He paused outside his room, his hand on the doorknob. He turned to me as I was closing the door.

'I wish you'd taken the chance when I suggested going out for dinner with me!' he said, his eyes wide with innocence. I felt my face flush and my heart beat a little faster. Why was he bringing this up again? Steven had shown no sign he was interested in me in months, if I thought about those early days again, *that kiss*, I was in danger of falling in love with him all over again, especially after the way he held me last night, dancing together. I shook the thought from my head and reminded myself of Chris, my safety net, my Knight in shining armour. But then I remembered what Ruth had said to me. Steven was there in front of me, real. Chris might as well be a computer programme, and he didn't want me either.

Steven was drifting towards me, a small smile tugging at the corners of his mouth as he watched my inner turmoil play out across my face. I smiled at him.

'Well, we agreed I would say no, until I knew I could trust you.' I nudged him playfully. He laughed out loud.

'So I'm your projects manager, you let me go out to represent your company, but you don't trust me?' he asked, amusement dancing in his eyes.

'That's business. Dinner is pleasure!' I grinned.

'Oh so I'd put you off your dinner, is that what you're saying?' His eyes were wide, laughing but trying to look offended. I blushed furiously.

'No! Well, maybe a little.' I laughed, nudging him

away from me. I turned back towards my room but he caught my hand.

'I invited you to Christmas dinner and you accepted. How is that different to coming out for dinner with me?' He cocked his head to one side watching me. I thought about his question for a moment and then smiled.

'Going out for dinner sounds like a date, but coming for Christmas dinner is your charitable deed for the year.' I smiled sweetly as he closed his eyes shaking his head.

'You are impossible. I give up.' He shrugged, defeated.

I closed my door gently and stared at it. My mind wandered to that kiss in the studio. My breath caught in my throat as I remembered it. The smell of him, his arms holding me, his fingers in my hair, the feel of his tongue, the taste of his mouth. 'Fuck it!' I grabbed the door handle and walked out.

There was no response when I knocked on his door so I made my way to the living quarters and stood outside the games room. I took a deep breath, knocked on the door, and pushed it open. Steven sat on the sofa with a PS3 controller in his hand. He turned to look at me, his face registering surprise.

'I hope I'm not interrupting, I was having PS3 withdrawal,' I smiled, nodding towards the controller in Steven's hand, Steven grinned and held it out to me.

'Not at all, I thought you were my mum coming to tell me off for spending too much time playing video games.'

My features shaped into a look of confusion. 'Is that even possible?' I asked grinning, taking the controller off him and dropping down next to him on the sofa.

Steven stretched his arm across the back of the sofa and sighed.

I looked up at him. I took in his beautiful face smiling down at me, his messy, thick hair shadowing his face. I felt his arm drop off the back of the sofa across my shoulder and before I could stop myself I'd leant forward and kissed him. Our lips pressed together and we both froze, unsure what to do next. I felt Steven's right hand touch my face, sending shivers of desire coursing through me. His lips parted, catching my bottom lip and tracing his tongue across it lightly, asking permission to enter, I opened my mouth slightly and his tongue met mine inside. Our eyes held each other's gaze as we kissed, exploring each other's mouth. His hand moved to my hair sending shots of electricity through my nerves, tingling in my scalp and down my spine. I could feel myself becoming aroused and I knew I had to stop, but I was scared to stop, scared what would happen next, and scared because I didn't want to stop. I wanted this, it felt right, no matter what reservations I had, this, right now felt right. I squirmed and felt him smile against my mouth. I pulled away and searched his face.

'I wasn't expecting that,' he whispered. I blushed, remembering that I had started it. I looked down at my hands.

'I'm sorry,' I blustered, pushing myself up from the sofa. Steven grabbed my arm.

'Don't run off, Ols,' he said quietly, standing up and putting his arms around me. I felt his face bury itself in my hair, kissing my head. I inhaled sharply as I thought about kissing him again.

I felt his hand around my neck, his thumb brushing across my cheek, gently tilting my face up towards him.

'Look, Ols, I don't know what you're feeling right now, but I need you to know that my feelings for you have never changed, so you know what I want.' His eyes bored into mine looking for agreement. 'I think, or at least I hope, you feel the same?' he whispered, staring once more into my eyes.

I squeezed my eyes shut and nodded. I opened one eye shyly and he laughed. 'What? You don't want to admit you want me?' he asked, searching my face, amusement evident in his eyes. I remembered how I had felt when everything was lost and remembered my promise. If by some miracle he still wanted me then I was his. I nodded and a huge smile broke across my face. Steven laughed and pulled me to him, hugging me tightly. I reached up to his face drawing it to me and kissed him.

'I should go get ready for dinner.' I smiled, pulling away from him. He grinned down at me.

'So you are going to have dinner with me then?'

'Ah, Steven, Olivia, there you are.' Mrs Teller pushed champagne flutes into our hands. 'Your grandmother was asking for you,' she added in a lower voice. Steven led me over to the sofa next to his gran.

'Merry Christmas, Gran.' He kissed her cheek and sat down next to me. 'This is Olivia.' He rested his hand on my knee. His gran scrutinised me openly before nodding.

'Nice to meet you, my dear.' She turned her attention to Steven. 'It's about time you brought a girl home.' She spoke sternly, making Steven laugh.

'I wasn't going to bring just any girl home, Gran, I was waiting till I found the right one.' He shrugged innocently, his eyes wide, apologetic. The old woman chuckled.

'Do I need to buy a new hat?' She laughed, her eyes moving between both of us.

'Maybe,' he whispered conspiratorially and she grinned. 'I'll make sure you get plenty of warning.' He tapped his nose, making her chuckle again. He turned to me and clinked his champagne flute against mine.

The whole conversation felt surreal, one minute I was just his boss and the next minute we're practically walking down the aisle. I realised suddenly that being here felt much more natural since our relationship had developed, I felt like I belonged, like I was a part of the family. Not just his lonely boss, for whom he had felt sorry. I smiled to myself. I couldn't believe how happy I felt. The more I looked at him the more I wanted him. I was seeing him with fresh eyes, seeing him properly without the constant reminder not to feel anything for him. I could openly acknowledge how I felt. It was as though I'd been given the best Christmas present in the world.

'So, Olivia, what do you do for a living?' Steven's grandmother asked me after the turkey had been carved and distributed.

'I do the same as Steven, pretty much.' I helped myself to some roast potatoes.

'You work at the same company, you mean?' She turned to Steven. 'Steven, don't you do something with computers?'

'Yes, Gran, I make games and programmes for computers.'

'So clever.' She smiled proudly, returning her attention to me. 'So you work for Steven, then?' She looked back at him, 'Bit of a cliché isn't it, Steven, shagging your secretary?'

Steven choked on his turkey, and I smacked him hard on the back. Cheeky bastard, I thought, is that what he's told people?

'Actually no, Steven works for me, I'm *his* boss.'

'You're his boss?' She looked horrified. 'I thought you were his girlfriend.'

I glanced up at Steven and raised an eyebrow, inviting him to respond.

'Yes, Gran, Ols is my girlfriend, but she is also my boss. Actually, she only agreed to be my girlfriend today. You know, I've been pursuing her for so long I'm surprised she hasn't sacked me for sexual harassment.'

There was a murmur of surprise around the table and I realised his parents had both assumed we were together already. I noticed concerned glances being exchanged across the table and felt myself blush.

'When Steven first asked me out, I wanted to say yes,

but I was scared that if it didn't work out it could get awkward at work. We agreed to take some time to get to know each other properly but then so much time passed I thought he'd lost interest and I stopped worrying about it. I had no idea he still felt the same way until this morning.' I explained.

'And of course who could say no to all this?' His Gran agreed, her tone was displeased and I felt irritation shoot through me. They could keep their big old draughty house with no phone reception – it was the kissing I couldn't say no to.

'I'm not a gold-digger, if that's what you're thinking.' I mumbled under my breath. I didn't want to cause a scene or be confrontational but Steven heard me and spoke up for me.

'Olivia is not just my boss, she owns the company. She has enough of her own gold to be completely disinterested in mine.'

'Nonsense, look at her clothes, if she's rich surely she would dress better?'

'I disagree,' I said bravely. 'Sure, having money gives us more freedom to buy the things we like, but I'm not going to spend money on things I don't want or need just because I can. I'm not into those expensive designer fashions, of course if I had known about this place before we left London I would have bought something appropriate in order to fit in, but I wouldn't have been comfortable at all, this is me with or without money.' I saw his gran purse her lips and went in for the kill, 'there are far more important things to be attracted to than wealth.'

I noticed Mr Teller smirk to himself and nod approvingly at his wife. He seemed pleased I was arguing with his mother-in law, perhaps she was something of a battleaxe. It seemed my newfound confidence was paying off in more ways than one.

It was almost 9 p.m. by the time we all went our separate ways.. So much food had been consumed and we were all ready to lie down. Steven took me to the games room and we settled on the sofa.

I watched him, smiling at the twinkle in his eye. He took my face in his hands, pressing his lips to mine. 'I love doing this.' He sighed, kissing me again, 'I wanted to do this every day since I started working for you.' He kissed me again. I giggled.

'Even on day one when I was rude to you?' I reminded him. He nodded.

'I wanted to kiss you in my interview, Olivia. I knew, the instant I saw you.'

'I guess I knew that Friday night, after I helped you escape from Melissa.'

I giggled at the memory, it all seemed so long ago now.

'I recorded the *Doctor Who* Christmas special if you want to watch it?' He suggested.

'I thought you would never ask!' I grinned. 'The beginning of the end, but I think I can cope with David Tennant leaving now that I've got my own Mr Right,' I said, kissing him.

By the time the programme ended, I was overcome with tiredness and yawned, covering my face with my hands. I blinked up at his smiling face.

'Come on,' he said, 'it's been a long day, we'll say goodnight to everyone.'

My heart leapt into my mouth. Was he expecting us to sleep together? I wasn't prepared for that yet. I mentally checked through my suitcase and confirmed I had nothing vaguely sexy to wear to bed – I couldn't have Steven see me in comfortable underwear, not the first time. Butterflies descended to my stomach and I felt sick. I felt his hand on my lower back guiding me towards the stairs and through my butterflies, I felt the first stirring of desire. Would it really matter if I didn't have sexy underwear? *Yes!* I doubted if Steven would notice, much less care. But I cared; I wanted to feel sexy, attractive, ready for him. I was ready for him now.

Steven threw his arm casually across my shoulder and I snaked my arm around his waist as we slipped through the passageway towards the bedrooms and then paused at the top of the stairs.

'Can I get you anything? I fancy a hot chocolate before I go to sleep, would you like a warm drink?' I couldn't imagine Steven wanting hot chocolate before bed. I found it unbelievably cute, and smiled up at him. I realised that while he was making drinks I could be disposing of my unattractive underwear, removing any unnecessary embarrassment should anything happen between us tonight. I nodded.

'That would be nice, thank you.' He kissed me quickly on the lips and skipped down the stairs.

I slipped into my room and leant against the door. My heart was pounding, excitement was building up mixed with fear and nerves and desire.

I took off my boots and socks and pulled out my pyjamas from under the pillow. They were plain black, nothing fancy but nothing too hideous either. I removed my huge pants and my less-than-glamorous bra and pulled the pyjamas on over my naked body.

I sat in front of the mirror and scrutinised my appearance. My skin had a warm glow from a mixture of the warmth of the open fire and the wine I had consumed with dinner. My mind drifted to my Friday-night fantasy and I felt a warmth spread through me as I pictured Steven standing behind me, kissing my neck, lifting me onto him. I jumped as the door opened shaking me from my thoughts. I watched Steven in the mirror as he walked into the room carrying two mugs and then spun myself around to face him, holding out my hand for my mug of hot chocolate. I took a sip, never breaking eye contact with him. He copied me.

'Oh wow, that's amazing, did you make this?' I gasped, placing my mug on the table next to his.

He grinned down at me. 'It's the first thing Mrs Reynolds taught me to make. I'm quietly proud of my hot chocolate,' he said modestly. He dropped down on to the day bed opposite me and pushed off his shoes. He undid his tie and slid it from his collar and unbuttoned his waistcoat.

'It's always nice to take the costume off at the end of the day.' He sighed happily.

'Costume?'

'This smart stuff, it looks good but it's not soft and cosy.' He was right about it looking good, I'd always loved his dress sense; his fitted suits, his tight jeans, his shirt and tie.

'Why do you wear it then, if it's not comfortable?'

'I like how it looks, and I like to have a distinction between my formal work clothes and my personal life.' He shrugged.

'Well, just so you know I don't expect you to dress smart for work.' I smiled. 'In fact, I'd find it much less distracting if you looked less attractive in the office.' I grinned.

'Oh you think I look hot in my smart work costume?' He raised an eyebrow and smirked at me, his eyes bright with humour.

'I imagine you'd look hot in –' I scanned the room for inspiration and spotted the plastic bag of presents '– a bin bag.' I giggled.

'A bin bag?' He followed my gaze and moved to the bag, tipping the presents out onto the floor, 'now how exactly do you imagine I'd wear this? Toga-style perhaps?' I shook my head and wrinkled my nose – a toga just conjured up images of rugby players in the student union.

'I was thinking more like a sarong.' I laughed at the look on his face, a mixture of disgust and amusement.

'Show me,' he whispered, and I felt my stomach turn itself upside down in excitement. There was only one way this was heading. I stood up and walked towards him, his eyes caught my gaze, the amusement evident as he smiled at me, waiting.

I reached out to unbutton his shirt, slowly, deliberately, not wanting to fumble in my desire to undress him. I slid my hands beneath the material and over his shoulders, tracing the contours of his arms and removing the sleeves from over his hands. I was so close to him, his skin was smooth, lightly tanned and taut, his stomach muscles rippled as his breathing became shallower. A small smattering of hair covered his chest. I breathed in his scent and pressed my lips to him, trailing kisses across to his nipple and surrounding it with my lips, my tongue teasing the little mound. He caught his breath and I heard the bin bag drop to the floor as his hands reached round me, pulling me against him, stroking my back as his hands lifted my top exposing my skin, I raised my arms as he pulled the top over my head and dropped it to the floor, returning my hands to his body and running them across the smooth skin of his chest, tracing the contours of his back and moving down towards his bottom. I slipped my hand beneath the waistband of his trousers.

I felt his hands in my hair, his thumbs caressing my cheeks as he gently pulled my head up to face him. Immediately his mouth covered my lips, his tongue darting into my mouth to find mine as they twirled around each other. He sucked on my lower lip, his teeth grazing, creating sensation after sensation that spread through my body. His hands moved down my spine, leaving a trail of heat as they descended my lower back.

Oh my God, that tickled! I felt a giggle bubbling up

inside me and buried my face into his chest. He cupped my bottom, squeezing it playfully before suddenly lifting me. I wrapped my legs around his waist as he carried me to the edge of the bed, laying me down gently where he rained kisses all over my face, marking a path from my lips along my jawline to my ear and down my neck. He ran his tongue along my collarbone and weaved his fingers into my hair as his lips locked around my nipple, teasing it with his tongue, his teeth gently pulling it as it hardened and extended under his touch. His fingers mirrored his action on my other nipple pinching and twisting, until they were both hard. I gasped with the overload of sensation as ripples of desire flooded through me, beating a path to the centre of my pleasure.

His hands moved lower, his tongue circling my belly button and I giggled as his hair tickled my skin. He looked up at me grinning.

'Is this OK?' He whispered. He looked so handsome, smiling up at me, his eyes full of lust and desire. *Yes! Don't stop, for God's sake!* I nodded, closing my eyes as he lifted my legs onto his shoulders and pulled my trousers down from under me. His hands moved slowly along my skin, his lips planting soft kisses along my inner thigh, I gasped as his nose pressed lightly against my clitoris and involuntarily squeezed my thighs together. He yelped as his face was squashed against my other thigh. He moved his hand, his thumb running up the inside of my leg, gently prising my legs apart and taking a deep breath.

'Sorry,' I gasped.

He grinned and moved his thumb gently across my clitoris in small circular movements. *Too hard,* my body instinctively shrunk away from him and he stopped, he watched me with interest as he touched me lightly, like a feather. I jumped as it tickled me, *too soft,* he changed his movement and as my body adjusted I felt pleasure shoot through me. I closed my eyes and relaxed. *Well that's new, was he paying attention to my reactions?* I gasped again as his finger found its way into my opening, sinking inside me while his thumb continued to rub against me. I couldn't describe the sensations, my body felt electric, my skin tingled, all my nerves rerouting to one place in my body. I stretched my arms out, grasping for something to hold on to, and felt his hand take mine, our fingers tangled together as I squeezed.

My hips started moving against the rhythm of his finger as I created some friction, I could feel my orgasm building and I knew I was close but I didn't want it to end, I wanted this to last forever. I felt his tongue running along the length of my clitoris, flicking needles of pleasure through my lower body as his fingers moved inside me, picking up speed. I arched my back and tensed my thighs as my orgasm came crashing through me, my hips bucking quickly against his hand as he kissed my stomach and thighs, cooling calming kisses as my body finally relaxed. I watched fascinated as he slowly pulled his finger from inside me, his eyes holding mine as he raised his hand to his mouth and sucked my juice off his finger. I screwed up my face in mild disgust and then laughed. It seemed ridiculous, the sort of thing you'd expect from a porno but not in real life. He raised his eyebrows in surprise.

I smiled back at him as I lay there waiting for my breathing to slow, I knew I had to return the favour but I was just so sleepy now. *How long can I put this off?* I wondered sleepily. I could feel him watching me as his hand stroked my stomach, trailing fingers making their way to my breasts. I groaned inwardly, and I held out my hands for him to pull me up. He held me against him as I covered his mouth with mine, tasting myself on him, I sucked his top lip between mine and teased my tongue down his neck, trailing kisses across his chest, mirroring his earlier actions. I caught his nipple between my teeth, flicking my tongue over the flat edge as it hardened in my mouth. I moved to the other nipple, curling my tongue around it as it stiffened.

My hands dropped to the fastening on his trousers, loosening the waistband and sliding my hands inside his underpants, forcing them both over his bottom and down his thighs. I dropped to my knees as I pulled his pants down to his ankles and ran my hands up the back of his legs up to his thighs to squeeze his bottom. Reaching up to trail kisses up his inner thighs, his hands snaked into my hair, twisting it around his fingers as his breathing became shallow. *I hope I do this right.* He gasped as my tongue ran up the length of his erection, tasting the tip of the shaft and running back down again. He moaned gently as I flattened my tongue, pressing firmly as I ran up to the top and opened my mouth to pull him inside me, my lips tight around his hardness as I moved him deep into my mouth and slowly out. He gasped and my tongue flicked across the head and back down the side as I drew him inside me again. *I'm doing something right.* His hips bucked as his hands tightened in my hair, holding my head as I released him again. He moaned as he pulled himself away from my lips and tugged me to my feet, covering my mouth with his. His hands crushing me against him.

He stepped out of his trousers and pushed me onto the bed. I watched as he retrieved a foil packet from his trouser pocket and shivered with anticipation as he rolled the condom onto his penis and climbed on to the bed, moving my legs apart as he reached over me, his face level with mine, his arms holding himself above me, his eyes holding mine, searching for permission. I lifted my face to his, catching his mouth with mine and pulling him towards me, his tongue filling my mouth as his hand held my face. I wrapped my legs around his waist, and stared into his eyes, waiting for him to enter me. I felt this hand trace a pattern across my clitoris and I gasped, as he sank his finger inside me, opening me up, preparing me. *Not well enough though. Oh. My. God.* I gasped as he pushed his way inside me, stretching me around him, I closed my eyes, the momentary pain coursed through me. He held himself still, concern filling his face as doubt flashed in his eyes.

'Am I hurting you?' He whispered. I blinked, not wanting him to stop, but not wanting to lie to him.

'It's been a long time.' I smiled, gasping again as he moved inside me.

'Do you want me to stop?'

Yes! I shook my head, I just needed to get this first time out of the way and then it would all be fine, but jeez, it hurt, I obviously hadn't been practising enough with the vibrator, *or I underestimated the size of his cock!*

'I'll go slowly.' He kissed me gently as he moved slowly inside, the pain subsided as my body accommodated him and I began to move my hips in rhythm with his movements, his eyes held my gaze as he picked up speed, the sensations building up inside me as I met him thrust for thrust. I could feel a warmth spreading through me with each push as he hit deeper.

He pulled out of me and pulled me upright, my legs still wrapped around his waist. He lifted me onto him and sank into me again, I felt full, the sensation of his invasion more intense. He thrust into me, his arms wrapped around me, holding me to him. His mouth caught my nipple and sucked, teasing me with his tongue and picking up pace with his thrusts. I tensed my thighs around him and bucked my hips, matching his rhythm. I felt an unfamiliar sensation building inside me and gasped, *I think I'm going to pee myself,* the faster and deeper he thrust, the closer I felt to urinating. I couldn't believe it was happening. I cried out as I tensed my muscles trying to control my bladder, it pushed him over the edge, his arms tightened around me as he made one final thrust, tipping his orgasm into me, he gasped, tensing his whole body as it rushed out of him. His body held me still and my bladder returned to normal. *Shit, did I wet myself? Or is that what a penetrative orgasm feels like?* I had no frame of reference, had it even felt good? I wasn't sure, perhaps, apart from the fear of peeing myself. *That's going to take some practice.*

I met his gaze as our breathing slowed. His hands reached for my face, his lips planting kisses all over me. He lay me down as he pulled out of me and drew me into his arms, cradling me, his hand stroking my hair as he kissed my temple.

'Wow,' he whispered. I looked up at him, trying to catch my breath and grinned.

'Wow indeed.' I laughed. 'First my project, then my business, and now my heart. I'm trusting you with my entire life, you realise that?' He nodded solemnly. Tightening his arms around me, I was aware of the feeling of his flesh against mine and I squirmed against him, enjoying the sensation. I couldn't believe it was happening but there we were enjoying a post-coital embrace. I realised I hadn't felt self-conscious or embarrassed at all, I just felt desire, *and a smidgen of pain and discomfort.* I realised that all my past fears were ridiculous, this was Steven, the one man I really trusted. Why had it taken me so long to realise that he was The One? He had never given me any reason to doubt him.

I glanced up at him and found him watching me, a small smile on his face.

'What are you thinking?' He whispered curiously, 'your facial expression has gone through so many changes in the last minute.' I laughed, embarrassed that he had been watching me so closely but secretly pleased that he was paying so much attention.

'I just had an epiphany I guess, realised something I should've known all along.'

'And what was it?' His expression was questioning but

his eyes were still smiling.

'I realised that you're The One.' I whispered and fell asleep.

Chapter Thirty-five

A knock at my door woke me with a start. I looked around me in a panic, scared we would get caught in bed together but Steven was nowhere to be seen. I rolled my eyes at my own stupidity. It made sense that he would have slipped away to his own room after I fell asleep. I liked that I fell asleep in his arms. I smiled as I hugged myself. I still couldn't believe everything that happened yesterday. I finally realised how I felt about Steven, found out he felt the same and had sex for the first time in nearly six years. I watched the door open expecting Rose and gasped when Steven appeared around the door. He was wearing boxer shorts and nothing else. Something stirred inside me as I admired his body.

'Hey, sleepyhead,' he teased me, his eyes full of humour. I grinned back at him, 'I didn't want Rose walking in on us so I went and made the tea myself, told her we were both already up and packing.'

'What time did you go to bed in the end?' I was curious how long I'd been sleeping in his arms before he left me.

'I didn't, I slept here all night, you were so tired even my snoring didn't wake you up.'

'I don't believe for a second that you snore. Mr Perfect at Everything.' *Perhaps this was his way of saying I was snoring.*

'Hey I gotta have some flaws, why not snoring?' His face was serious, but the twinkle in his eye betrayed his humour.

I snuggled deep under the covers and hugged myself again, I was so pleased he had stayed all night. Our first night together. *So much for taking it slow.* I didn't care, I'd wasted enough time and I didn't want to waste another second.

'What's the plan today?'

'I want to be on the road by noon, try and get us home before it gets dark. Tonight I'm taking you out for dinner and I'm not taking no for an answer.'

I pouted. 'Oh I see, you think you're the boss of me, do you?'

'Well you get to be the boss at work, seems only fair that I get to be the boss at home.' He grinned.

I considered this for a moment, and agreed. My mind briefly wandered to Chris, his soft, commanding voice as he told me what to do. I shook my head to clear the memory.

Steven placed two mugs of tea on the bedside table and crawled inside the covers, lifting his arm to invite me under as he rested it across my shoulder. His hand idly stroked my arm as I reached across to rest my hand on his stomach. My face was tantalisingly close to his nipple and without thinking I stuck out my tongue to see if I could touch it. I smiled to myself as I saw it tighten up and felt his arm tighten around me.

I casually moved my hand across his stomach, sliding down as I went from side to side. I felt his body tense as I touched him and suddenly he was on me, pinning me down under his weight as his lips found mine, his tongue invading my mouth. My hands slid under his shorts, pulling them down urgently, my desire for him overwhelming me. I didn't care about the foreplay, I just want to feel him inside me again, our bodies intertwined, becoming one.

'Are you sure?' He whispered, I kissed him urgently in response, desire welling up inside me. The sight of him was enough to arouse me and the feel of his soft, smooth skin beneath my hand was too much to bear, I needed him inside me. He pulled away and leant over the side of the bed, fumbling with his trousers. I heard the sound of a foil packet as he tore it open and gazed up at him in anticipation. He kicked off his shorts and crawled towards me, his intense gaze holding mine. My breath caught in my throat as I took in his features, his piercing eyes full of lust, the tiny smile playing at the corners of his mouth, the smattering of shadow across his jaw and his hair, flopped over his face, casting a shadow across one side. He looked beautiful, dangerous, and sexy as hell.

'Turn over,' he whispered. My muscles clenched with longing as I heard his quiet voice, commanding me. My heart thumped in my chest as the natural comparison hit me but I shook it off. I rolled onto my stomach and shivered as I felt Steven hover above me, trailing kisses along my back. I felt his knees parting my legs as he settled between them. 'Push up,' he instructed, and I pushed myself up onto my hands and knees. I felt him stroking my bottom and my muscles tensed as shivers of anticipation coursed through my nerves, sending tingles up my spine. I felt his soft lips pressing against the small of my back, his kisses following the path down to my bottom, I squirmed with embarrassment as I felt his tongue exploring my anus, *gross, there's no way I'm doing that to him, what if he farts in my face?*

Suddenly I felt a bubble of laughter rise inside me and my shoulders started shaking as I tried to suppress it but the giggle burst forth loudly. I sensed him rise up and sit back on his feet.

'What are you laughing at?'

I collapsed onto my stomach and rolled over to look at him, 'Nothing, I'm sorry, please carry on.' I placed my legs either side of him.

'Are you laughing at me? Am I doing something wrong?' He looked uncertain, I'd never seen Steven look unsure of himself.

'No, it was just something popped into my head, it was

silly, please forget it.'

He leant over me again his lips pressing against me, his tongue flickering across my clitoris. A bubble of laughter threatened again and my stomach tensed.

'Seriously, Ols, what's so funny?'

'It's really juvenile,' I protested.

'Well you do like to remind me how young I am, so I'll probably find it hilarious.' He was getting irritated and I felt bad. This was not going as I had expected.

'I'm sorry, OK? I just found myself picturing the look on your face if I'd farted while you were down there.' I cringed as I said it, 'I mean obviously I wouldn't cos I don't do that sort of thing,' I smiled innocently.

Steven stared at me as he digested my words, I held my breath waiting for him to respond, when suddenly a laugh snorted out of his nose and he fell forward giggling, his shoulders heaving with mirth.

'So you do find it funny?' I giggled.

'Yes, but only once I pictured your face if I did it to you.'

'You wouldn't dare do it to me.' I said, my mouth wide in surprise.

'Wouldn't I?'

'Not when I've got your most prized possession between my teeth, no!' I smiled smugly.

We gazed at each other, little smiles betraying our effort to stop laughing. *Is there anything in the world funnier than farting?* Finally I nodded towards my lower body and raised my eyebrow. He smiled, shaking his head and slowly moved down my body, trailing kisses past my belly button, my stomach convulsed with laughter again and he sat up.

'OK we're done here.' He lay down next to me and threw his arm across his face. I couldn't tell if he was still amused or pissed off. Either way I wasn't done yet. I climbed across him, straddling him and locking my lips to his, he moved his arm away from his eyes to look at me with interest, perhaps he hadn't expected me to take the lead. I lifted my body up and positioned myself above him and sank onto him. *Fuck!* I held myself still allowing my body to accommodate him before I started moving. It was different, directing the pace, I lifted myself almost fully off him and lowered myself slowly down his full length, I experimented and tried it fast and full, he watched me with interest as my hands cupped my own breasts, my thumbs circling around my nipples, squeezing them as I built up a rhythm, my orgasm starting to build up. I could see him getting frustrated as his hands grabbed at my hips to try and set the pace.

He pushed me off him onto the bed and positioned himself behind me. I gasped as he slammed into me, stretching and filling me. He pulled slowly out of me until he was almost free then slammed into me once more. I cried out. Again he repeated his slow torture until gradually he picked up speed. His hands holding my hips, pulling me towards him as he thrust into me. He reached across me, his arm wrapping itself around to caress my breasts as his rhythm picked up pace. I felt his fingers pinching my nipples as ripples of electricity coursed through my body, the familiar pool of desire building up as he hammered away at his own orgasm, I felt the need to pee again and tensed my muscles, he slammed into me one last time holding himself deep inside me as he cried out, his orgasm rushing out of him. He pulled me backwards into a kneeling position sat on his knees and held me tight, kissing my shoulder and massaging my breasts. I let my head fall back onto his shoulder and laughed quietly. *Should I tell him I'm not done yet?* I listened to the sound of our panting breaths as they gradually returned to normal before I raised myself off him and rolled onto my side facing him. He smiled down at me tenderly.

'Does it hurt?'

I nodded. He closed his eyes, guilt filling his face.

'It's been a while, it's a good hurt.' I explained, his face relaxed.

'I asked Rose to run me a bath. I thought it might help, I wasn't expecting us to do this again so soon.' He smiled down at me.

'Well, you will climb into my bed mostly naked.' I shrugged. No matter how my body felt after my re-deflowering, there was no stopping arousal when it hit and the desire to satisfy that itch.

Steven handed me my cup of tea and pulled on his shorts. I felt a stab of disappointment that he was preparing to get up, I wanted to stay there all day, cocooned in this beautiful room. I sipped my tea as I watched him, admiring the view. His arms and back looked strong, though slim, his muscles were evident beneath his smooth skin. Seeing him in the office every day was distracting enough already, what would it be like now that I know what is under his clothes?

He found his jeans and pushed his arms through his shirt. He had retrieved a bathrobe from his room and swung it around my shoulders. I pushed my arms into the sleeves and took his hands as he pulled me off the bed. My legs wobbled. The muscles were trembling after the exertion. I took a step forward and stopped. Steven steadied me, his eyes sparkling with amusement.

'Did I make you weak at the knees?'

I smacked him lightly on the arm, 'No, it's just my ageing limbs aren't as flexible as they used to be.' My muscles ached and my body felt stiff.

He lead me to the door, opening it and popped his head out, checking for signs of life before pulling me across the hall to his bedroom, 'Perimeter's clear,' he whispered.

'Copy that,' I glanced around as we passed through the door. The room was the same size as mine but an additional door at the end revealed an en-suite bathroom.

Steam from the freshly drawn bath filled the room. Steven held my hand as I stepped into the bath.

I felt my muscles relax and loosen as the warmth of the water spread through me. I closed my eyes and sighed. I heard the bathroom door close and the lock click and opened my eyes.

'Scoot forward,' he instructed as he climbed in behind me, squeezing his legs either side of me and pulling me back to lean against his chest.

I closed my eyes, enjoying the feel of his arms around me. The warm water relaxed my muscles and soothed my aches. I felt tired but content.

'Well I didn't imagine Christmas with your family to turn out like this.' I sighed happily.

Steven squeezed me, kissing my temple.

'No, me neither. I wish I'd brought you here months ago,' he teased. My mouth fell open in surprise.

'You don't really think that?' I asked, concern evident on my face as I pushed myself away from him and turned to meet his gaze. He shook his head smiling.

'I know you don't care about any of that stuff, Olivia. Truth is, I realised on Friday night that you had moved on, the guy on the dance-floor, Chris calling you from America, I was jealous. I hoped bringing you here would make you think about me again, see me in a different way, not just as your employee. Then I was planning to start asking you out for dinner until you eventually gave in. Then I was going to woo the fuck out of you till you fell into my arms.' *Woo?*

Steven leant forward and kissed me, his mouth covering mine as our tongues danced slowly, his hands held my face gently as he kissed the tip of my nose, his eyes meeting mine, full of love and passion.

I couldn't wait to get home, suddenly, the thought of being alone with Steven with nobody watching us was everything I wanted. I was excited about us going out on a date and being able to hang out together, finally secure in our feelings for each other and our freedom to be together.

I threw my belongings into my case and carried it downstairs to the hall. Steven's bag was already waiting by the side door and I stood mine next to it, smiling at the realisation he was as eager to get home as I was, I guessed for the same reason.

The whole family were sat around the table which, as before, was filled with hot plates of bacon, sausages, toast, scrambled egg, mushrooms, beans, jugs of orange juice, and pots of tea and coffee. Steven pulled out the chair next to him as I made my way around the table, brushing my fingers across his shoulder as I passed him. He grinned at me as I sat down, like we were sharing a secret. I noticed the family were a lot less formally dressed than they had been the previous two days. I finally felt like I fitted in.

'Ah, finally on our last day I've got the right clothes with me.' I laughed.

'Olivia, did you sleep well?' Mrs Teller asked. I glanced up at Steven who was smiling to himself but avoiding my eye.

'Like a baby.' I grinned, helping myself to some toast, 'I had such a nice time yesterday, thank you for letting me gate crash your Christmas.'

Mrs Teller waved her hand dismissively.

'Nonsense, it's been a pleasure to have you here. What time are you heading off?' She asked turning to Steven.

'After breakfast, I think. I want to be back before it gets dark.' I felt Steven's hand on my thigh and smiled.

'Well I hope you'll visit us again soon, Olivia.' Mr Teller smiled kindly at me, 'and if not soon then at least the next formal occasion.'

I raised my eyebrows questioningly, waiting for an explanation.

'I'll email you our social diary.' Steven promised.

I still had a lot to learn about his family and the expectations of the household. I found it exciting to think about formal parties and events though, having no family and no social life to speak of, I found the idea suddenly appealed to me.

The air was frosty and the ground was slippery with patches of ice. Steven held my arm to steady me as we crossed the courtyard to the car. The engine was already running and the heaters had warmed the car up. I shivered momentarily as the warmth hit me but quickly felt myself relax.

'Where are you taking me for dinner?' I asked, my mind quickly leaving the house and turning to home, 'is there a dress code I should be aware of?' I asked sternly.

'I thought we could go to Callum's,' he replied, 'should be able to get a table regardless of whether it's booked up.'

I nodded. I had liked Callum and I wanted to thank him for our Christmas party.

'We've done this in the wrong order, haven't we?' Steven glanced at me, waiting for my explanation, 'first you take me home to meet your parents, then we have sex, and finally we're going on our first date.'

He laughed.

'Do you remember what you said to me before you fell asleep last night?' He asked suddenly. I shook my head frowning. I barely remembered anything other than the strange second orgasm, 'you said you'd realised I was The One.' He smiled. My eyes widened and my face flushed with heat.

'Oh, so we're on the same page then?' I asked. He nodded laughing.

'So I guess it doesn't matter what order we did it in. I mean dating just helps us work out if we want to have sex right? And I already knew that, I've been imagining it for months.'

'Are you imagining it now?' I asked quietly, I looked up at him, a hint of a smile on my lips as he glanced down at me. He slowed the car down and let it roll to a stop. We'd only been driving for five minutes and were still on the driveway of the manor, hidden from view of the house and the road by the orchard. Steven switched off the engine and turned to face me, reaching out to touch my face, he smiled.

'You should know that, as a man, I think about sex on an hourly basis and while I intend to lose entire evenings, mornings, and afternoons making love to you, I also think a lot about just fucking you quick and hard, usually at work on your desk. So yes, I am imagining it now. I'm thinking about pulling you onto my knee and fucking you quickly so that I can concentrate on driving us home.'

I felt the familiar surge of desire rush through me and pool on the floor of my pelvis. I squirmed in my seat. Holding his gaze I saw the sparkle in his eye. Did he actually want me to fuck him in the car? Excitement and arousal coursed through me. Holding his gaze I braced myself against the back of the seat, lifting myself up, and quickly undid my jeans, pulling them down over my hips and right down to my knees. His eyes widened as he watched me, a smile starting to spread slowly across his face. He copied my movement, sighing with relief as his erection sprung free from his jeans. He unclipped our seat belts and reached across to me, his hand running up my thigh as we kissed, his fingers skimming my clitoris as he eased my legs apart. His finger found my opening and he smiled as he felt how ready I was for him.

He pushed his seat back as far as it would go and pulled me on to him. I heard the rip of the foil packet and the familiar sound of him rolling on the condom. I wondered if I should go on the pill, I'd have to discuss it with him at some point. I felt him lift me and then I was consumed by the fullness of him sinking himself into me. I cried out – I was still tender from earlier but I soon forgot about that as he started moving inside me. I held onto the steering wheel for support, my feet on the floor allowing me some freedom to move my body up and down his length. It felt different, me directing the pace. He pulled me back against his body, the change of angle forcing him deeper inside me. I gasped as I felt him hammering against my insides, the pressure building up as I felt the familiar wave of sensation rising ready to break and crash. He unzipped my coat and slipped his right hand inside, squeezing my left breast urgently, trying to apply pressure to my nipple, I was close. His left hand held my face, his tongue finding my mouth as he pounded into me faster, harder. The need to pee returned but I ignored it, instead of trying to suppress it I rode it, relaxing my muscles until I was tipped over the edge, my orgasm exploded with a squeal of laughter and he allowed himself to reach his climax. We both moaned in unison, our breath gradually slowing at the same time. His arms wrapped around me as he kissed my neck, his arms and legs squeezing against me as if wringing out every drop of his juice.

He supported me as I raised myself off him and pulled up my jeans. The exciting moment replaced by an awkward tangle of limbs, my jeans got caught on the gear stick as I scooted across to my seat and I became aware of the dampness spreading uncomfortably into my underwear.

Steven started the engine, leaning over he kissed me once more and started driving.

'I had no idea you were so insatiable, Ols.' He grinned.

'Neither did I.' I replied. I noticed Steven's grin get wider. I adjusted the back of my seat and leant back, closing my eyes. I suddenly felt exhausted and drifted to sleep.

Chapter Thirty-six

The phone was ringing when I entered the flat and I smiled to myself, knowing full well it would be Ruth. I had sent her a text message to tell her about Steven and I knew she would be over as soon as I arrived home to hear all the details.

'Hello?'

'Oh good, you're home. I'm coming over.' She said quickly before hanging up.

I shook my head laughing as I replaced the receiver and made my way to the kitchen to stick the kettle on.

After I had taken my bag to the bedroom and unpacked my make-up and toiletries, I filled the washing machine, made two cups of tea, and settled down on the sofa.

I heard a car door slam outside and glanced out of the window as Ruth hurried up the driveway to my front door. She let herself in and burst into my living room, breathless and excited.

'I want to hear everything.' She announced. She sat down on the edge of the armchair and looked at me, 'you look so happy.' She beamed. I returned her smile.

'I am. It was like a fairy tale.'

'Yeah he suits being Prince Charming. So how did it happen? Did you have sex?' She noticed the blush spread across my face, 'You did! Oh my God this is huge, what was it like?'

'OK, OK.' I laughed. 'Too many questions, what do you want to know first?' I asked.

Ruth thought about it for a while, struggling between wanting the full chronological story and wanting to hear about the sex.

'OK start from the beginning. How did you end up spending Christmas with him?'

'Ah, an easy question. We had our Christmas night out on Friday and basically I had forgotten to plan anything but luckily Steven reminded me on the Monday and managed to get something sorted at short notice to spare my embarrassment. But then after a few drinks I admitted I'd forgotten and explained why I don't much bother with Christmas. Steven was horrified at the thought of me spending Christmas Day alone and insisted I spend it with his family.'

'And you agreed to it, just like that?' Ruth wasn't convinced.

'Well no, I said I'd think about it. But then Chris rang me, we had a bit of a row actually, turns out he doesn't think we should meet, said it wouldn't be fair. I got on my high horse and accused him of just using me like I was some kind of free porn.' I felt myself flushing with embarrassment, I was vaguely aware that thinking about Chris made me feel guilty now, 'so all weekend I was feeling depressed and lonely and when Steven reissued his invitation I decided to accept, I figured being around people would stop me wallowing in self-pity.'

'Does Chris know?'

I shook my head, 'No, unless Steven has told him.'

'How do you feel about the cyber vampire now anyway?' She asked, noticing the change in my attitude.

'I think I feel guilty. Not about his feelings, but about Steven, every time I remember the cybersex I feel cheap and disgusting.'

'But why? You weren't doing anything wrong, last week you seemed really excited by the whole thing, planning to go and meet him.' She searched my face for an answer, 'I mean I am relieved that things with the real life human, the very attractive might I add, Steven have worked out as they should have done all along, but why the change of attitude towards Chris?'

'Because he's Steven's friend. He's seen me in ways that only Steven should see me.' I shrugged miserably.

'But you're a grown woman with past relationships, Steven won't expect to be the first man to see you naked. You don't feel guilty about Brian having seen you naked.'

'No I just feel a mild sense of disgust that Brian saw me naked.' I laughed, making a show of shuddering my whole body, 'I just think this is different. How would you feel if you found out that Andrew and I had been indulging in cybersex before you two got together?'

'As long as it wasn't happening after we got together what does it matter?' She asked, her voice slightly tight. I glared at her, 'OK, I'd want to scratch the image of my naked husband off your eyes.' She agreed.

'So you see? I think Steven will hate it and it makes me feel really guilty. I guess I really thought that there was no chance for us, otherwise I wouldn't have been so thoughtless.'

'It sounded like Chris was pretty persuasive, don't beat yourself up about it. Steven's hardly been an angel.' She reminded me. I didn't want to think about Melissa but it was obvious to what Ruth was referring.

'I think I should tell him.' I whispered.

'Are you sure that's such a good idea?' She asked, there was no mocking to her voice or surprise, just concern.

I nodded, 'I don't want there to be any secrets.'

'So when will you tell him?'

I shrugged, 'I don't know because on the other hand the sex is really good, I don't want to risk losing that just yet.' I explained laughing.

'Better than the cybersex?' She teased.

'I was scared nothing would be like he described, but it was, and all the better for being Steven, someone I know and trust,' I blushed, 'and love.' I added.

'Olly loves Steven, Olly loves Steven.' Ruth sang at me. I threw a cushion at her, laughing.

'Of course it's also entirely possible he will find the whole thing quite a turn on.' I suggested blushing.

'Now that sounds like Chris talking.' Ruth admonished me, 'so what's happening tonight?'

'We are going on our first date.' I grinned.

'What are you going to wear?'

I glanced at Ruth's shoes – she was wearing reassuringly uncomfortable high heels and I breathed a sigh of relief that I wasn't about to be dragged off to buy a first date outfit.

'I hadn't thought about it – care to check out my wardrobe?' I invited. She was already halfway to the door before I finished speaking.

I was ready and watching out for his arrival by 7 p.m. It had taken a while but Ruth had eventually found something she was happy with letting me leave the flat in. I was wearing a knee length, black pencil skirt, one of my few smart items that I occasionally wore to work meetings, which she had matched up with a black chiffon blouse over a red satin vest. The red shimmered through the chiffon. She had glared at me, hands on hips, when I tried to pull on my knee-high flat boots.

'I know you have dressy shoes, Olly, you haven't thrown any clothes away since 2001 so I know you still have the ones from your May Ball.'

I'd sighed theatrically and scrambled under the bed to find them. My feet were killing me already and I'd had to practice walking for an hour before I felt confident I wouldn't fall over. But they looked good, they made my boring work skirt look sexy.

'You know, we will have to do some serious shopping if you guys are going to keep going on dates, I thought you two were all about staying in playing video games.'

'I certainly hope we will be, I don't think my feet could take too many nights out.' I complained, wincing as the shoes pinched my toes.

I hadn't yet told Ruth about Thornton Manor, I was going to wait until Steven sent me their social diary so I could present Ruth with the gift of shopping. She would know exactly what to wear for these engagements. For a moment I envied her the natural ability to dress well.

Out of the window I saw Steven's car pull up in front of the building, I checked my make-up one last time in the hall mirror and waited for the chime of the doorbell.

He smiled at me when I opened the door, his eyes twinkling with pleasure as he took in my appearance. He leant forward to kiss me, a brief touch of his lips against mine as he walked past me into the flat and made his way upstairs.

'What time is the table booked for?' I asked, I suddenly felt shy and nervous at the idea of us going on a date. Ridiculous considering everything else we had already done together in the last twenty-four hours.

'Whenever we want. Callum has reserved us a table for the evening, said to just turn up.'

His eyes met mine, a small smile tugging at the corner of his mouth. He looked effortlessly handsome in his fitted jeans, white shirt, and waistcoat. My stomach did a somersault as I realised how much I wanted him.

'Do you want to head straight off or do you want a drink or something before we go?'

He closed the gap between us, his hands reaching out for my face.

'Maybe something before we go,' he whispered, his mouth covering mine.

My entire body flushed with desire, my legs wobbled, and I wrapped my arms around him, holding onto him. His hands were in my hair, his thumbs tracing the sides of my face as his tongue danced with mine, his teeth grazing at my lip and his eyes staring into mine.

I felt him smile against my mouth as we pulled apart.

'Shall we make a move then?' He asked pulling open the door. I was breathless with wanting and frustration. He grinned at my surprise, 'Don't worry, we'll pick this up again later.'

'Is this some clever plan to make me think about nothing else all evening so you can bring me home and have your wicked way with me?' I asked irritably.

'Not at all, I'm just hungry.' He grinned at me again, 'Why? Are you thinking about it now, Ols?' He teased.

I gazed steadily into his eyes, a small smile playing across my lips. 'I've been thinking about it all day.'

Chapter Thirty-seven

Callum's was crowded. Every table as far as I could see was filled with couples enjoying a post-Christmas meal. Perhaps they had been separated for the big day and wanted to share a special evening together. I felt a fizz of excitement in my belly as I thought about Christmas Day. I had relived the moment when he told me his feelings hadn't changed over and over again. His glances throughout the day, his hands idly resting on my knee. But besides the joy of finally being together, Christmas had been a magical day. I had become accustomed to spending it alone, no longer caring about the day itself. Steven had given me the gift of Christmas again. A family Christmas. The realisation that I would be expected to spend Christmas at Thornton Manor every year was a welcome obligation. Already I was picturing our children running around playing hide and seek.

Callum was approaching us, his arms open wide, a big grin on his face.

'Wow, Steven, why didn't you tell me who your date was?' He exclaimed, kissing me on the cheek, 'Olivia, how are you?'

'I'm good thank you, Callum. How was your Christmas?' I asked, smiling back at him.

'It was so nice to have a day off, but ironically, there's no rest in the restaurant business. Come, I saved you the best table in the house.' He wound his way through the tables towards the back corner of the restaurant and indicated a booth. It was circular, large enough to fit ten people, with a cushioned bench running around the entire thing.

We slid onto the seat across from each other and grinned up at Callum, who was opening a bottle of champagne. A waiter placed three wine flutes on our table and Callum poured the bubbling liquid.

'A toast,' he announced holding up his glass, 'Olivia, when Steven told me he needed a table because he had a date I thought, good, he's finally getting over Olivia, but when you walked in I was even happier. I'm so glad you finally put him out of his misery, he's been propping up my bar for far too long.'

I expected Steven to be irritated or embarrassed but he just smiled at his friend, I flushed at the realisation that it didn't matter to him, he was content enough for me to know that he had been hurting as much as I had, more even. I raised my glass.

'Well I hope his happiness doesn't affect your profit margin.' I grinned.

'I hope it will improve my profit margin, romantic meals are more expensive than shots of tequila.'

'Well I'm not much of a cook so eating here will get my vote.' I whispered conspiratorially.

Callum handed us both a menu and left us alone to decide.

I was aware of him watching me as I looked through the menu and for a moment I felt self-conscious until I remembered it was Steven, he wasn't judging me. It felt strange to be so assured of his feelings for me. My thoughts drifted to Chris. What would Steven think about that? I was dreading that conversation. Would he be shocked? Disgusted? Betrayed? He might be turned on. I wondered briefly whether Steven and I would ever have cybersex. I couldn't imagine doing that, performing for Steven, but then I never imagined I'd do that at all a few months ago. Was it the anonymity of Chris that made it OK? The fact that I couldn't see him made it seem as though he wasn't really there. Could I behave like that if I could see someone watching me?

I continued to read the menu, aware of his eyes on me, idly raising my left hand to my face, my fingers caressing my right cheek and my thumb across my left. As I scrutinised the menu I slowly moved my thumb across my lips, drawing the lower lip down and slowly licking my thumb with the tip of my tongue. I heard Steven slowly exhale and fidget in his seat I sensed him moving towards me across the table. *He likes to watch.*

I wrapped my lips halfway around my thumb and slowly pulled it out, tracing a damp line across my chin and allowing my hand to brush across my breast on its way to the table. I drummed my finger loudly on the menu.

'I know what I want.' I said innocently, glancing up at him. His was face inches away from mine, his dark eyes filled with lust.

'So do I,' he whispered. Leaning over the table, his mouth covered mine, sucking gently on my bottom lip, his tongue darting into my mouth, dancing with mine. His hands were in my hair, his thumbs caressing my face.

'Do you guys want to eat anything from the menu tonight or just each other?' Callum teased, causing us to jump apart suddenly. An embarrassed flush crept across my cheeks but Steven just grinned at him.

'Jealous?' he asked.

'Yeah, obviously.' Callum grinned. 'The girl of my dreams never wants to kiss me back.'

I glanced at Steven, who was watching me, his eyes sparkling with amusement. I really wanted to kiss him again. I wanted Callum to go away so we could get back to kissing. I felt frustrated and slightly appalled at my desire to behave like a teenager in such a public place. Perhaps this is why Callum put us in the far corner of the restaurant!

He topped up our champagne glasses and took our orders and finally, after what felt like hours but realistically was only a matter of minutes, he walked away.

We watched each other, a small smile tugging at the corners of Steven's mouth, his eyes boring into me. I slid around the bench towards him as he watched me, amusement evident in his face.

'So, first date, what are we supposed to talk about?' I asked curiously.

'I believe we are supposed to get to know each other a little,' he explained.

'Right. And if we already know each other a lot?' I asked, placing my hand on his leg and leaning into him as he put his arm around me.

'Then I guess we can just kiss,' he whispered into my ear, his tongue tracing a path from my earlobe to my jawline, across my cheek, and finding my mouth. I reached up to touch his face, my hand weaving into his hair as we kissed. My desire for him was overwhelming, blocking out all sense of our location, the people around us, nothing mattered except us.

We were interrupted by the sound of plates being placed on the table.

'Don't mind me, you two just carry on.' Callum teased before walking away. Steven's arm stayed across my shoulder, pulling me into him, his fingers playing with my hair.

Reluctantly I pulled away and moved back to my place; picking up my cutlery I tried to concentrate on my food. He was watching me when I glanced up at him, smiling.

'You know we may need to hire more staff,' I said suddenly, 'because I don't know how much work either one of us will get done if we're in the same office together every day.'

'Well then it's a good job you have your own office, isn't it?'

'God, I thought you were distracting enough as it was, strutting around in your cool clothes with your handsome face and your sideburns and your toned, slim body, making me want to kiss you. Now that I can kiss you, how am I supposed to ever do anything else?'

'I guess you'll be sending me to more conferences then?'

'Oh I don't know if that's a good idea, you'll bring in more work that I haven't got time to do because I'm too busy thinking about kissing you.'

'Well it'll give you a sense of how frustrated I've felt since I joined Inspired,' he said, smiling. 'All that nonsense about being my boss, not trusting me. I wish I had just told you everything, I knew you were the one for me, I should've realised that my background wouldn't matter.'

'That day when you kissed me.' I shook my head remembering it, 'I replayed that over and over so many times, just thinking about it was enough to turn me on.' I blushed as I admitted that, but I felt comfortable telling him, it was Steven after all.

'I'm so glad all that confusion is behind us.' He grinned.

'Me too.'

We decided to skip dessert. We said our goodbyes to Callum, hailed a cab outside the restaurant, and made our way back to my flat.

I checked the fridge for drinks. 'Do you want a beer?' I called towards the hallway where Steven was hanging up our coats.

Suddenly I was aware of him behind me, his hands on my shoulders, his lips brushing against my neck. I cocked my head to one side, giving him more room, and moaned as his tongue began to trace circular patterns across my neck and bare shoulder. I felt him growing hard as he pressed himself into the small of my back. His hands moved across my body, cupping my breasts, his thumbs rubbing circles across my nipples. I turned my body to face him, searching out his mouth with mine and tracing the contours of his body with my hands. He picked me up and sat me on the edge of the counter.

A moment of *déjà vu* hit me as I remembered the story I described to Chris, I pictured it in my mind and smiled to myself as I opened my eyes and looked at Steven, the embodiment of the man I'd described. I had never been certain how Chris looked at all, but when pushed to describe how I imagined him I'd simply described how I wanted him to look. And here was that man right in front me. My perfect man, everything I'd ever wanted, had been right there all along and now he was right here in my arms. Happiness washed over me along with desire and longing. I wrapped my legs around his waist, pulling him to me as my hands moved to the fastening on his jeans. His erection sprung forward from the heavy material and his face relaxed as he opened his eyes to look at me, his lips brushing against mine as he encased his length inside a condom. Still kissing me he pushed my skirt up, his hands running up my thigh beneath the material to catch my thong and pull it down.

He wrapped my legs back around his waist and pulled me to the very edge of the counter before pushing himself inside me. I gasped, still tender but so ready for him, he filled me, stretching me, the feeling was exquisite. Slowly he pulled away from me before slamming back in, he rolled his hips as he pulled away and quickly slammed in, again and again, hammering away at my pleasure, pushing me to the edge and holding me there ready to break. I tensed my thighs around him, bucking my hips to meet his thrusts, driving him further and further into me as my orgasm built up until finally I crashed, riding the crest of the wave until my climax subsided. He moaned out loud as his orgasm rushed into me, squeezing every drop of his climax out of his spent body.

I wrapped my arms around him, cradling his head against my chest and kissing his forehead. His lips found mine and we kissed slowly, long exploratory kisses as our heartbeats slowed and our breath returned to normal.

He looked into my eyes as he pulled out of me.

'So, did you want a beer?' I asked smiling.

'Oh, no, have you got any wine?' I shook my head, 'OK, I'll run the shop and get a bottle, any preference?'

'Something pink.' I said smiling as he fastened up his jeans. I jumped down and straightened my skirt. No one would ever know by looking at us that we had just had sex on the kitchen counter. I followed him to the hall and watched him shrug on his coat.

He reached out to caress my face and planted a soft kiss on my lips.

'I think I'm giving you a bad impression, my love,' he frowned, 'I promise you tonight, I am going to make tantalisingly slow love to you.' He grinned, kissing me again. I felt my body flush with anticipation. It didn't matter how fast or slow it was, I was enjoying every second of it, the arousal, the kissing, just being in such close proximity to Steven, his scent, the feel of his skin, it was all intoxicating.

I ran to my bedroom after he left and straightened up the room. I rummaged through my underwear drawer and found the new underwear Ruth and I had chosen a few weeks earlier. Only one set was still unworn, I didn't want to wear something that Chris had seen, I wanted something that only Steven would see.

I quickly removed my skirt and top and wriggled into the underwear. The bodice was made from maroon satin with a black lace covering, the satin shimmering beneath the lace. Ribbon was woven throughout the edges of the cups and along the hem. The thong was black lace with the same maroon ribbon edging.

I studied my reflection in the mirror and wondered if

Steven would like it. *Well, I'd do me!* I grinned at myself and grabbed my silk dressing gown, pulling it on as I made my way back to the living room.

I curled up on the sofa and eyed the laptop. I felt the skin on my neck prickle with discomfort. It was stupid, but I felt guilty. I couldn't decide whether I felt guilty about what I'd done and how Steven would feel if he knew about it, or if I felt guilty about Chris. Should I give him a heads up about me and Steven?

I glanced at the clock. Steven would be back soon, but I decided I had time to make a quick call to Chris and let him know what had happened. I opened up FaceTime and created a connection to Chris. I saw the connection icon and heard a faint ringing. I waited for the screen to change but nothing happened. The ringing noise sounded louder suddenly until I realised it wasn't the computer. The ringing noise was coming from the hallway, drowning out the sound from the laptop. I followed the sound and found Steven's phone on the hall table.

Idiot, who goes out without his phone? Curiosity got the better of me, there was so much about Steven I still didn't know and I wondered who was ringing him at this time of night. I picked up his phone and checked the caller ID:

Olivia Jones wants to FaceTime with you.

Chapter Thirty-eight

I was still staring at his phone when he pushed open the door to my flat, clutching a bottle of wine.

'Oh I wondered where I'd left it,' he laughed with relief when he saw me holding it. He frowned when he saw my expression.

'Get out,' I hissed.

'What? Ols, what's going on?'

I pushed the still ringing phone into his chest and pushed him towards the door, 'just get away from me.'

Steven took hold of his phone and looked at the screen. The colour drained from his face when he saw the caller ID message.

'Liv.'

'Don't you call me Liv. I mean it, Steven, get out.' I scowled at him as he took a step towards me, 'Now!' I screamed.

He held his hands up and grabbed his coat.

'I'm really sorry, Ols, I can explain.'

I turned my back on him and waited for him to leave. I heard the door click shut and then flung myself on the sofa and burst into tears.

The following morning I heard the phone ringing in the kitchen, and reluctantly dragged myself out of bed.

'What happened?' Ruth said as soon as I picked up the phone.

'What do you mean?'

'Your text message last night just said 'I hate him.' Who? Steven?'

'We came home from Callum's last night and Steven

left to go to the corner shop to buy a bottle of wine and I decided to FaceTime Chris.'

'Why?'

'I don't know, it's not important. The important thing is that Steven left his phone behind and when I tried to call Chris the call went to Steven's phone.'

'No! Steven is your cyber vampire?' Her voice registered the same shock I'd felt last night.

'It would seem so. He came back and I kicked him out. I haven't spoken to him since. Although I've had about ten text messages from him and several missed calls.'

'Well that explains the unidentifiable photos. Wow. I can't believe it.'

'I can't believe he did that to me. So much for trying to prove I could trust him.' I sighed miserably.

'Did he explain why he did it?'

'I didn't give him the chance.'

'He might have a good explanation.'

'I've thought about this all night and I can't think of a single reason that he could give me that would be acceptable.'

'Give it a few days and see how you feel. You'll have to face him sooner or later.'

I sniffed sadly, 'I just can't believe it. I lost both of them in one instant.'

'Or looking at it another way, you get to keep both of them.' Ruth pointed out. She was right as always; I had felt conflicted at times, frustrated that I couldn't be with Chris but wanting Steven too, I'd felt guilty and ashamed about Chris because of how Steven might feel if he found out. Turns out he knew all along. All the things I loved about each of them I could have because they were both the same person.

I shook my head, 'I just feel so stupid.' I whispered.

'You shouldn't feel stupid, Olly,' she reassured me, 'but until you speak to him, you can't know what his intention was and you'll drive yourself insane making assumptions.'

She knew me too well. I would wallow in self-pity, imagining he'd planned it all from the start, with some hidden agenda that would ruin me. I ended the call and put the kettle on. Tea – the nation's healer. I glanced over at my laptop and decided to shut it down, unplug it, and put it away on the bookshelf. I turned off my mobile and put it with the laptop, Ruth would call my landline if she wanted to get in touch and I didn't want to hear from anyone else. Finally I settled on the sofa, turned on the TV and PlayStation, and loaded up *Lego Batman*. A big part of me wanted to punch Steven in the face, but I would settle for bashing Lego bricks instead. I destroyed every Lego building I could see and when there was nothing left to break, I punched Robin. Part of me liked making my character punch his assistant: it was as close as I was going to get to doing it in real life.

Chapter Thirty-nine

It was four days before I felt human again. I woke up that morning and realised I needed to shower. My armpits smelled like curry and my hair was so greasy my head slid down the headboard every time I propped myself up against it. I felt disgusting. Pull yourself together, for goodness sake! I ordered myself. I was behaving like I had been dumped; heartbroken and alone. I hadn't been dumped – I'd been duped.

I had spent three very cathartic days pummelling the hell out of a variety of video game characters, watched some TV box sets, and ordered takeaway each night. Chris would have been horrified at my diet, *if he existed that is*. But now I'd exhausted all my hibernation options and felt like I needed to get out. I was ready to face the world again.

I felt almost happy as I rounded the corner towards the old school. I was pleased to see cars in the car park, as much as I loved the place there's nothing creepier than an old, empty primary school. I wasn't planning to stay long, I'd started sketching some ideas for a game and I wanted to collect the ideas so I could do some planning before we started back in the new year.

As I made my way along the corridor I heard a chorus of voices floating out from the choir room and smiled to myself. Hearing the choir always gave me goosebumps, something about the harmonies and the collection of voices all working together felt magical. I'd always wished I could sing. *Can't be good at everything, unlike some people.* I shook the thought from my head, I didn't want to think about how perfect Steven was right now.

I unlocked my office door and slipped into my room. I loved my office. The checkerboard floor, the prints on the wall. I sat down on the sofa and closed my eyes. I'd always loved coming here to work, but over the last few months it had become my favourite place to be and I knew that was partly down to Steven. The first few weeks had been difficult, so distracting but when Melissa came along and Chris was taking care of my sudden sexual urges, something more important developed between Steven and I. We grew to understand each other, trust and respect one another.

I was distracted from my thoughts by the phone ringing. I frowned, *we're closed!* As I reached over to answer it the ringing stopped. The connection light was lit up under line number two. Someone had answered the call. *Someone else is here.* My heart started thumping and a prickle of discomfort ran up the back of my neck. *Steven.* It could only be Steven, no one else had a key to the main room. I crept over to the door and crouched down to peek through the keyhole. Sure enough there was Steven sat at his desk. His hair had that wilted look he had when he was anxious and worried; flopped lifelessly to one side covering half of his face. He hadn't shaved and his face had a pretty impressive beard forming. It had never occurred to me that he might shave every day, *no wonder I didn't recognise him on camera.* He was wearing his glasses too, I'd never seen him wearing glasses before, except on the webcam. *Well it worked for Superman I suppose.*

I listened carefully to his conversation:

'No we are closed for the holidays, but I wanted to get some work done.' Steven was explaining to someone, 'No not at all, she doesn't know I'm here, I came of my own free will.' He paused, listening to the caller, then his eyebrows shot up and his eyes narrowed before he frowned. 'Wow, gosh – that's, well, I'm really flattered,

Celine.'

Celine O'Hara? A rep from Ignition Games, one of the largest developers in the UK.

'I'd have to give it some thought; I certainly haven't had any desire to leave Inspired.' He paused. 'Wow, that's a very generous offer. I don't really know what to say.'

She'd offered him a job? I could feel panic rising. We had come so far in such a short time but that was all down to Steven, how would we manage without him?

'I don't know what you mean,' he said suddenly, I could see him frowning. 'Callum's? Yes why?' He paused again. 'Boxing Night?' He closed his eyes as the penny dropped. Someone had seen us together. But so what? 'I go in most nights, Callum is my best friend and I often join him for a closing drink.' He shrugged. 'Drowning my sorrows? Wow, you've gone to great lengths to get something on me, I'm flattered.' He laughed, then his face grew serious. 'I suppose it could get awkward, you may be right, and it is a very generous package. I need time to think it over, though.'

I couldn't believe what I was hearing. He was going to leave us. I felt sick and so confused, the thought of Steven leaving was horrible. It hadn't even occurred to me that he might leave Inspired because of all this. He'd probably take all my clients too, I thought bitterly. I could feel tears threatening and I wanted to get as far away as possible. I gathered up my sketches as quickly as I could, trying to stuff them into my bag as I made my way to the door, I slipped out of the door and into the corridor and quietly pulled the door shut behind me.

'Liv?' *Shit!* Steven was opening the door to the main office as I was turning the key in my lock. I didn't know if he had heard me or if this was a coincidence. I didn't really want to speak to him to find out. 'Will you let me explain, please?'

'So you can make some more stuff up? Tell me more

things that I want to hear?' I pulled the keys out of my door and popped them into my bag, straightening the strap on my shoulder as I walked away. He grabbed my arm and I stared at his hand at my elbow.

'Are you ever going to speak to me again, Liv?'

I stared at his hand. I really didn't have an answer for his question. Part of me pictured a time in the future when all this was behind us, but I couldn't see the scenario where I forgave him. I shrugged, 'Perhaps Celine O'Hara can cheer you up. When are you leaving us?'

His mouth fell open and he loosened his grip on my arm. I took my chance and hurried away.

Chapter Forty

'So which is it then? You never want to see him again or you don't want to lose him?' Ruth asked, confused. She was waving a hot curling tong around like she was conducting an orchestra just inches from my ear. It was New Year's Eve. I hated New Year's Eve. But Ruth was insistent that I join her and Andrew at a local party being thrown by someone Andrew worked with. 'It'll be fun,' she'd wheedled, 'and it's walking distance from home.' I really wasn't in the mood for a party.

'Personally I don't want to see him, but professionally, he's had a significant impact on Inspired, if I lose him I lose my charming spokesperson who brings us all our work in.'

'Not all your work, Olly, you were managing just fine on your own.' She reminded me.

'Yes but now I have six members of staff, I don't bring in that much work alone to pay them all.'

'But your output is significantly bigger than it was which means you'll be more noticeable, customers will come looking for you.' She shrugged, 'and don't forget that there are other charming men in the world, hire a schmoozy sales guy to go to all your conferences.'

The thought of sending someone else out in my name horrified me, especially if he didn't know anything about programming. Steven was the perfect poster boy for Inspired, he could really sell us because he was passionate about our products and heavily involved in making them. A rare thing, someone who spent his days plugged in to a computer who could also engage effortlessly with the public. He was irreplaceable. I slumped in my seat and yelped as the section of hair being coiled around the curling tong left a dull ache in my scalp.

'Keep still and stop slouching,' she laughed, 'so how do you reconcile these two major parts of your life?'

'I don't know. It doesn't really matter anyway, he'll go off to Ignition, I won't have him distracting me in the office any more and in time I can just forget he ever existed.'

'And what will you do about the gaping hole in your heart?' I glanced up at her stern face in the mirror and shrugged. 'You're behaving as though he cheated on you or dumped you, Olly. But the way you described him in the office yesterday he looked miserable, he's obviously hurting as much as you, worse probably because this is his fault, he had everything he wanted, he's been pursuing you by any means necessary since he joined Inspired and finally he had you. And just like that it's gone because you discovered the path he'd been taking to win you and you didn't like it.'

I frowned. It was as though Ruth wanted me to forgive him. 'Why are you suddenly on his side?'

'I'm not, I just don't want you to lose him out of stubbornness. You haven't even given him a chance to explain yet. All I'm saying is that you're acting like you lost him, *both of them*, but he's right there, pining away because he wants you and you won't speak to him.'

'So why's he running away to Ignition if he's so innocent?'

'You don't know for sure that he's leaving, you heard one side of a conversation. Maybe he's thinking about it because he needs an escape plan if you won't forgive him.'

'Do you think I should forgive him?'

'I think you have to remember that he's a good-looking boy, and you know the pretty ones are stupid. You made it clear you're really pissed off about it, now let him make it up to you and then go fuck his brains out and forget it ever happened.' She smirked, 'At least until his next trip away and you decide to get the webcam out for old times' sake!'

I laughed then, 'I couldn't do it, when I saw him that one time, felt him looking at me, I felt so self-conscious. Knowing it's Steven ...' I trailed off.

'The guy you love? The guy you just spent a passionate Christmas night and Boxing Day with?'

'Yes, knowing it's Steven, I don't think I could do that now. I think I enjoyed the naughtiness of it, the anonymity of this strange, almost non-existent man. I think Steven represented something more innocent, real, and pure. I can't bear to think of Steven seeing me in that way.'

'Why can't he be both? You want your man to think you're sexy, surely? As well as loving you and sharing your interests, he's your best friend but also a hot-blooded male who looks at you and gets a raging hard on,' she grinned, 'when Andrew goes away, I want to know he's thinking about me and not checking out anyone else while I'm out of sight. Make him want to go back to his hotel room to call you instead of propping up the bar and flirting with loose women.'

I was silent while I digested this suggestion, Ruth finished my hair and started rummaging through my wardrobe for something suitable for me to wear.

The party was in full swing when we arrived, lots of people were milling around, music was coming from one room, the noise of lots of people all talking at once was drifting in from another room. I just wanted to find a quiet corner to sit down and nurse a drink. Preferably near the buffet table.

I spotted the food in the kitchen and made a bee line towards it.

'Hey, Olivia,' I heard the surprise in his voice and turned around, I wasn't expecting to see anyone I knew at this party. It was Callum.

'Oh hey, what are you doing here? I'd have thought your place would be rammed tonight?'

'It is, but we also agreed to cater this party so I volunteered to come here. I didn't want to spend my New Year's Eve working, this job will finish as soon as I pull this last piece of cling film off, and then I can help myself to a drink and go party!' He grinned at me as the cling film peeled away from the tray of chicken signalling the end of his shift. 'So, Olivia, I know it's none of my business but what happened?'

I raised my eyebrows questioningly, 'What do you mean?'

'Well, he's been drowning his sorrows the last three nights, you promised me romantic meals.' He smiled kindly. 'You don't have to tell me of course, but you seemed so happy the other night.'

I frowned despite myself, I didn't really like being asked about it, I certainly couldn't tell Callum what had happened, I was relieved that he didn't know though, at least Steven hadn't told him what he'd done – or what I'd done.

'You can tell when he's happy because his hair is all big and hard but right now it's all limp and floppy.' He grinned, I laughed at his description and realised he was right. 'I mean look at it,' he continued, nodding his head. I felt my blood rushing to my head as I turned to follow his gaze, I could hear my heart pounding. There he was, through the clearing of people I spotted him, sat in the corner idly tearing the label off his bottle of beer. I was looking for a quiet corner and he'd beaten me to it. He had shaved and swapped his glasses for lenses but his hair was flopped over to one side, covering half his face, like the Phantom of the Opera. His white shirt was unbuttoned at the neck and untucked. His sleeves were rolled up revealing his strong arms. His jeans were scuffed around the edges. He looked strangely normal, but not like Steven.

He'd forgotten to put his costume on. I felt my heart break, *am I the cause of his misery?* I fought against my desire to go and comfort him, surely he deserved to feel bad, he'd done a bad thing, he'd hurt me, tricked me. I looked at Callum sadly. 'He told me that he's the one who did wrong, so I can't imagine how miserable you feel if you're the one who's been hurt.'

I reached for a couple of beers and nodding I made my way over to Steven. Between Ruth's calm reasoning and Callum's comments I was beginning to see this whole situation differently. I realised one thing for sure, I didn't want to lose this man from my life. I loved him, even if I did want to smash his face in at the moment.

I flopped down on the sofa next to him. He didn't look at me. I watched him for a little while but he didn't seem to notice, he just stared into space and picked at the label on the bottle. 'Here,' I said holding out a bottle to him. He looked at the bottle and frowned, is eyes flicked up to my face and away again as he took the beer. Then he lifted his head as he realised who I was.

'Liv?'

'I got your messages,' I said.

'Can we talk about it?' He asked, uncertainly.

'You mean about the revelation that you've been lying to me all this time?'

He sighed.

'You're right, I have been lying to you, and I'm sorry. At first I just wanted to get to know you better, learn some things that might help me to woo you.'

I suppressed the urge to giggle at the word woo and waited for him to continue. He turned to face me, his knee moving up onto the sofa between us and his arm resting across the back of the sofa.

'Then I wanted to help you, you had all these ridiculous insecurities and I saw them as barriers to you giving us a chance. So I used my conversations with you as Chris to try and help you.'

'And the sex?'

'Well in my defence, I never suggested you take your clothes off, I just told you what I would be doing if I'd been there with you, slow dancing.' His eyes moved to my face again and registered the look of anger at his words. 'It got out of hand, Liv, and I am sorry. But when Melissa came between us, I guess I was clinging on to the only way I could be with you. When I realised you were falling for Chris, I knew I had to end it, especially when the Melissa problem was resolved and there was nothing else standing in our way except for Chris. I was actually a bit jealous.' He laughed slightly at the irony of being jealous of himself.

I was silent for a moment, replaying his words, the way he described it didn't seem too bad. It wasn't as though he had concocted some elaborate scheme to trick me – he'd just wanted to help. 'I suppose this is where you tell me that you're sorry and if you could go back and change it you would, that you wish you hadn't done it?' I asked scornfully. Steven frowned and shook his head.

'No. I don't regret it. You wouldn't have had any of those conversations with me because I'm your employee and you liked me, even though it was against your better judgement and you didn't want me to know your insecurities. But you wanted to feel good about yourself and I wanted to help you do that. Pretending to be someone else was the only way I could get close enough to help you,' he paused and caught my eye, 'it did help you, didn't it?'

I admired his honesty, there was no apology there, just statement of fact. *How dare he blame the sex on me*, but realistically it was true, he hadn't suggested I do anything, I'd been caught up in the moment and he just carried it on. I felt mortified that I had been so, *what's the word?* Liberated. *Slutty.* He was right too, I had changed, my self-esteem was much better than it ever had been and I felt more independent and free from my repression. I nodded, sighing in defeat.

'Yes, you did help me.'

'I'm sorry if I've hurt you, OK? I didn't set out to do that, I just wanted to be closer to you somehow.'

I turned to face him, matching his position on the sofa, our knees lightly touching, my head fell against the back, and I felt his hand move slightly to touch my hair. I closed my eyes as little tingles started running from my scalp down my neck and along my spine.

'It's nearly midnight, Liv,' he whispered gently, 'I don't expect you to forgive and forget but what if we start again?'

I opened my eyes slowly and smiled. 'For the sake of Auld Lang Syne?'

I was aware suddenly of the music going off and the TV was switched on, the chimes of Big Ben were counting down the stroke of midnight as the party goers all started shouting, 'Ten!'

I glanced at Steven and felt my heart soften, he looked less miserable and more hopeful, the change in him made me feel happier.

'Nine!'

He held my gaze as he leant closer towards me.

'Eight!'

His fingers brushed against my shoulder, sending currents of pleasure coursing down my spine, I felt a giggle threaten as the tingles reached my lower back.

'Seven!'

My hand touched his knee lightly.

'Six!'

He reached up to touch my face.

'Five!'

My hand slid up his thigh as we moved closer to each other.

'Four!'

His fingers weaved into my hair as his thumb stroked my cheek.

'Three!'

My hand snaked around his waist.

'Two!'

I felt his breath on my face as I closed my eyes.

'One!'

His nose brushed against mine.

'Happy New Year!'

Our lips pressed together tentatively, my defences crumbled, and I let him invade. His tongue found mine and slowly they danced together like old lovers, comfortable with each other's routine. His thumb caressed my cheek as my hand moved to his face, weaving my fingers into his hair as I tugged at his top lip. He tasted of beer and peanuts and Steven, his lips were warm and soft and gentle. I opened my eyes to look at him and found him watching me, his eyes were smiling, that spark of light had returned. He pulled away and gazed at me, contently.

'Happy New Year, Liv.'

'To fresh starts.' I agreed.

'You must have questions?'

'I thought you wanted a fresh start, brush it under the carpet and forget about it?'

Steven shook his head, 'I want no secrets between us, I want you to be able talk about anything and everything with me. You have questions, ask them.'

I nodded. 'OK. Where did the American accent come from?'

'It's the only accent I can do, I needed to disguise my voice somehow.'

'And all those girls you used to take home every weekend at uni.' I said frowning.

He laughed. 'A slight exaggeration. Wanted you to think I was more desirable than I am so you'd want to snap me up.'

'Why do you call me Liv now, instead of Olly?'

'I told you, Olly is a horrible name,' he smiled.

'I quite like you calling me Ols, makes me feel young, but I like Liv too, it makes me feel feminine and grown up.'

'Well then I'll be sure to use both with equal measure,' his eyes were smiling and the familiar twitch was apparent at the corner of his mouth.

'How much did Ignition offer you to leave us?' My eyes narrowed as I recalled the phone call from the previous day. His eyes widened and he smiled.

'Not enough, I can assure you.'

'But there is a price?' I was stunned, I hadn't thought money would be of concern to him.

'No,' he shook his head smiling, 'I'm not going anywhere, Ols, but it's very nice to see you're worried about it.'

'Worried? Who's worried? I could replace you like that,' I snapped my fingers together and made a loud popping noise.

He laughed, 'What about in your bed? Would you replace me there just as quickly?'

'Well I haven't so far,' I grinned. I wanted to change the subject, this had descended too quickly into familiar territory, 'Who are you? Steven or Chris?'

'Both, the perfect combination of nerd and perv.' He winked at me lasciviously.

I shrugged. 'OK, but you're not a fitness instructor.'

'No, but I have one, he made up your diet plan for me and provided me with lots of his sexploits – he likes to kiss and tell.'

'So those all really happened?' I asked, wide-eyed.

Steven nodded. 'Oh yes.' He leant closer to whisper conspiratorially. 'And that Jacuzzi is a five-minute walk from your flat, just so you know.'

Something inside me snapped, and I felt desire gathering in the pit of my stomach. Easy now, I told myself, don't rush it. 'Interesting, I have been quite keen to sink into that Jacuzzi.' I grinned. Or I could rush it – either way is fine.

'Well, not that you need it, but if you want me to continue to help you with your fitness I could take you to the gym with me. That unisex changing room is always empty.'

I felt a warm glow spread through me. The accent had gone but that teasing, suggestive voice was evident in his words. I'd thought it would feel strange to talk with Steven the way I'd talked with Chris but it was just the same. My mind wandered back to Boxing Day, in the car on the driveway, our date, I'd already been more open about sex with Steven than I had imagined, perhaps that was his doing, or perhaps it was me. I gave in, there was no point in pretending otherwise, I wanted Steven and Chris and lucky for me they were both here rolled up in one very handsome package. Besides which, I had lost entire days dreaming about that Jacuzzi.

'When can we go?' I asked, and just like that, our romance was back on track.

The Suited To You Trilogy
by
Demelza Hart

For more of our titles please visit our website

www.xcitebooks.com

7493207R00191

Printed in Great Britain
by Amazon.co.uk, Ltd.,
Marston Gate.